Also by
KATELYN DETWEILER

The UNDOING
Of THISTLE TATE

❧⟫⟪❧

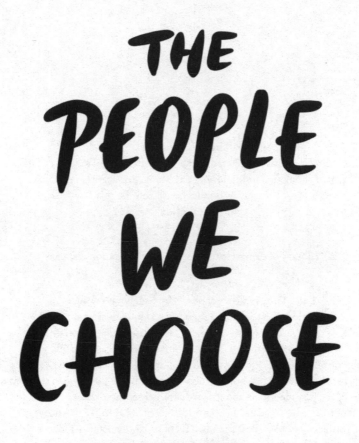

THE
PEOPLE
WE
CHOOSE

KATELYN
DETWEILER

MARGARET FERGUSON BOOKS
HOLIDAY HOUSE · NEW YORK

Margaret Ferguson Books
Copyright © 2021 by Katelyn Detweiler
All Rights Reserved
HOLIDAY HOUSE is registered in the U.S. Patent and Trademark Office.
Printed and bound in March 2021 at Maple Press, York, PA, USA.
www.holidayhouse.com
First Edition
1 3 5 7 9 10 8 6 4 2

Library of Congress Cataloging-in-Publication Data

Names: Detweiler, Katelyn, author.
Title: The people we choose / by Katelyn Detweiler.
Description: First edition. | New York : Holiday House, [2021]
"A Margaret Ferguson Book." | Audience: Ages 14 and up.
Audience: Grades 10–12. | Summary: Seventeen-year-old
Calliope Silversmith's lifelong friendships are transformed when she starts
dating new neighbor, Max, but her life is turned upside-down when she learns
the identity of the sperm donor her mothers chose.
Identifiers: LCCN 2020034226 | ISBN 9780823446643 (hardcover)
Subjects: CYAC: Best friends—Fiction. | Friendship—Fiction.
Lesbian mothers—Fiction. | Identity—Fiction.
Sperm donors—Fiction. | Families—Fiction.
Classification: LCC PZ7.1.D48 Peo 2021 | DDC [Fic]—dc23
LC record available at https://lccn.loc.gov/2020034226

ISBN: 978-0-8234-4664-3 (hardcover)

＞＞ ＜＜

To Danny and Alfie,
the people I will choose,
every day, always.

＞＞ ＜＜

THE
PEOPLE
WE
CHOOSE

Chapter One

AT first I wonder if he's a mirage.

The air certainly seems hot enough.

Rustling branches along the tree line, and then two legs, two arms, one head. The pieces come together to make a boy, and that boy walks across our wild grassy lawn and up to where I sit on the porch.

I put down my dog-eared copy of *Sense and Sensibility* to take him in. Long limbs and warm brown skin, black T-shirt and black cutoff jeans. His clothes are splattered in streaks of bright paint, golds and blues and reds and greens and purples, like *he* is the painting. He is the work of art.

I'm out here early today because I needed to breathe. Mama and Mimmy are firm believers in open windows and fans, even during the first heat wave of the summer. They only have air conditioners at Hot Mama Flow, their yoga studio—with aerobics classes and weight-machine circuits, too, because yoga isn't popular enough to sustain an entire business in our small town of Green Woods, Pennsylvania. And even there they keep the AC off for most classes. "A little hot yoga is good for the soul," Mama says, usually as she's upside down, balancing on her hands, legs in a split, as if gravity is not an actual thing. And maybe for Mama it's not.

"I was looking for some sign of life," the boy says, his voice somehow deeply growly but sweetly musical at the same time. "I just moved in next door. If you can call it *next door* when there's five minutes of woods between us. I mean, Jesus. How is this only an hour outside of Philly? I feel like I'm lost in some kind of West Virginia wilderness."

I raise my eyebrows. He looks less art worthy now. And it's really more like ninety minutes most days because of traffic, at least during rush hours, but I don't correct him.

"So anyway," he starts. Stops. Runs one hand through his tight-cropped curls. "Sorry. I'm Max. Should have started with that."

"Calliope."

"That's an interesting name."

"My moms are big on mythology." I emphasize *moms* and say it like a challenge. It's a hard habit to break, maybe because Green Woods still has some people clinging to the Dark Ages. But Max doesn't react.

"That's cool. I like it. I don't actually know why my parents named me Max. My mom does love a good T.J.Maxx deal, but I hope that's not the reason."

"Uh-oh. The closest T.J.Maxx is a forty-minute drive from us. Will your mom survive out here? You can assure her we do get mail. Much faster since they ditched the horse and buggy last year. Mail trucks now, can you believe it?" I smile, kicking back in my midnight-colored rocking chair. Right between Mama's sky-blue chair and Mimmy's sunny-yellow one. The wooden slats of the porch floor creak. Our little stone house was built sometime in the early 1800s—or so the Realtor said when Mama and Mimmy bought it before I was born, and I believe it because every last piece of it feels old and persnickety.

Max squints up at me with dark amber eyes and laughs. "I get it. I was trash-talking your home before I even introduced myself. Not the best way to meet a new neighbor. My mom would tweak my ear for that one. So maybe don't tell her?"

I shrug. I don't love his attitude. But it's not every day I get to meet someone who hasn't spent their whole life here.

"Let's start over," he says, taking it upon himself to climb the porch steps. He sits on Mama's chair, like it was put there just for him.

"I hope all that paint is dry. Mama will ruin you if you mess with her favorite chair."

He looks down at his shorts. "Oh right. I was painting my bedroom walls this morning. I was just going to do normal boring gray on all of them, but then I had this vision of our apartment view, so I painted a mural of my old bedroom window and the scene outside it on one wall. We lived in the tallest building on our block, so I got a peek of the Philly skyline right when the sun comes up. That's always my favorite time to paint." He grins at me, bright white teeth with a small gap in the middle. It's a really good smile.

"Why did you move here then? If you love Philly so much?"

The whole porch seems to shift around us with that one question. The good smile disappears.

"Family stuff," he says. There is an extra-bold black period at the end of his sentence.

"I'm sorry," I say, because I'm not sure what other response there is. "But Green Woods isn't so awful. I promise. You'll get used to it. There's plenty of good to go with the bad." I glance above me at the sprawling canopy of deep green leaves that line the woods surrounding our house—dark and dense, swallowing us up from the rest of the town. "Just close your eyes for a minute."

He looks like he wants to ask why, but doesn't.

"Just sit there and listen," I say. "Breathe."

I close my eyes, too, even though I know all the sounds and smells as well as I know my own fingers and toes: the soft rumble of the creek that coils behind our meadow of a yard, the buzz of cicadas and grasshoppers and the sea of other insects that come to life every summer, the heady scents of damp soil and wildflowers and freshly cut grass.

"I bet you didn't have all this in Philly, did you?"

"Nope." He sighs. "Definitely not."

I sneak a peek through lowered lids. He's leaning back in the chair with his eyes still closed, arms spread open. Like he is drawing it all in, this day, this porch, these woods.

Our old landline phone rings from inside, and his eyes flip open. He looks around, like maybe he's in a dream. But then his gaze falls on me, and he blinks again, like worlds have clicked back into place.

I let the call go to voice mail. Only robots call that number these days.

"I actually came over here for sugar," he says, laughing. "Which sounds like a bad line from an old TV show. But my mom and I found everything for coffee this morning except the sugar, and there's no way I'm drinking that stuff unsweetened. Dad's got the car for a Philly trip today and I have no clue what direction the store is in or if I can even get there on foot. I won't talk down on your town—*our* town, wow—anymore, but . . . there's something to be said for having three bodegas within a block of your home. I'll leave it at that."

"It's nice to have trees on every side of your house, too. And no people. Except for neighbors that are a five-minute walk away."

"I guess we'll see about that."

"Uh-huh. And I hate to say it . . . but you walked in the wrong direction. My moms refuse to keep white sugar in the house. The devil's drug, as they say. We mostly use stevia, and sometimes agave or honey or maple syrup. I could pour some stevia into a cup for you if you want?"

His mouth drops open in disbelief. "So you're telling me . . . if I'd gone five minutes the other way I'd be walking home with bags of deathly but delicious sugar right now?"

"Actually, no. That's an old Boy Scout camp that no one uses anymore. If there's sugar there, you wouldn't want to use it. Maybe ten minutes north through the woods. I think you'd hit the Coopers' house then. And they are the jackpot because Mrs. Cooper runs the school's biannual bake sale. She's fully loaded, I'm sure."

"Do you have a compass on you?"

"Nope. I usually just lick my finger and see where the wind's blowing."

"Whoa. Really?"

"No, not really. That was a joke. But I *can* use the sun and the moon and the stars. Plus, I've lived here for seventeen years. I've walked through the woods once or twice."

"Are you saying you want to be my escort?" The really good smile is back.

"No thanks, but I can point you in the right direction so you have at least a fifty percent chance of making it there on your own."

"You have better things to be doing then?"

I don't. I'm working at Hot Mama Flow this summer—odd hours here and there at the front desk, whenever the moms need me to fill in gaps for their regular employees—but not today. Mimmy and Mama are both at the studio now, as they are most days, rotating with the rest of their staff between teaching, training, desk work, cleaning.

My only plan for today was to read on the porch for as long as I could bear it, then call my best friends, Ginger and Noah, to see if they want to come sweat here with me. Fill up the new inflatable turtle kiddie pool in the backyard with ice water and eat Mimmy's homemade strawberry basil ice pops, while we complain about having nothing to do all summer except work and sit in my yard eating ice pops. The same thing we did last year, and the year before that, and so forth, only with a pool this time. One of my better ideas, I'd say, bringing back the kiddie pool for the first time in a decade. We spend most of our time together at my house in "the country"—their term, as if living in Green Woods proper with a few streetlights and sidewalks somehow makes them actually urban.

"Maybe not, but I'd rather do nothing on this hot porch than trek through hot woods with a stranger."

"Well, we're not technically strangers anymore. We're neighbors and potential new best friends. Besides, those woods look pretty thick and shady if you ask me. I bet it's much cooler in there. And filled with all sorts of weird bugs and animals that a city slicker like me can't deal with alone."

"Bad news. I've had the same two best friends since I was out of the womb. Ginger and Noah. That's how it works in Green Woods. Total cliché story, too, our moms all meeting at Lamaze class. We were destined prebirth."

"Huh." He pauses, his face suddenly serious. "Well, looks like you and Ginger and Noah might just find yourselves in a quartet now."

Before I have time to respond, his pocket starts blaring music.

"*Ghostbusters* theme?"

"You got it," he says, grinning as he slides his phone out. "Hey, Mom!"

I pretend to go back to *Sense and Sensibility*, but I don't read a word. I'm watching Max over the edges of the book. Watching that grin fade, a small frown taking its place.

He ends the call after a minute, and I put my book back down. "Mom needs me. My thirteen-year-old sister, Marlow, is on a rampage because her vast collection of shoes is nowhere to be found, so I need to go through the Mount Everest of boxes in the garage to save the day. I'm going to have to chug the coffee down straight. Desperate times. But you are *not* off the hook."

"Oh?" I brace my feet against the porch.

"Nope. We're going for that walk in the woods." He stands up, salutes me, and takes all three porch steps in one leap.

I watch until he disappears back into the woods alongside our house, the wild trees eating him alive. Until it's almost like I did imagine him after all. A trick of light and heat.

It's hard to refocus on my book after that. I've read *Sense and Sensibility* so many times—too many times, probably, given how many books exist in the world. Maybe because as an only child, I've always been envious of the Dashwood girls. My copy of *Little Women* is just as exhausted looking, filled with rips and scribbles and food stains. I used to dream about being a March sister— minus civil wars and scarlet fever and other such unpleasantries, of course.

I use my last reserves of energy in this heat to make sure the bird feeder in our backyard is full, and then I top off the birdbath, too. The birds in these woods need the relief as much as I do.

I curl up in the hammock after, the shadiest place in the backyard. And sure enough, soon I hear tires rolling down our long gravel driveway, and a moment later Ginger slides in next to me. I forgot to call her. Noah, too. Not that I ever have to call either of them to make plans. They just appear.

"Hey," she says, lazily turning over to smile at me. Thousands of little freckles shine like copper glitter on her pale skin, and her hair is lit up a blinding golden white from the sun. So bright I need to squint just to face her. I find her eyes, the greenest I've seen in real life. If I hadn't woken up next to her a thousand times at sleepovers, I'd never believe she didn't wear contacts.

"They didn't need me at the diner today and my mom was annoying the hell out of me. Not even air-conditioning made staying home more attractive. I'd rather drown in my own sweat over here with you."

"I'm sorry. About your mom."

"Yeah, well. Same old Sophie. She *casually* mentioned setting me up with the son of my aunt's sister-in-law's cousin or something like that. The woman just can't help herself."

I was born first, the early baby. Ginger was second, right on schedule for the first and only time in her life. Noah came out late, two weeks after his due date—a September birthday, which meant when the question of kindergarten came up, our moms decided to keep all of us summer babies together, always the oldest kids in our class. Our families understood we couldn't be separated at that point. Noah's mom, Beverly, still pops over sometimes for a glass of wine on the porch, but Mama and Mimmy's friendship with Sophie faded over the years. It turned out they didn't have much in common other than their pregnancy timeline.

"I would have come sooner but I was waiting for my leopard nails to dry." She flutters her fingers in my face, the light catching on her shiny collection of mood rings and crystal bracelets. "Noah's here, too. In the kitchen, whipping up some iced green tea for us. He was talking about cutting up some ginger and limes for infusing when I left him. How did we get so lucky?"

"I don't know. Our parents conceived around the same moon cycle?"

She ignores me. "I'm telling you, some girl is going to swoop in and snap him up, and where will that leave us? Hm? Making our own infused tea? Ugh. In case you forgot, I'm not straight, so it's not my duty to lock him in to a monogamous romantic relationship. And besides, we both know I'm not the one his sweet, soulful heart wants, no matter which way I sway. Also, can I say, very objectively, that our boy is growing into quite a heartthrob. He's got that whole skinny-but-ripped thing going on. It's bizarre."

I don't bother responding. The three of us had our yellow-poop-drenched diapers changed side by side. We played mermaid and merman in the tub together until we turned five and our moms decided it was perhaps time to acknowledge our different genitalia.

Noah is a brother to us. I understand as well as anyone that family isn't always about blood.

"People moved into the old Jackson house," I say, knowing Ginger will quickly latch onto this sparkly new tidbit dangling in front of her. Max didn't have to say where he moved into, because it's the only empty house in a five-minute radius.

"Oh my god, *what?* Hanging out with the ghosties? Yikes. I guess no one warned them. I don't think I could live in a house where humans have died."

"Lots of people die in houses, Ginger. That's not so unusual. And Mr. Jackson seemed pretty ancient." He's the old recluse who had died there when we were kids. The police found his body during a check-in after he stopped picking up the newspaper from the top of his driveway. He—and the house—had become a source of all kinds of popular local lore.

"Not Mr. Jackson, though I don't fancy the idea of meeting his ghost either. I mean whoever was murdered. Before him. Or *while* he lived there."

"We don't know for sure that happened."

"We don't know for sure that it *didn't* happen."

I shake my head. Sigh. "Anyway. Not the point. There's a boy who moved in, maybe our grade. He came over asking for sugar this morning."

She giggles, a light, bubbly sound. "Sugar? For real? That's actually a thing people do?"

"Apparently."

"Fascinating." She lifts her eyebrows, two perfectly symmetrical white-blond arches. "What was he like?"

I shrug. "Not sure yet. But he wants to be best friends with us."

"Did you tell him it's a pretty exclusive club? Tied forever to our moms' vaginas?"

"Ew, Ginger. Unnecessary visual. But yes. I did express it, though more politely."

"Well, I suppose we can give him a chance to earn it." She pauses. "Is he pretty?"

There's no point in lying. "Very pretty."

"Worth breaking the rule for?"

"Ginger! No! I am not—"

She exhales loudly, cutting me off. "I know, I know. It doesn't matter if he's very pretty. Or very charming, sweet, smart, funny, talented, et cetera et cetera. You aren't dating anyone before college."

I reach out and pinch her elbow. "Yes, and it's a good rule. A *great* rule."

A rule that served various helpful purposes. I could focus on friends, family, school. Avoid the drama and heartbreak that goes along with dating in high school—especially a small school like ours, where relationships are often like a messy overlapping Venn diagram. But the primary purpose—the one I absolutely never say out loud, and the reason I came up with the rule in the first place—is because of Noah. I can avoid the idea of dating *him* specifically if I make it clear I'm not dating anyone period. He'd slipped an anonymous Valentine's Day card in my locker sophomore year, but "anonymous" isn't possible after a decade and a half of seeing your best friend's handwriting. *You are the most beautiful human in the world.* I knew the loops and slants of his letters as well as I knew my own. But it was obvious without the card anyway. Had been for a while, really. The way he looked at me was evidence enough. I never acknowledged that I knew—that I'd recognize his words anywhere. Instead, I declared my rule the very next day: No dating until college. To be fair, I had never dated even before I came up with the rule. No one had ever asked. But there was no one I wanted to ask me either.

"It's an arbitrary rule." She pinches me back with those fresh leopard nails, the tips fittingly sharp and clawlike.

I wince and rub the half-moon imprints on my wrist. "It's not arbitrary. And it's more important now than ever. We only have one year left in Green Woods together. *One.* I intend to use my time wisely. You and Noah. My moms. College applications. The Environmental Club—which, now that I'm president this year, I fully expect you to join. So, yes, actual important things. Not a meaningless relationship that'll inevitably end anyway when it's time for long distance." And I *do* believe in all of these reasons. They're good ones. Just not the only ones.

"Uh-huh. And have I ever told you that you seriously over-think everything?"

"Oh, at least a million and two times before today, I'd say."

"Well, then let's make it a million and three. Because you do. Overthink. Just let life happen sometimes, okay?"

I shake my head, and Ginger knows me well enough to move on. "Anyway, in other news, I think Penelope Park smiled at me a little... I don't know, wistfully, yesterday when I went to buy some almond butter and fluff at the store. She was checking me out—at the register, I mean, but maybe actually checking me out, too—and our hands touched for a good three seconds when she handed me the receipt."

"Not to be a buzzkill, but isn't Penelope still with Ethan? And... potentially straight?"

"Well, right, that's why I said the smile was a little *wistful*, like she maybe wants to be with me but is still too ensnared in the oppressive chains of her heteronormative lifestyle to break away quite yet. But maybe she will. I can be patient. It's hard to come out when there are only two confirmed lesbians in a school of, oh, you know, *five hundred* students."

The kitchen door opens before I can respond, and Noah steps outside slowly, balancing a pitcher of tea and three glasses on a wooden tray. He's dressed like he usually is, plain white T-shirt and dark denim shorts, battered gray slip-on sneakers. In the cold months it switches to dark jeans and a sweater over a white T-shirt. He has the kind of fair skin that somehow turns a deep tan after one summer day in the sun—whereas I go straight to pink—and he already has that bronze glow now. His thick golden-brown hair is curling up in the humidity, looking purposefully, artfully messy, but I know he's never touched a dab of product in his life.

He smiles wide when he sees me watching him.

Ginger looks between us and sighs dramatically. "What a shame."

"What's a shame?" Noah asks as he puts down the tray on the picnic table. He pours two tall glasses of tea and then delivers them to us in the hammock.

"Oh, nothing important," Ginger says, waving him off as she lifts the glass to her bright red lips and takes a sip. "Mm. Excellent infusion. I do have a real affinity for all things *ginger*, not surprisingly."

"I was just telling her," I say, "about the new neighbors that

moved into the Jackson house. It's a shame, isn't it? A nice, innocent family picking such a sad place for a home."

"Seriously?" Noah looks off toward the woods, as if he might
actually make out the Jackson house behind all the trees. "Someone is really living there?"

"Yep. I met one of them, a boy around our age. Max."

"Yeah? Well, we'll have to be extra nice to Max. Show him
Green Woods isn't all scary and gloomy like that house. Boring,
maybe. But the scariest thing about Green Woods is the lack of
good food options. Or maybe the fact that even a mediocre hospi-
tal is thirty minutes away." He turns back to the table, pours himself a glass of tea.

"That house is definitely scary," Ginger says, crunching on a
piece of ice. "Especially since the roof has looked on the verge of
collapse for the last decade or so."

"That's probably a bit dramatic. Maybe just the porch roof,"
I say, and then I taste the tea. Ginger's right. The ginger-lime
combo is excellent. Maybe Noah's best yet.

I sit up taller in the hammock and raise my glass. "Let's toast."

Ginger raises her glass up next to mine, and Noah comes over
to join us.

"To summer," I say, "and to the beginning of our last year
together."

"We'll always be together," Noah says. "I'm pretty sure we
don't need Green Woods High for that."

"But it will be different."

Ginger clinks my glass hard. "To embracing different. Because that can be a good thing."

I clink back harder. "But to keeping our friendships the same. No matter what."

"Always," Ginger says.

"Always," Noah echoes.

We tilt our heads back and drink.

Always.

Chapter Two

"**I'M** feeling celebratory today," Mimmy says the next morning, putting a stack of fluffy blueberry pancakes in front of me. Sun streams in through the lacy buttercup-yellow curtains, making circles of light dance around our old wooden kitchen table. "Mama and I got coverage for the opening shift at the studio, for one. And it's officially the first Saturday of the summer. A few happy months of sunshine ahead, and then our baby girl is a senior. A *senior*."

"Jesus Christ, we're old," Mama says, coming up behind her with a bottle of maple syrup—the real stuff, of course. It's a festive morning in the Silversmith house. "Feels like just yesterday she was sliding out of our uteri, doesn't it, Mimmy? Almost makes my eyes damp."

Uteri, always. Never uterus. Though Mimmy is the one who technically carried me for nine months and pushed me out into the world. I've seen photos of her bump, so I know that much. But they refuse to say whose egg was responsible for creating me— whose egg was used to make the embryo, my petri-dish beginning. It's supposed to be a forever mystery, which one, Mimmy or Mama, has half of my genetic code. They won the sperm bank lottery, apparently, because it's completely impossible to tell whose egg spawned me—the donor must have a weirdly precise blend of both my moms' features. I have Mimmy's light freck-les and permanently tangled auburn hair, Mama's blue eyes and slightly upturned nose, which she calls a ski slope and I call a pig snout. I have Mimmy's squeaky laugh, Mama's strong yoga arms. Mimmy's dimples, Mama's pointed ears. I like to bake and create like Mimmy, but she's softer than me, dreamier and more medi-tative. I'm not as tough as Mama either, but I'm type A like she is, a planner and an overthinker—as Ginger likes to remind me. I'm miraculously a perfect fusion of them both.

Mimmy was once upon a time a Silver, Mama was a Smith.

But we're all Silversmiths now.

"At least we have almost a month until she's eighteen," Mama says, digging out a blueberry from the top pancake on my plate. "We can still baby her."

"Don't you have your own pancakes to plunder?" I pretend to slap her hand away, but she catches my fingers in hers—all ten of them together, long and slender and big knuckled, I can hardly tell which are hers, which are mine. "You took the best blueberry."

"Mimmy still has mine on the griddle. We both love you enough to give you the first ones, so don't you dare complain to me."

"Do you and Ginger and Noah have any plans today?" Mimmy asks, sipping from her mug of foamy green matcha with one hand as she flips pancakes with the other. "It's gorgeous out there. Maybe you should have a picnic at the lake? I made some hummus last night and picked a handful of tomatoes and peppers from the garden."

"Ginger's around, I think, but Noah's busy. He's taking an

intensive all-day private cello lesson on Saturdays at a studio in Philly this summer. Prep for college auditions."

Mama and then Mimmy settle in at the table with their pancakes, and the conversation moves on around me: studio schedules and garden supplies and the merits of veggie burgers versus salmon burgers for the grill tonight. I eat my pancakes in a contented silence, picking all the blueberries out first. I pour more syrup into the holes and watch the dark amber sunrays skim to the edge of the plate.

"I will forever blame Frank for your sweet tooth and odd eating habits," Mama says, swiping the syrup bottle from my hand. "This is why we only have pancakes on special occasions."

Frank. The donor.

His name's not really Frank. Or maybe it is, I have no clue. I've been calling him Frank, though, for as long as I knew that half of me logically must have come from someone else. The legend goes that Mama was always listening to Frank Zappa when I was little—she still does sometimes, though the nickname has ruined the music for her, she says—and one day I asked if he was my daddy and that's why she loved him so much. That was when I learned to never say *daddy* again, because whoever this man is, wherever he might be—he's not my *daddy*. Being a daddy is about much more than DNA. But *donor* sounded too cold, like I'm a science experiment from a lab—even if, yes, that's what in vitro fertilization actually means—so Frank stuck.

"When I'm eighteen, I'm buying my own supply of syrup, and you can't tell me not to."

"Speaking of eighteen, and Frank, and the decision you'll have to make—whether or not you want to be in touch..." Mimmy squeezes my hand and gives me a very meaningful look.

"That again, Margo? Seriously, Frank could have died years ago," Mama says, her eyes focused intently on her pancakes.

Mimmy and I sigh at the same time. We've heard this argument before. "Well," I say, "he could have chosen to be an anonymous donor. But he didn't. And you could have picked an anonymous donor to use for me. But you didn't." *Just in case*, they say. *Just in case* of what exactly, I'm not sure. I don't think they're sure either. Maybe access to future medical information. Or maybe it just felt too final to close that door for good. "You picked someone who was willing to be contacted. When I turned eighteen. If he's still alive."

I might not even request any information about him. A month from now, or anytime ever. Because then what? We talk on the phone? I search for him online? Pore over photos that come up, dissecting eyes, lips, cheekbones, ears, to find something that looks slightly like mine?

Mama impales a blueberry with her fork. "That may be true, but—"

"Can we talk about something else?" I interrupt, tapping my fork against Mama's plate so she's forced to look up at me. "Aren't we supposed to be celebrating?"

"Sorry. I do come on strong, don't I?" She grins. "Part of my charm. Can't deny it."

"Mm-hmm, whatever you say, sweets," Mimmy says. She

rolls her eyes, but in a loving way. She'll never be immune to Mama's charms. "Oh, I have something else to talk about! I went for a walk this morning, and I saw a car pull out of the driveway next door—the old Jackson place. I wonder what that was about? Could someone actually be moving in?"

I glance toward the window. "Yes. A family—they already moved in. I met the son. Max."

"Oh?" Mimmy asks. "When?"

"He came by yesterday morning. Asking for sugar. I forgot to tell you last night."

"Sugar!" Mama laughs incredulously. She scoops a forkful of dry, unsyruped pancake into her mouth.

"Yes, *sugar*. I had to regretfully inform him that sugar wasn't allowed in our home."

"So what was he like? It's hard to imagine anyone besides Mr. Jackson living there. I assumed at this point that house was permanently abandoned." Mama tilts her head, likely considering all potential cons of this development. "At least if they're terrible, we have a sturdy army of trees between us."

"I'm not sure we need an army. He seemed friendly enough."

"Maybe we should bake something for them?" Mimmy says. "Welcome them to Green Woods. It can't be easy, living in that house."

That house.

My skin prickles at the way she says it, even though it's already ninety degrees in our kitchen.

"There's nothing wrong with that house," Mama says,

shaking her head. "It's just an innocent dilapidated pile of dust and stone and I'm glad someone outside of this silly town can clean it back up. Otherwise it might as well be knocked down so the animals can have more room to play."

Mimmy doesn't seem convinced. "Maybe the stories aren't all true. But I don't have a good feeling when I drive by there. I swear my bones can feel it. The sadness."

We all quietly continue eating after that.

Mimmy looks like she's still thinking about ghosts. And Mama looks like she's mentally planning out poses for her weekend classes.

I wait until I've cleared every last golden pool, running my finger against the plate and licking it clean. And then I say: "You're right, Mimmy. It's a good idea to bake something for the new neighbors."

I walk into the shadowy trees later that afternoon.

I'm carrying a plate of Mimmy's signature dessert, peach cobbler bars, with a tiny bowl of homemade maple-tofu whipped cream on the side. She'd walked me through the recipe before she and Mama left for the studio. Hopefully it's at least half as good as hers. Half as good would still be far better than anyone else's peach cobbler bars.

The woods become thicker and duskier as I get close, branches dipping low across my path. Leaves muffle the sound of the creek that runs behind both of our properties. I am alone. The only creature on this planet.

But then a ray of sun filters in. The trees open up slowly, one by one, like the woods are laying down a leafy golden trail for me.

One more step, and there it is, a hulking stack of old stones and wooden beams. The Jackson house. Looking just as decrepit and foreboding as I remembered. Even the meadow it sits in seems washed out, like every natural color has been bleached from too much exposure to the sun. Noah never understood our squeamishness, but after Mr. Jackson died, Ginger and I used to dare each other to see who would get closer to the house. She touched the front door once with the tip of her pinkie. I couldn't even make it up the porch steps. It's been a few years, though, since we cared about the house. Or cared enough to pretend to be brave.

But I'm brave today.

My feet skitter purposefully across the dull green grass, broken up with patches of cracked dirt and debris, rotting remains of old leaves and weeds. There's a light scent of smoke in the air. I don't see any cars, though the garage door is closed.

The first porch step is fine, but the second one gives as I step down, and I hop quickly to the third and onto the porch. Empty windows watch me. I can't hear anything besides my own breath.

I knock three times. Wait. Knock again, louder. I even try what looks like an old rusty doorbell, but I can't tell if it chimes inside the house.

No one comes.

I don't leave the dessert on the steps. Animals might eat it, after all.

Maybe I'll try again tomorrow.

*   *   *

An owl hoots outside my windows that night. My owl.

Calling out to another bird. Serenading the stars. I see this particular great horned owl sometimes, yellow-eyed and resolutely somber-faced up in the high branches. I like to believe she guards our clearing by night.

My bedroom is in the attic, planked wooden floors and rough plaster walls, the ceiling slanted on both sides with a steep point in the middle. Mama and Noah both have to stoop when they come inside. If I wear a bun, my hair snags on the rafters. Ginger's hair, too. Only Mimmy fits just right.

From the big round window over my bed, I see leaves and branches and sky. My moms tried to keep me in the bedroom downstairs next to theirs, but I'd always wanted this. So when I turned twelve, I moved up here. My bird's nest. A tower in the clouds. The walls are covered in photos—some snipped from old magazines, others professional prints I've ordered, framed and unframed, a total mishmash of animals, trees, insects, mountains, lakes, rivers, oceans. Pictures that I've seen and thought: this is our world and I'm lucky enough to live in it.

The owl hoots again.

Ginger is sound asleep on a cot across the room. There's a breeze coming in the windows, making the curtains rustle. I listen to the rhythmic hum of the fan, Ginger's soft in-and-out breaths. I should feel sleepier than I do.

I lie in bed, my feet at the wall, my head on the pillow—the headboard perfectly positioned in the middle of the room so I can see out the round window. The pale sliver of yellow moon smiles down at me through the trees.

There's a row of small wooden drawers built into the wall next to my bed, mostly filled with treasures from outside— heart-shaped stones and dried flowers and bits of old pottery and glass that Mama and Mimmy and I have unearthed while gardening. I reach for the bottom drawer, my fingers wrapping around the pocket-size green notebook I've kept there for as long as I can remember. Because I can't shake this morning's breakfast conversation.

My moms don't know about this notebook. Neither does Ginger or Noah.

Mostly it's lists of things I'd tell Frank if I ever had the chance. Questions I'd want to ask him. There are notes about Mama and Mimmy, too, speculations about which one's blood I have pumping through my own veins. Midnight scribbling usually fueled by some kind of disagreement, like Mama telling me I couldn't die my hair purple, so of course that night Mimmy seemed like the better candidate to be Biological Mom. But some nights, even without any arguing, I couldn't help but think about Frank before I fell asleep. Does he have a wife? A husband? Other kids? Does he live somewhere close or somewhere on the other side of the world? He'd been here, in Pennsylvania, at least once. To go to the cryobank near Philly, do his business in a little plastic cup, walk away with money in his hands. But that was almost two decades ago. Now? He could be anywhere. Including buried underground or piled up neatly inside a little metal urn.

I grab a pen from my nightstand. *Cons*, I write, squinting at the page in the dim moonlight. There are a lot of them, surely.

1. Hurting Mama's and Mimmy's feelings, even if Mimmy would support my decision.

2. Making them both feel like they're not enough for me. Like this family, us, isn't enough.

3. Complicating and confusing everything.

4. Feeling crushed/disillusioned/broken if I find out that Frank: is dead; is a horrible human being; doesn't care even a tiny little 0.01% bit that I exist. Being dead might be better than being horrible. (Though maybe I'm horrible for even thinking that, which makes the genetic odds of him being horrible, too, more likely...)

5.

Other cons? That can't be it. Though I suppose hurting Mama's and Mimmy's hearts or hurting my own heart are both two fairly big potential risks.

But to keep it balanced and fair, just in case: *Pros*.

1. Learning more about who I am and who/where I came from.

2. Answering some of the questions in this stupid notebook so I can sleep better at night instead of doing things

like this, such as: Am I the only one? Or do I have half-siblings? Why did Frank donate? Does Frank wonder about me? Does Frank love nature documentaries as much as I do? Does Frank hate fake fast food burgers, too? Does Frank have blue eyes like mine? Does Frank have the same scary dreams about flying over a never-ending icy ocean? Do any of these dumb questions even matter? But if they don't, why do I keep asking them???

3. No more worrying/wondering about the truth because I'll know and whatever it is can't be that bad because it won't change anything about my life with Mama and Mimmy.

Because no matter what, I don't actually want him *in* my life. It's not about that. No. I don't need him to start playing dad. It's just about knowing. Scratching an itch.

I put the pen down. I can't decide anything for a month anyway.

I shove the notebook away and slide the wooden drawer shut.

Chapter Three

IT would be blasphemous to let peach cobbler go to waste.

After Ginger goes home the next morning, I try again.

The sun is hidden behind a vast wall of steely gray clouds. I can smell the rain, even if it's not here quite yet. Hopefully we'll have at least a temporary break from the heat.

I pause in front of Max's porch, staring up at the house. Waiting for what, I'm not sure. Maybe for someone or something to lurch out at me from behind hedges that clearly haven't been trimmed in decades. They tower above me like strange, amorphous green monsters. But then I hear a voice inside. I step on the first stair, expertly move straight to the third and onto the porch.

It only takes one knock before the door swings open.

A girl stares up at me. She's petite, but if Max hadn't told me his sister was thirteen, I would have assumed she could be our age. She must spend hours studying YouTube makeup tutorials, because her cheeks and eyes and lips look airbrushed, they're so perfect. Even Ginger would be in awe. Thick black-and-blond box braids dangle down her back. She's wearing a pink dress that is definitely too cool for a Sunday morning in Green Woods and matching sandals that lace halfway up her legs.

I feel overwhelmingly plain in comparison. Plain blue cotton dress. Plain white slip-on sneakers. Plain face with no makeup.

"You found your shoes," I say.

She looks down to her feet, then back at me, frowning. "Who are you?"

"Oh, sorry. I'm Calliope. Your neighbor." I wave toward the woods between our houses. "Max came by the other day."

Her frown eases. Slightly. "Right. You're the weirdos who don't believe in sugar."

I laugh. "That would be my family, yes."

"I'm Marlow. So...what's that, then?" She points at the plate of cobbler in my hands. "Dessert with no sugar? Sounds *delicious.*"

"No white sugar. Luckily my moms do believe in honey. In moderation, of course."

"Marlow?" Max materializes from the dark hallway behind her. He's wearing glasses today, half-rim frames, black and silver, looking like he's walked straight out of a Warby Parker shoot. "And...oh, hey, Calliope." He grins. "I knew you wanted to be friends."

"You got me. I'm here with a welcome-to-the-neighborhood present. It's my mom's cobbler recipe."

"Super, thanks. I can't wait to try that. Hey, Marlow, can you take the plate and put it in the kitchen, please?"

"Why can't you?" She leans her hip against the doorframe.

"Because I'm just about to explore the woods with my new friend. Gotta get to know the neighborhood and all that."

She raises one thin, perfectly arched black brow. "But Dad said to unpack and—"

Max cuts her off with a glance. "It's fine. I won't be gone long. Okay?"

"Whatever." Marlow grabs the plate, her gold nails glittering, and turns away from me, disappearing into the house.

"She's not always that rude, promise. She just doesn't want to be here. I'm not sure any of us really *want* to be here." Max catches himself this time. Winces. "No offense. Just the truth."

"Then why did you move?" I ask again, and immediately regret it. *Family stuff*, he'd said before. Meaning: not my business.

He looks up at the sagging porch roof, all splintered wood and rusting gutters. "Long story. But there was family drama in Philly, and my parents wanted a fresh start for all of us. So, anyway . . . Green Woods. Here we are. This marvelous old shack."

I watch as he skips the second and first steps altogether, leaping gracefully into the tufts of grass. I quickly follow. He pauses for a beat to glance back at the house, his lips curling down. "We came for a family cleaning day before we moved our stuff in, but this place needs a lot more than some Mr. Clean and a dustrag. My dad talks like he's going to fix it all up, make it nice and shiny, but . . . yeah, let's just say my hopes are low. Thank god I only have one year left before college. Poor Marlow."

I don't know what to say. I don't have the heart to tell him that the house his family chose for their fresh start is a town legend— and not for happy reasons. So I walk and take the lead instead, pushing aside some low-hanging branches as we dip back into the woods.

It may be shadier here in the leafy shadows, but it somehow feels like the sun shines brighter than it does over the Jackson house.

"Did you really want the neighborhood tour, or would you rather I drive you somewhere for sugar and a little taste of civilization? It's going to rain soon."

"Honestly, anywhere that's not *home* right now sounds great to me."

"I'll give you the abbreviated tour then, at least until it starts pouring."

We walk without talking for a few minutes until we reach a towering oak. "This," I say, stopping, "is my favorite tree in the woods."

"Favorite tree, huh? Can't say I've ever had one of those. What gives this one the edge?"

I motion for him to follow me to the other side of the trunk, so thick we could easily both hide behind it.

"See this perfect hole at the bottom?" I motion toward the opening at the base of the tree, a neat arch from the ground up to nearly my waist. "My moms refused to build a tree house for me when I was little—Mama is deathly afraid of heights, though she pretends not to be afraid of anything. But Ginger and Noah and I had this at least. We even slept out here a few times. We couldn't all fit at once so we'd rotate."

"You *slept* out here?" Max's jaw drops. He looks genuinely horrified. "In a dirty tree hole where squirrels and beetles and spiders and god knows what else were crawling on you all night?"

His hands slap at his arms, fighting off invisible critters. "That's disgusting."

"I'm sure it's challenging for a city boy such as you to understand. But we survived, and somehow we even managed to avoid any rabies."

"It's a miracle you're still standing here. So . . . *this* is the neighborhood? Maybe I don't need senior year and a diploma after all."

"Probably not if you want to be an artist." I lean back against my tree, bark scraping at my shoulders. "Is that what you want to do?"

"My mom says I can only do art if it's a double major—the second major needs to be something practical so I can have a *real career*. She majored in history, and has hated every job she ever had, which is why she has no job right now. So . . . clearly trying to fix her mistakes through me. Though my dad studied philosophy before law school—an equally meaningless major—and he's turned out to be, well . . ." He kicks at a dead branch, snapping it in two. It's clear he doesn't intend to finish the sentence.

"I'm a senior, too," I say, to carry on the conversation. "I'm thinking about environmental studies or biology or ecology— some practical way to appreciate nature. Maybe with a dual major in education so I can teach kids about these things, help them to care, too. Making a permanent decision about colleges and majors feels so scary, though. Sometimes I think maybe I'd rather just live in tree holes and eat acorns and berries for the rest of my life than be an actual adult human."

"Sounds about right for a Green Woods girl."

"I was joking. We're not really all backwards, you know." The words come out sharp. I'm not sorry.

Max sighs, taking a step closer to me. "You're right. I'm being a huge prick again, aren't I? Blame my parents—they never took me on a single camping trip growing up. We went to the Jersey Shore when we wanted a little nature."

"I feel sorry for you then."

"And come on, who wants to move away right before senior year? Imagine if you had to leave your girl Ginger and this Noah dude behind. Do dances and sports and stuff all on your own and watch your old friends' lives go on without you. And realize it's that easy for them to fill the Calliope-sized hole you'd left behind. Trust me. Not fun."

"I don't really do dances and sports and stuff. Mostly Environmental Club and peer tutoring. But I take your point."

"Great. So . . . we're friends again?"

"Best." I roll my eyes and start walking, deeper into the woods as they curve around the back of my house. We cross over the two wide logs that act as a bridge over the narrow creek. What slivers of sky I can see are a sickly looking gray. We should turn around before the rain starts. But there's one more thing I want to show Max. We start up an incline—not too steep, but still enough for both of us to be panting within a few minutes.

The trees in front of us slowly start to thin, tall pines lined up against the pale light. I push ahead faster. "It's hard to tell with the woods blocking the view, but we're actually pretty high up here."

We step out into the clearing, the edge of a long chain of hills.

It's a delicate patchwork world beneath us, the skinny line of Main Street weaving through the heart of our town. Clusters of homes, a few church spires, farmland sectioned off in orderly rows.

I wave my hand grandly. The Vanna White of Green Woods. "Welcome to your new home, Max. Officially. You can even see the Walmart Supercenter and the movie theater if you squint hard enough. Don't get too excited, though. It only has one screen, so pickings are slim. But sometimes that's better than driving thirty minutes for more options."

"Wow. I think my neighborhood in Philly was bigger than your entire town, but—"

"Really? That's all you can say? You're an *artist*. This view isn't nothing."

"Hey," Max says, reaching for me, his warm fingers brushing against my wrist. "You didn't let me finish. *But*...it's a pretty spectacular view. Definitely more green than I've seen in a long time. Who knew there were farms like this so close to the city? Huh."

"You're a funny one."

"Yeah? Why's that?"

"I'm supposed to be the simple country girl. But it turns out you're actually the sheltered one."

"Maybe that's a little bit true. When you live in the city, it can feel like you don't need anything more."

We're silent for a moment. Staring out. "I know this view right here isn't what you expected your senior year to look like," I finally say. "But do you really want to waste the whole year being miserable?"

"Thank you," Max says. I glance over to gauge whether he's being sarcastic, but his eyes are lost over the valley. "I needed to hear that. I'm sure I'll find the good in living this country life."

I smile.

"So," he starts. Pauses. "You and this Noah of yours, are you two...?"

"Dating?" I laugh. And then I think about Noah and his feelings and I instantly want to take the laugh back. He deserves better. "No. We're too close to date. And to save you from asking, I'm not dating Ginger, either. I'm not going to date *anyone* until after graduation."

"Oh?" He turns to face me, brows raised. "And why is that?"

I repeat the words I've said endlessly to my moms and Ginger and Noah: "Too many other things to focus on first. Friends. Family. School. My entire future. And what's the point, anyway? Everyone is going their separate ways soon enough."

"So... your mind skips ahead to the ending before there's a chance for a beginning?"

I shrug and fiddle with the strap of my dress. "Something like that."

"Maybe you just haven't met the right person."

"Maybe not, but even still it would be the right person at the wrong time. So—not happening."

"Hm," he says, nodding. "Got it."

A thick drop of rain hits my bare shoulder. Another lands on my cheek. I tilt my face up.

"I love the way it sounds." Max closes his eyes. The splashes are quickly becoming a steady stream. "The rain on the leaves. My mom had a noise machine that made a sound just like this in our old apartment. She won't need it here, I guess."

He pulls his glasses off, makes a few pointless swipes with his T-shirt before he pockets them in his shorts.

"Good thing these are mostly just a cool accessory," he says, grinning.

"We should probably go." I'm already turning toward the path. "Heads up, the hill can get slippery in the rain. Odds are high you'll be sliding your way down."

Noah comes over for dinner that night. It's just us, which doesn't happen very often. Mama and Mimmy are hosting a workshop on inversions at the studio, and Ginger has the evening shift at the diner. It's nice to have the quality time.

I coat the salmon in soy sauce and a generous squeeze of sriracha. Noah chops up kale and tomatoes from our garden, tosses them into a pan already sizzling with diced shallots. I bump him aside so I can put the salmon into the oven, and he sighs, pretending to be put out. I take longer than I need to, arranging it to be just so on the rack before I step back. Noah shakes his head, rolling his eyes. I pull myself up to sit on the counter, watching as he goes back to stirring.

"How was the fancy cello lesson yesterday?" I ask.

"Hard, but good, I guess. I feel like I have so much to do if I have any hope of getting into a decent music school."

I dangle my feet, kick him gently with my bare toes. "Well, you're the best cellist I've ever heard in real life, so I have faith."

"We live in Green Woods." He glances over at me, smirking. "I'm the only cellist in the school."

"I still have faith." And I do. He's *good*. Good enough to make me cry sometimes when he plays. "You just have to find a partner and you could absolutely give 2CELLOS a run for their money. Maybe you'll fall in love with another cellist at college, and then you can travel the world together playing. The romance would add to the allure."

He laughs, but more of a *ha* than a *ha ha*. "Yeah. Maybe."

"Seriously though, you'll land somewhere great. Just promise you'll remember me and Ginger when you move to some glamorous, faraway city."

"You two can always move to the glamorous, faraway city, too. *If* that happens. Ginger could be my publicist. She's a good blend of charming and stubborn. Like a friendly pit bull. People don't like to say no to her."

"Yeah, and what about me? You know I'd shrivel up and waste away in a city. Visiting is one thing. But *living* in one? It'd be like ripping the roots from a tree."

"We'll find you a nice quiet suburb nearby, don't worry."

"Or maybe you can just fly me in on your private jet to visit sometimes. A direct line from my cave in the woods to your big-city skyscraper."

"A private jet? Am I suddenly Jay-Z in this scenario? Did I marry someone from the Kardashian family?"

"Um, no, you would *never* marry a reality star. That's just how much I believe in you and your ability to become magnificently wealthy with that talent of yours. All on your own."

"I hope that's not why you keep me around."

"Nah. I keep you around for the cooking. Clearly."

He tosses a handful of kale stems at my face.

The conversation moves along to other things—Noah's part-time job making hoagies at Wawa and his favorite people-watching anecdotes of the week, a ranked list of the worst horror movies he's made me and Ginger endure, whether or not we should use Mimmy's prefrozen dough to make ginger cookies for dessert.

I am taking the salmon out of the oven when the doorbell chimes. It's a full, resonating sound, and I jump, almost dropping the hot pan. I forget the bell is there usually. Ginger and Noah always come right in.

"I'll get it," Noah says, already on his way toward the front hallway. I put the pan down on the stovetop and pull the oven mitts off my hands.

I hear the door open. Then a brief snippet of a pause, the space of two blinks. The rest of the house is silent, waiting with me. "Hey?" Noah says. I can hear the question mark at the end, but probably because I know him so well.

"Oh, hey. You must be Noah."

Max.

"I'm Calliope's new neighbor. Max."

"Oh! Max. Of course. Calliope told us about you. Welcome to the neighborhood."

Hands slap, presumably some type of complex male handshake.

"Yeah, thanks. I heard all about you, too. The mom club and everything."

The door closes and footsteps start down the hallway.

I immediately regret the faded Green Woods Middle School T-shirt and cutoff sweatpants I threw on earlier. Not because I'm trying to impress Max—but because no one but my moms and Ginger and Noah need to see me in my ratty old pajamas.

Noah turns the hallway corner and steps into the kitchen, Max right behind him.

Max smiles at me. I smile back.

"So where's Ginger?" he asks, leaning against the counter. Making himself instantly at home. "I need to meet her, then my introduction to Green Woods will feel complete."

"She's waitressing. You'll have to win her over another day."

His eyes land on the salmon, the pan of vegetables. "Oh, sorry. Am I interrupting? I can come back later. Or not."

"Why don't you eat with us," I say. Even though there's not really that much food.

"You sure?" Max looks at Noah. Noah nods. "Cool. We haven't done any real shopping yet, so the only food at home is canned or boxed. Actual food would be nice."

Noah asks Max where he lived before, what grade he's in. Polite small talk.

I pull out plates and start divvying up little thirds of food while Noah fills three glasses with water. I can feel Max watching us move together: the way I step back to let Noah into the sink, the way Noah helps me balance the hot pan as I scrape out every last sliver of shallot.

"I'm impressed," he says. "I mostly make eggs and grilled cheese. But you two are like an old married couple. You must do this all the time."

"My moms care about food. *Good* food. But Noah's even better than me in the kitchen," I add. "A valuable life skill around here because we don't have a lot of takeout options. You'll have to get used to it, too, city boy."

He laughs loudly, and it feels so good to hear that sound, like finding a twenty-dollar bill on the sidewalk. "Nah, I just have to come over here. One more point for the new neighborhood. First that scenic view, then the dessert you brought over—I may have forgotten to share it and accidentally ate the whole thing for lunch." He lifts the empty plate in his hand, which I didn't notice when he came in. "So yeah, Green Woods is crushing it today. Philly? Bye."

"What view?" Noah asks. He's watching Max closely, his thick brows pinched in a V.

"The top of the hill. We were up there today right when the rain hit. I nearly expired in the mud when I slid and fell on the way down."

"Got it. I'm glad you survived."

Noah is quieter than usual while we eat. He's never the

chattiest in our trio—that's Ginger's role, obviously, while I land somewhere in the middle, and Noah spends a lot of time listening to us banter with an amused grin on his face. But tonight he studies his plate as if the wild Alaskan salmon is deeply fascinating. I try to pull him in at first, telling Max about what a magician Noah is on the cello, and how our moms used to swap our clothes when we were little—I was bigger than him the first two years, and then he doubled up on me. Noah smiles at that at least, but he doesn't add much of anything to the conversation.

Max is animated, though, talking about his old neighborhood in Philly, asking questions about teachers, cafeteria food, classes and teachers to avoid, and it's easy to focus on him. It's easy to talk, easy to listen.

Easy to imagine our trio becoming a quartet after all.

Chapter Four

"**YOU** do realize you could ask for my number," I say, opening the screen door for Max. It's pouring rain again. "Save yourself a muddy walk through the woods. I'm not always here with no plans."

"Really?" He whips his head back and forth, fat droplets of water streaming from his hair. One splashes against my cheek. I don't brush it away. It feels nice, cool. The air is thick and muggy, a heavy curtain that even the rain can't draw aside.

"Actually, I had a desk shift at my moms' studio this morning and then took a class with Mimmy, so I just got home. You lucked out." I look down at my bright rainbow-striped yoga pants and neon-blue sports bra. It felt perfectly acceptable at the studio— most women practice in their sports bras, even the ones using their senior discount. Mama encourages it. She's all about stoking that fierce confidence, that sense of our own divinity. But right now I wish I'd thrown on a T-shirt after class. Mama would be disappointed in me. Or maybe not, given I'm in a bra in front of our new neighbor.

"I definitely lucked out." Coming from another teenage male, that could be suggestive. But Max doesn't seem to notice the extra dose of skin and cleavage, or if he does, he tactfully keeps his eyes on mine. "Do you want to come over to my house today? My mom is so relieved I've made a friend already, and she's asking to meet you. She said she'd offer to host you and your moms for dinner, but she's too embarrassed by the state of our house right now. Someday. You can just come by for a little, though, say hi. If you want. No worries if you have lots of other big plans this afternoon . . ."

I don't want to step inside Max's house, but I don't know how to say that.

If we're going to be friends, a visit there is inevitable.

And besides, it's all town gossip. I hope.

"Yeah, okay," I say, "but let me hop in the shower first. I need to wash yoga off of me."

"Sure, whatever you need to do. I'll just wait here on the porch, if that's okay. Maybe the rain gods will give us a break by the time you're ready."

I nod and then walk up the stairs, into the bathroom. I let the water run much colder than usual, shocking my hot skin with its sharpness as I step into the old claw-foot tub. The half-open window alongside the shower looks out over our porch roof, and rain is streaming in sideways through the screen.

I rush through the shower. Turn the water off. And then I hear it—Max, singing. Low and slow, a song I don't recognize. I close my eyes and listen. Certain words catch—*love* and *please* and *sorry, so sorry*. His voice is warm and beautiful and unexpected.

The song comes to an end and I pull myself out of the tub and away from the window, into my room to change. I put on a black romper and pull my wet hair into a messy side braid, then smear a dollop of coconut oil on my lips for one last casual finishing touch.

My phone has been rapid-fire chirping, and I check it after tugging on my red rain boots. A text exchange between Noah and Ginger, planning a movie night for later today—at my house, our assumed meeting place—compiling a long list, one horror movie for Noah for every rom-com Ginger picks. I'll chime in when I get home. I leave my phone on the dresser and head downstairs to the porch.

Max is sitting on Mimmy's yellow rocking chair, swaying gently back and forth with his eyes closed. He startles when the screen door flaps behind me, jumps up to stand. The porch creaks loudly under his feet.

"You look nice," he says. "Though you looked nice before, too."

"And you have a nice voice."

"Oh god, you heard that?" He pretends to grimace, but he looks secretly pleased.

"Don't act like you're embarrassed."

He chuckles. "So, we're making a dash for it? Do you want to grab some umbrellas?"

"Nah, umbrellas will just catch on the branches and slow us down."

Without waiting for him to respond, I leap from the porch onto the slick grass and shoot off toward the woods. A few seconds pass before Max lets out a hearty *whoop* and sets off behind me.

We slip not so gracefully between the trees, laughing and shouting as we switch leads, until Max loses a sneaker in the mud and slides dramatically, catching himself with his hands just before he fully face-plants in a puddle. It's an impressive show of strength, but still—Max zero, rain two. I slow down, glance back to make sure he's okay as he shoves his filthy shoe back onto his foot—and then he springs right back up, grinning wider than ever, unfazed. But I'm too far ahead to lose now. Max's house is peeking out between sheets of rain and soggy leaves, and I push myself through to the clearing, arms raised above my head in victory. I keep moving until I'm on the porch, so determined to be first under the roof that I briefly forget to be anxious.

The Jackson home is well suited for this day. It's somehow less sinister looking in the rain—like maybe it's the contrast with yellow sunlight and blue sky that ordinarily makes the house so fearsome. I take a deep breath to refill my lungs, and there's a sharp whiff of rot and decay beneath the smell of fresh summer rain and wet earth.

"That wasn't a fair race," Max says, panting as he hops onto the porch behind me. "You had rain boots *and* you know the path better. There will definitely be a rematch."

I shrug and smooth down my hair, wringing out the end of my braid. "Whatever will make you feel better about yourself. Next time it rains, maybe you should stay inside?"

Before he can respond, the front door opens with a creak and a woman I presume must be Max's mom appears on the porch. Her skin is a darker brown than his, but she has his amber eyes and high-cut cheekbones. She's tall like Max, probably within an inch or so of his height. But when she smiles at me, it's not full and easy like his, not as happy.

"So. This must be the wonderful Calliope my son can't stop talking about?"

"I won't even try to deny that," Max says as he steps up next to me.

"Come in," his mom says, reaching out, slipping her arm loosely around my damp shoulder. "I'll get some towels. I just unearthed our extras this morning."

"Thanks, Mrs. . . ." I realize I don't know Max's last name. We haven't gotten to that stage of the friendship yet.

"Joanie. Please just call me Joanie."

We take our muddy shoes off and step inside.

My eyes adjust gradually to the dim foyer around us. It's two stories high with vaulted beams and mostly bare still, except for a few stacks of cardboard boxes and a dusty gold-framed mirror hanging on the wall opposite an old wardrobe. Stairs rise in front of us, wide wooden boards with banisters that were probably very elegant back in the day, carved deeply with twisting vines and leaves. But now the stairs sag tiredly to the left and only a few slats still hold up the banisters, like a grin missing most of its teeth—a crooked jack-o'-lantern with no eyes.

"Home sweet home." The way Joanie says it, it doesn't sound like she thinks it's all that sweet. "You two get cozy in the kitchen while I grab those towels. The kitchen is our only room that's fully set up. We have our priorities. Oh, and Max? Please wash those filthy paws of yours before you touch anything. I would have thought you were a little old to still be making mud pies. How sweet."

She smiles again, a slightly happier one this time, and then she starts up the steps, favoring the right side.

"*Mud pies.*" Max shakes his head as he turns to me. "I bet you made lots of those growing up, am I right?"

"It's a strong possibility that my childhood involved making intricate mud pies, yes."

"Knew it," Max says, laughing. Before I can think of a witty comeback, he walks off toward a door at the end of the hallway, and I follow him. Most of the kitchen looks like it hasn't been touched in years—chipped blue cabinet doors, scratched and sliced wooden countertops, a stove that's missing half of its burners. Stained linoleum tiles on the floor, paint strips flaking from the ceiling. There's no dishwasher that I can see. But there's a bright white refrigerator and a shiny black microwave. Some hints of the modern era.

"There's a new stove coming this week," Max says, watching me take it all in. "It's a work in progress."

"No, it's...charming."

"You're a bad liar." He turns on the faucet and applies a liberal amount of soap to his hands before scrubbing.

Joanie walks in then and drops a plush black towel around my shoulders, gently tucking it under my braid so it cradles my neck. "There you go, sweetie. Don't ever say there's no luxury in this old house." She moves aside, handing a second towel to Max, and then she opens the refrigerator door. "We don't have the fridge stocked yet, but I can offer you some cheese and crackers and pickles that made the trip here with us. I'm determined to get to the store this afternoon. Would you believe we *still* don't have sugar?" She shakes her head, staring vacantly into the empty refrigerator racks.

"I'm fine, Joanie, really. Don't worry about me."

"After you made my son the delicious dessert that he didn't share with me?" She kicks the door shut. "I insist. Marlow locks herself in her room all day, and I'm just so glad one of my kids isn't brooding right now."

Joanie asks pleasantries about Green Woods and my moms as she slices the pale orange cheese and spreads it on a plate with Ritz crackers and a few neon-green pickle wedges. Like Max, she doesn't seem fazed by the fact that I have two moms and no dad.

"Okay then," she says finally, setting down the plate on a round, polished kitchen table that clearly came with them from Philadelphia. "I'll leave you to it. I just wanted to make sure my boy wasn't making you up. Who knows what sorts of creatures and fairies live in those wild woods? We have our fair share of weird just in this house, that's for sure."

I look at her, willing her to elaborate. But she's already turned her back to me, walking toward the hallway door. I wait until she's on the steps to ask Max, "What kinds of weird things?"

He looks down at the plate. "Nothing. We're just used to a much newer apartment building. This house never shuts up. Creaks and groans and rattles. Like it's settling into its own death-bed or something. It just takes getting used to, that's all."

We quietly chew our cheese and pickles and crackers.

"What?" Max asks.

"What do you mean what?"

"You have something on your mind. I can tell. You have something to say about this house, but you're nervous for some reason."

"I don't know what you mean."

"Like I said—bad liar. I've only known you for a few days and I can already tell. You squinch your eyes up a little. Like this." He dramatically squints, flickering his eyelids.

"That is definitely not something I ever do."

He watches me as I slowly eat a cracker.

"Okay. Fine. Listen, it's just . . . there have always been stories about this house. Ginger and I used to freak ourselves out with it when we were younger. Daring each other to step on the porch, touch the door, dumb stuff like that. It's the local spooky haunted house. Every small town probably has one."

"What were the stories?"

I glance around the room, at the cracked window above the sink, the peeling yellow floral wallpaper. The dripping faucet, one loud *plink* every three seconds.

"People always said that someone was killed here. I don't know. No two versions of the story were ever the same. Ginger and Noah and I tried to look through newspaper archives in the library once, but we couldn't find anything. There was an old man who lived here when I was a kid. A total hermit. He died—of old age, probably. Nothing dramatic."

"Hmm," Max says. He chews the last bite of his cheese-pickle-cracker sandwich slowly before speaking again. "You finished?"

I nod.

He steps away from the table and cracks open the side kitchen door. I follow him into a closed-in glass structure that was once a sunroom, but now, with half of the glass panels gone, it's more like a back porch. There are two rusty lawn chairs set up side by side on the cracked-tile floor. Max sits in one. I sit in the other. My seat is missing two slats, and my bottom is balancing precariously in the middle.

We're both silent, listening to the rain clink against the metal roof above us.

I glance over at Max and he smiles, but his eyes look sad. Maybe—probably—because of what I said about his new home. *Good job, Calliope.* As if this place wasn't already bad enough. Throw a murder story in, too, why don't you?

I close my eyes and pretend we're anywhere but the Jackson house.

"Oh, sweet *lord*," Ginger whispers, though not quietly enough. Max and Noah are in the living room, only one thin wall away from us. Mama and Mimmy are out of the house for their monthly book club. "I am so glad you invited the new boy to movie night. You were right. He's *very* pretty."

"You didn't really need more lemonade, did you?" I ask.

"Nope. But seriously, whether you like it or not, you two have some kind of intense chemistry. He's cute and artsy and funny, and seems like your type—not that I knew what your type was before today. It sounds cliché, I know, but it's true. There's something there."

"I don't know what you're talking about." I busy myself with the lemonade pitcher, stirring in a few more chunks of sliced strawberries and a handful of raspberries.

Ginger chuckles. "*Oh*-kay. Whatever you say."

"I'm being friendly to a neighbor. He's the new kid in school for senior year."

"Very altruistic of you, being the welcoming party. That's all there is to it, I guess."

"That *is* all. And really, the three of us should be working on our friend-making skills. We won't have built-in womb buddies at college."

"I'm perfectly capable of making friends, thank you." She plucks a few raspberries from the pitcher and pops them in her mouth. "But Noah will be relieved to hear there's nothing going on between you two. Poor baby boy. He's looked so terrified all night, and I don't think it had anything to do with the cheap and gratuitous gore on the TV screen."

My stomach pinches. "He'd be okay. Even if I was interested in dating Max."

Ginger cocks her head, those green eyes squinting hard at me. "You sure about that, sweet thing?"

Before I can answer, Max interrupts us from the kitchen doorway.

"I knew it," he says. "The lemonade refreshing was all an

elaborate excuse to talk about me." He leans against the door-frame, looking like he belongs there, like it's not odd at all that he's suddenly a part of our group. "Please, don't keep me in suspense. Did I get the Ginger seal of approval? Am I officially a part of the crew?"

Ginger laughs, stepping away from me. She hoists herself up to sit on the counter, studying Max with raised eyebrows. "I'm not one for rash judgments. I might need all summer to decide."

He lets out a low whistle. "That's intense. I was nervous about making it into the Art Club, but I guess this will be the real test."

"I'm pretty sure anyone enrolled in an art class is allowed to be in the club, so actually that one won't be a test at all. And besides, if you're joining any club, it has to be Calliope's. Help her petition for solar panels and a plastic-straw ban and whatever else is on her agenda for the Environmental Club this year." Ginger pauses, then says, "So why did you move out here to a haunted house in the middle of bumblefuck anyway?"

I try to catch Ginger's eye, but she's too intent on Max to notice me.

"Well, according to old Green Woods lore, anyway," she continues when he doesn't immediately respond. "But who knows? You could say better than anyone at this point."

Max rubs his hand along the back of his neck, slowly, deliberating. He finally says, "I don't know about any ghosts living there. But a few brave humans must have come in and out over the last few years, based on the beer cans and food wrappers that were scattered around the floor. Nice welcome to the new home. That wasn't you two, was it, partying in an old abandoned house?"

He's skipped past the *why* of the move. Luckily Ginger's far more interested in the ghosts.

"I can assure you, that was not our trash," Ginger says, laughing. "We were always way too terrified to make it past the porch on our paranormal investigations. Calliope was the biggest wimp of the three of us."

"She's exaggerating," I say. "Don't listen to her." I scowl at Ginger, and this time she notices. She sticks her tongue out at me in response.

"Interesting." Max cocks his head, studying me. "Maybe that's why Calliope seemed nervous coming over today, even in broad daylight. And yours truly took it upon himself to personally destroy all cobwebs, so it wasn't that either."

"I didn't not want to be there," I say, too loudly maybe.

Max raises his right brow, smirking. "Mm-hmm."

"I promise. I'll go over there anytime."

Ginger slides off the counter. "I'm going to go check on Noah, and you two can finish up that lemonade freshening. Seriously. I actually do want more."

I turn back to the pitcher after Ginger leaves, busy myself with adding a few more raspberries to replace the ones she stole.

"Silversmith?" Max asks. "Is that your last name?"

I glance over to see him studying an old article featuring Hot Mama Flow taped to the refrigerator door.

"Yep. Mimmy was a Silver. Mama was a Smith. They lucked out with two names that worked as a combo. They would have been flipping coins otherwise."

"I like that. Your family is totally its own. Different than everyone who came before."

He's looking at the article still, a serious expression on his face.

"What's yours?" I ask.

"Martz."

Max Martz. I nod. "Solid name. I like the alliteration."

He's quiet for a moment before he turns back to me, that serious expression replaced with a smile. "Calliope Silversmith, would you go on a totally platonic non-date with me tomorrow?"

An easy question. I don't need time to consider.

"Yes."

Chapter Five

THE sun comes out the next day, blindingly bright. A good omen, I hope.

Not that I should be worried about a *non-date*, as Max put it.

But I've never flown solo, even platonically speaking. Maybe because I've had the same best friends since I was zero years old. We have other school friends, sure. Acquaintances. Ginger and Noah more so than me. But no one I hang out with unless Ginger and Noah are there, too. We're a package deal, the three of us.

This is new.

I do a few sun salutations and headstands to get the blood flowing, then take an extra-long shower. After I've brushed through my tangles and laid out three—very casual—dresses to choose from tonight, I head to my moms' room for their laundry. My eye catches on their bureau, Mimmy's favorite bottle of perfume. It's teeny tiny and yet disgustingly expensive, for special occasions only. Mama once said it's a crime for anyone to spend that kind of money on a few drops of synthetic chemicals. But she buys it for Mimmy every year like clockwork, on the day that was once their official dating anniversary, and that seven years ago became their official wedding anniversary. Or, more like a court-house marriage and a big party at the studio. Still, a *wedding*.

I have the strange urge to try some today. Just a splash.

I dab some on my wrists, sniff. Floral, earthy, wild.

"Calliope?"

I drop the bottle like it's a bag of cocaine, just as Mama steps into the room.

"Mama? Aren't you supposed to be at work?"

"Got home a few minutes ago. I gave away the rest of my classes today. I'm teaching back-to-back classes tomorrow and I wanted to get some things done around here. But...perfume, huh?" Mama puts down the yoga mat she carried in, perching her hands on her hips. "I know that's not for poor Noah's benefit."

"Why is everyone suddenly so concerned about Noah? He's not some lovesick puppy. He gets it." He *should* at least. I hope he does by now.

She gives me a sad smile. "Regardless, it's not your fault. As long as you two communicate honestly about it, you'll figure it out. But if the perfume's not for Noah...?"

"It's not *for* anybody." I flop down onto their king-size water-bed, enjoying the satisfying tidal roll that moves under me. "I'm just hanging out with the new neighbor. Max. Not a big deal. He came over with Ginger and Noah last night while you and Mimmy were at book club."

"I'm sorry I missed that. I hope he'll be picking you up tonight." It's not a question, the way she says it. He *will* be picking me up.

"Okay. But it's not a date, so no interrogation necessary."

"It's still a boy spending alone time with my little girl, and I'm allowed some curiosity. I'll be excited to meet him later," Mama says, very definitively. She turns away, moves the perfume bottle back to its rightful place on the bureau. I grab the laundry basket and leave the room.

Mama must have shared my news when Mimmy got home from the studio. They both hover in the living room, watching an episode of *I Love Lucy*. Mimmy's favorite—the great chocolate-wrapping debacle. I join them, because it's impossible to pass up on Lucy, and because she's a nice distraction.

Max had told me to be ready at six. The doorbell chimes at 5:57, startling us all. I jump up and move toward the front hallway. Mama and Mimmy stay seated on the sofa, but their eyes are definitely not on Lucy anymore.

I open the door and Max is there, a wide smile on his face.

"Hey, neighbor," he says. "You look nice. Though I liked the drenched-and-mud-soaked look, too. It's a tie." I'm glad he didn't say he preferred the yoga-sports-bra look. Mama might have had words.

"Thanks. You look nice, too." *Nice* isn't adequate. He looks much better than nice in his crisp short-sleeved white button-up shirt, tight dark blue jeans, and those glasses that only make the gold flecks in his eyes pop brighter. "Want to come in for a minute? My moms are excited to meet you."

"Of course." His eyes light up. He stands a little straighter, growing at least an inch. He is pure confidence.

"Well, hello there, neighbor!" Mimmy hops up from the sofa, rushing over to Max. She grabs his hands and wrings them effusively. "I'm Mimmy to Calliope, but you can call me Margo. I hear you approved of my cobbler recipe? That's a good start for you and me. A *very* good start."

Max pumps his hands and arms in sync with hers, kindly reciprocating the overzealous shake. "We lived near one of the best bakeries in all of Philly, I swear, and your bars were better than anything I ever ate from there. Must have been that stovia stuff you use. Who needs sugar anyway, Margo, am I right?"

I don't have the heart to tell him it's *stevia*, not *stovia*, and fortunately even Mama somehow resists a jab. Though I hear a quiet snicker behind me.

"And I'm Stella," Mama says, stepping next to Mimmy. She extends one arm, much more stoically, and Max transitions from Mimmy's hands to hers. "To be candid with you, Max, I'm the tougher mom. The one to be wary of."

"Ha ha." Mimmy elbows her. "She's kidding. She's acts hard, but she's really softer than a month-old peach. Don't you worry about her."

"I can confirm that Mama's a major softie," I chime in. "I caught her crying at an episode of *Queer Eye* last week when she thought I was out with Ginger. My only regret is not recording it before I started laughing my ass off."

Mama shakes her head. "I refuse to confirm that claim."

"And notice that she also won't deny it," Mimmy says, patting Mama's shoulder affectionately. "Anyway, we'll let you kids go light up the streets of Green Woods. But Max, we'll have to have your family over for dinner sometime. Welcome them properly."

"That would be nice, thank you."

We say our goodbyes and head out to the porch. There's a banged-up dark-mossy-green car in the driveway. One door is a completely different shade, more Easter-mint pastel.

Max notices me staring. "Yep, that's our sweet chariot for the night. My parents bought a second, newer car this weekend, now that we're country folk who need wheels to get around, but this is still my favorite. Dad always said there was no point in having a nice car in the city if you didn't buy a parking space. We got a new scrape every week. I like to see all the dings and dents as Philly leaving her mark. Each one tells a story."

"That's very artistic of you."

"It is, isn't it?" He hops down the porch steps. "What about you? Do you have a car? Hard not to around here, I would think. Like being a clipped bird."

"My moms and I share two cars, too," I say, following him down the path to our driveway. "Usually they try to work the same hours at the studio, so I get the free car. Otherwise, I can ride my bike into town. Or beg Ginger or Noah to drive me. They're both spoiled having their own cars, so it's only fair they share their good fortune with their best friend."

"Well, my mom barely drives. So sign me and this green dream machine up to chauffer you, too." He opens the minty passenger door and grandly gestures for me to enter. "It would be our honor."

As he strolls to his side of the car, I see Mama's face peeping out from behind the kitchen curtains. I stick my tongue out, and the curtain falls back in place.

"Your moms seem cool," Max says as he starts up the car. "That Stella's got some fire. I like it."

"Mama's definitely a character. She's not really that hard to please, though, as long as someone is a decent person who thinks for themselves."

Max starts slowly down our long driveway, the gravel crunching loudly under his tires. "Okay. So I have a question," he says, eyes flitting from the driveway to me, "and it might be totally rude and inappropriate and out of left field, in which case please just tell me to shut up and mind my own business and I will never ask another question like it again."

"Wow." I cross and uncross my legs, the cracked faux-leather interior sticking to my thighs. "That's quite a lead in. I'm dying to hear this question now."

"Right. Ha. Probably not the best intro." He pauses for a minute, turning left onto the main road. "But I'm just curious, wondering... is one of your moms your biological mom? Or... uh... neither? If you were adopted, that is."

"What do you think?"

He glances over. "What do *I* think?"

"Yeah. You've seen them both now. You've seen me. So, what do you think?"

"This feels like a terrible test that doesn't have any right answer."

"Well, you asked, and I'm turning the question around to you. It's my right to do that."

"True. Okay." He looks back and forth a few times,

squinting. His gaze on my lips, then my eyes, my nose, my chin. "You'd think as an artist I'd be better at this, but nope. I don't think you were adopted because you have Stella's blue eyes, but Margo's smile and freckles. And personality wise, I'd say you have some of Stella's sass, but you're warm and friendly like Margo. So you must be a genetic miracle. You're not one or the other—you're *both* of them." He dances his fingers on the steering wheel, grinning at the road ahead of us. "Am I right? Did I pass the test?"

Without thinking, I reach out and touch his wrist. "That was the best answer you could have given me."

He lets out a deep breath. "Really?"

"Yeah."

"Okay."

"The truth is, one of them *is* my biological mom. But I'm not sure if it's Mama or Mimmy. They don't want to tell me—it doesn't matter, they say. And they just happened to luck out and pick a sperm donor who was freakishly like whichever mom didn't actually contribute DNA."

"Wow."

"Yeah. I don't know anything about the donor. We just call him Frank. But I can find out, if I want. When I'm eighteen. Next month."

"So . . . will you? Find out then?"

"I'm not sure yet."

We're silent for a few minutes. Trees and houses blur past us. I take my hand off his wrist.

"I won't bring it up again," he says finally. "Unless you want to talk about it."

"I don't mind."

"Want me to tell you something hugely personal about my family so we're equal?"

"You don't have to do that."

"Nah, it's cool. So, I can officially tell you that dads aren't all they're cracked up to be. Mine cheated on my mom back in Philly. More than once. I'll spare you the gorier details—can't unload all the family drama at once."

"I'm sorry," I say, but I'm not sure if those are the right or best words.

He nods. "Thanks. Anyway, long story short, he begged her back, and they decided moving would be a fresh start for the whole family. But they're definitely not happy, so I didn't see the point in trying to fix things. I freaked out about leaving Philly. Threatened to move in with some friends so I could stay there. I didn't want to put Mom through that, though. Or Marlow. So I sucked it up and came along."

The car stops, and I realize we're in town, parked along Main Street. The bright neon sign for Mario's Pizzeria lights up my side of the car with a faint red-and-green glow.

"Don't worry. We're not eating inside. The photos I found online looked too depressing. But I did compare reviews for all four pizza places in town—a remarkable number, really, considering the only other option was Chinese or a deli—and Mario's came out tops. Your moms let you eat cheese, right?"

"Yes, they *let* me. Well, that's if Mama milked the cow and curdled it on her own."

His jaw drops.

"I'm kidding. Yes, cheese is great. I ate delicious cheese and pickle cracker sandwiches at your house, remember? My moms are pro–small farm and local and we're not big meat eaters at home, but even they occasionally can't resist some Mario's. Your assessment was good. Some people say Vinnie's is better, but the sauce is way too sweet."

"Great. Nailed it. I'll be right back. You wait here."

I watch him as he waits in the storefront, until the cashier must have called his name and he disappears from sight.

He gets back in the car a few minutes later with a pizza box and a paper bag, and we drive some more. I don't ask where to. I like the surprise of it all. I like that I'm in my same small, dusty town, but it feels exciting tonight. I don't recall ever feeling that way about Green Woods before.

We pull into the dirt lane that leads to the local lake. It's not much—a nature loop around the rocky beach, a few picnic tables, a grill I've never seen anyone use, a creaky set of swings, and a long dock for fishing. But twilight at the lake is far better than sitting in the plastic chairs at Mario's, where you can see every pore and stray eyebrow hair on your dining companion's face, thanks to the glaring fluorescent lights.

"I know it's kind of underwhelming for a first official friend outing," Max says, "but in all fairness, options within a reasonable driving range were limited. I needed to leave our woods, though. I had to escape my house's gravitational pull for at least a few hours."

I would want to escape, too, if I were him. Every day. "Nah, city boy did well. Trust me, I understand the Green Woods limitations. You do the best with what you have."

Max pulls a quilt from the back seat and I grab the food. It's a crowded night here, joggers running the loop, kids kicking balls and throwing Frisbees, couples sprawled on blankets. We wander around the path, dodging people and flying objects, until we find an empty grassy patch at the water's edge.

"Second-best view in town," he says, spreading the blanket.

"Eh. Third. I like our pond, personally. It's intensely green. You can just picture singing water pixies in frilly tulle skirts doing choreographed swims in it at night."

Max whistles, a perfect whistle, smooth and even, high but not screechy. "I gotta see this pond of yours. Sounds like a real-life Disney movie."

"Pretty much. My own little backyard fairy tale."

Max opens the box to reveal a large pesto and spinach and broccoli rabe pizza. *"Extra green,"* he says. "I assumed you would approve." And then he empties the bag—mozzarella sticks and marinara sauce for dipping, two glass bottles of Coke, and one massive chocolate cannoli.

We eat then, mostly in silence. I'm content with my pizza and people watching, and Max seems to be, too.

"Do you think you'll go to a college near here?" he asks, dipping his last sliver of crust in the marinara.

"Maybe? It's hard to say. I can't imagine being too far away from Mama and Mimmy. And I need to be near woods and fields. But I also can't imagine not seeing more of the world."

"It does seem like you kind of love it here. You're proud of it."

"Proud of some things. Mostly nature related. The closed-minded people? And the lack of good restaurants? Not so much. But this pizza is good. And some of the people are, too. A lot of them, actually. I probably don't spend enough time with anyone besides Ginger and Noah."

"And me now. Thank god I came along. You needed some diversity."

"And you. Yes."

"So, speaking of *diversity*, am I going to be the only Black kid in school?" He glances at the people scattered around us in the grass. "From what I can tell, it's a sea of white here."

I finish my half of the cannoli and wipe my hands on my legs. "No. I mean, not the *only* one. But it's definitely a sea of white, as you put it. White and Christian or white and not religious. Maybe we have a closet Wiccan or two. But there aren't a lot of outliers. We're pretty...limited. Definitely lacking in any real diversity."

"Got it. I assumed. No offense."

"None taken. Like I said. Proud of the trees and the pond and the lake and the fields."

"Ginger seems cool. And your moms. Noah, too, I guess, though I kind of got the feeling that he isn't psyched to have me around."

"That's not true," I say, the words too fast, slippery on my tongue.

His lips quirk. "You sure about that?"

"Yeah. He just takes a while to warm up to strangers."

"Whatever you say."

"Really. He's a great person. He just..."

"Is madly in love with you?"

I open my mouth. My throat constricts.

Max laughs. "Yep. Knew it."

"We've been best friends my whole life," I say quietly. "That's all it can ever be."

"I get it. It's a lot of history. Is he... part of the reason for your *rule*?"

"Noah knows I wouldn't date him with or without the rule. And maybe not dating anyone else either feels... easier somehow. But I can't live to protect his feelings. The rule is about what's best for me. Right now. Even if, maybe, he was a little bit of the reason. When I first came up with the rule." I've never admitted that before, not out loud.

"We don't have to talk about it anymore. It's not really my business. I was just curious. About Noah."

"It's okay. I don't mind talking about it." And then, before I can stop myself: "What about you? Did you date a lot in Philly?"

"Not a lot. But I dated. My last date was a few months ago at a way-overpriced and not particularly delicious Mediterranean restaurant that had a rat run out of the kitchen right in front of us mid-meal."

"Did the dinner conversation make up for the rat poop you ingested in your hummus?"

"Nah, the hummus was *way* better. No second date. To be honest, there usually wasn't."

"Why?"

He shrugs. "Maybe I'm more like you than I realized."

"Meaning?"

"Dating in high school can seem . . . silly, I guess. People fall in and out of love in a week. Then they date each other's best friends. Everyone talks about *forever* as if they actually believe any of the words they're saying."

"Whoa. I had you pegged as a total sweet-talking romantic. It turns out you're even more jaded than me."

His laugh is so loud people on nearby blankets turn to stare. "Not jaded. Just honest. Realistic. I don't have any rules against dating. I just haven't expected any of my dates to end up being my soul mate. That's all."

"That sounds reasonable enough."

"Thank you. We can cruise through senior year together single and above it all."

I lift my Coke bottle and so does he, our glasses clinking in solidarity.

He swigs the last of his Coke and lies back on the blanket, arms tucked behind his head.

I fall back, too.

The park is clearing around us, families packing up their bags and corralling screaming kids. Streetlights flick on along the perimeter of the path, dots of hazy light in the lengthening shadows. The last remnants of hot-pink sun are brushing against the tips of the trees as the moon moves to center stage.

"Park's closing." I jolt upright to see a heavily bearded park ranger hovering above us. "Gate closes after sunset." He folds his arms over his brown uniform—looking like a grown-up Boy Scout on a power trip—and gives us one last warning glance before moving on to the next blanket.

"Yes, sir," I say. Too obediently. Max chuckles under his breath. I jump to my feet, scurrying to pack up the food scraps and garbage.

"Even more reason to try out your pond next time," Max says, folding the blanket into a neat triangle. "I'm assuming you don't employ your own rangers there?"

I laugh. "We have Mama. No need to employ anyone else."

We drive home with the windows down, sweet summer air humming through the car. Fireflies flicker like fairy lights in the trees as we turn onto our road.

Max slowly pulls up to my house and parks the car. He taps his fingers against the steering wheel, slow thrumming beats. Crickets and cicadas chatter all around us, frogs croak, a lone bird sings.

"Thank you," he says, cutting through the noisy summer soundtrack.

"For what?"

"For hanging out with me tonight."

"Of course." I turn toward the door and reach for the handle, even though I'm not ready to say good night.

"This sounds cheesy as hell, but I'm saying it anyway."

I look back at Max. "I'm okay with cheesy."

"I miss home. Philly. The house is a disaster. My family's maybe an even bigger disaster—and that's saying something. But I'm glad I'm here now. I'm glad I met you."

Chapter Six

MAX and I don't make plans. We don't call or text. But the rest of the week when I'm not at work, we crisscross back and forth through the woods. We find each other. We walk, we talk, we watch TV and eat Mimmy's baked goods. His parents gave him the summer off from finding a job—a perk of moving against his will—so he has lots of hours to fill outside of his painting projects. And it seems like he wants to fill those hours with me.

Ginger joins us, too, sometimes. Noah's been busy. But I always invite them at least.

I want this summer to be about them. Us. Just like always.

But I want this summer to be about Max, too.

Friendship, old and new—or silver and gold, like that old song we sang in my Girl Scout days. There's nothing wrong with that.

It's been an endless Saturday morning working the reception desk at the yoga studio. It's only 10:53, and I've swiped the membership card of every mother in town I've known my whole life—including Noah's mom, Beverly—finished all the laundry, mopped the lobby and locker room, and color coded the printed schedule for next week with a rainbow of highlighters. Mama's in the middle of a brutal ninety-minute flow class, Salt-N-Pepa's "Push It" pulsing from her studio. Those more delicate yogis expecting soothing whispers and essential oils and quiet chanting music in the background would find themselves sorely disappointed in one of Mama's classes. Meditative, restorative yoga is Mimmy's department at Hot Mama Flow.

The phone rings, Mimmy checking in on her day off. "Everything going okay? Did you get the washer to work? The knob can be a little finnicky, I've been putting it right on the edge between permanent press and—"

"Mimmy," I say, sighing. I hop up to sit on the front desk, legs dangling over the construction-cone-orange *YOGA EVERY DAMN DAY* sign taped under the register. "You need to learn to enjoy your rare days away from this place. That's why I'm here. I got this. It's nothing but Zen here. Only one broken neck so far this morning. We're totally good."

"Oh, well, that's a relief! A broken neck, *psh*. A handstand is only exciting because of the risks! I broke my nose the first time I got up in the air." She's most likely grinning to herself as she rubs the tiny, entirely negligible bump on her nose, her war trophy she reminds me of at least once a week.

We say our goodbyes and I jump down from the counter, pick a few dead leaves off the fiddle-leaf fig tree next to me, wonder what in the world I'm going to do for six more hours. I should have brought a book.

I pull out my phone to text Ginger, but because we are cosmically connected, she chooses that exact moment to strut through the front door, a little tinny gong sounding as it opens and closes. She's in her typical yoga attire: animal-print leggings—a mashup of giraffe spots and zebra stripes—and a neon-pink sports bra.

"Hey, doll," she says, giving me a full-body squeeze. "I fig-ured you'd be bored by now. I had the predawn shift at the diner today and chugged way too much coffee for a nap. So lucky you, here I am."

"You know the next class doesn't start for an hour, though, right? I assume based on the fact that you're wearing a bra for a shirt that you're planning on actually sweating on a mat at some point."

"Eh, I don't really care. I was trying to fit in with the aesthetic, plus"—she wiggles her eyebrows, grinning at me—"you told me Penelope's mom comes in some weekends for classes. Maybe her lovely daughter will be getting tired of endless summer days."

"Mm-hmm, right, so not here to see me at all then?"

"Not true," she says, grabbing a spare yoga mat from the shelf by the counter and unrolling it on the floor. She plops down, mak-ing herself at home in the middle of the lobby. "Though I do feel like I've barely seen you this week."

"You've barely seen me? We had movie night Monday. You came over for lunch on Wednesday. And then we boiled ourselves in the hot pool for a few hours on Thursday."

"Okay, so yes, I technically *saw* you. But Max was there every time. I couldn't pry. Or talk about my raging cramps. Or the hot dream I had about making out with some random cheerleader behind the bleachers."

"You can talk about your period with Max—you talk about it all the time in front of Noah. And you can talk about your dreams, too."

"Firstly, Noah doesn't count. And, um, did you hear me say *cheerleader*? I'm not admitting that out loud to anyone else. It's not my brand."

I sit next to her on the yoga mat and stare her down. "What's definitely *not* your brand is to not speak your mind. Do you think I'm spending too much time with Max?"

She holds out her hand, studying her fingers—each nail a different shade of green. "No. I'm not saying that."

"I want to spend time with all three of you. That's the whole point."

"The whole point of not dating, you mean?" She smirks, batting her corn-silk lashes at me.

"We don't like each other like that."

"Sure, girlfriend. Whatever you say." Her smirk is still there, smirkier than ever. "I want you to have that alone time. I'm giving you that—with my blessing. Because if there's something there, you should admit it. *Embrace* it. Just give me some solo time once in a while to ramble on about secretive, sexy womanly things, okay?"

"Of course we can hang out, just you and me. But there's nothing to admit. I've known him for a *week*."

She waves her hand, dismissing the subject. "What about tomorrow? The Fourth? Are we still watching together from the top of the hill?" It's the best view in town for the Green Woods fireworks. The three of us go there every year for the holiday—a time-honored tradition.

My mouth drops. I look over at her. "You shouldn't even have to ask. The Fourth is sacred."

"Just checking. I hope Noah comes."

"Um. Why wouldn't he?"

"He's..."

"He's what? Don't tell me he has to work. I will personally drag him out of the sandwich line at Wawa if he's not at my house tomorrow evening."

She scoots closer to me, leans her head on my shoulder. I get a strong whiff of her trademark ginger-coconut shampoo. It smells endlessly better than Mimmy's overpriced perfume. "No, not work. I think it's just hard for him—having you spend time with another boy, even if it's *platonic*." I ignore the emphasis. "We tried to hang out yesterday just the two of us while you were at the studio, and it was like a tricycle with a wobbly flat tire on one of the back wheels. We could move, kind of, but not very gracefully and not for very long. I bowed out before we could crash. Lied and told him I felt a migraine coming on. I've never had a migraine in my life."

"Really?" I laugh. "Noah and I hang out one on one and it's fine. You've known him your whole life. How can it possibly be awkward?"

She jabs her pointy elbow into my side. "Trust me, it just is without you. You're our secret ingredient. Our magic sauce. Don't question it. It's a compliment."

"I'm honored, I guess. Even if it's weird to me."

"Anyway, moving on, you realize you turn eighteen this month? We should start planning for it now to make sure it's appropriately epic. What about a weekend in New York? Do you think the moms would be on board?"

"I don't know. And I don't care that much, honestly. It doesn't have to be a big deal. I'd rather wait and celebrate with you on your birthday. I don't mind sharing."

She lifts her head from my shoulder, studying me with narrowed eyes. "Come on. You know most people are hugely excited about turning eighteen, right? It's a momentous rite of passage."

I shrug, looking down. "It's not really that life changing."

"Uh-huh. Sure. Is there something you're not saying here, Calliope Silversmith? Because it seems to me like you have a weird grudge against this particular birthday."

"Maybe. Yes." I press my fingernails into the spongy yoga mat beneath us. "Eighteen means I can make contact with Frank. If I want."

Her eyes widen. "Oh. Right."

"What do you think I should do?"

She's silent for a moment. A silent Ginger is a rarity. "I don't know," she says finally. "I mean he's half of your DNA, sure, but he's also nothing in every other way that matters. You have the best parents in the universe."

I look up at her. "I know."

"You have to do what you need to do, Calliope."

Do I *need* to know who he is? Or do I *want* to? Is there a difference?

"Would you do it if you were me?" I ask.

"If I found out now that my dad wasn't really my dad, would I want to know the biological one? I don't know. Probably not. Maybe. I'd be afraid to hurt my dad. But it's totally different, because you've known all along. It was scientific and planned, not some lusty one-night stand."

"Yeah."

"You don't have to decide right now, but I don't think there's a wrong or right answer."

"I just... I don't know, I mean I could request to be in touch, and then go to meet him and find out he's a terrible asshole who hates everyone and everything and hits kittens and bunnies with bats in his spare time. Or I could wait years to do it, and then find out he died a little after my eighteenth birthday, doing something absurdly heroic, like saving a baby from a burning building, and I'll never have the chance to know him because I was too indecisive and afraid."

"Okay. No way did you come from a bat wielder. I can guarantee you that. You refuse to kill spiders. Plus, you can't play any sports. Bats are out."

We sit for a moment, both lost in our own thoughts.

"I think it's perfectly okay to be curious," she says at last, talking as quietly as I've ever heard Ginger talk. "It's nothing to be ashamed of. And it doesn't mean you don't love the moms enough. Margo would understand. Stella, too, even if she gets all hot about it at first. They'll get over it. Both of them." She wraps an arm around me, rubbing circles on my back. "Like I said, you don't have to decide this month. Or this year. Do it on your own time. But don't let it ruin your eighteenth birthday. Because that would be a goddamn shame."

It sounds so simple when she puts it like that. But it's not. It's not simple at all.

Because how can I possibly decide what's worse, wondering or knowing? I can't.

The gong sounds as the door swings open. It's our regular mailman, delivering a stack of bills and promotional flyers. I make small talk with him about the heat, the holiday tomorrow. After he leaves Ginger is watching me, and I'm relieved to hear Mama harmonizing the closing chant. Sweaty, dripping women start filing into the lobby, towels wrapped around their necks. Beverly stops to say hello on her way out, and Ginger keeps up the conversation for the both of us, luckily, describing an unruly drunk diner from the morning in vivid detail. I wonder if Noah has told Beverly about Max. If she's worried about any romantic inclinations.

Ginger hangs around until the next class starts—no Mrs. Park or Penelope, sadly—and then declares the coffee buzz is gone and she needs some sleep.

"I'm being forced into a family dinner out tonight for my parents' anniversary. Ugh. But I *will* see you tomorrow," she says, hugging me tight. "And tell Max he's not done winning me over yet. Maybe some delicious holiday treats will help the cause."

"I will pass that message on."

The afternoon is quiet without Ginger. Too quiet.

Mama chats with me between classes, Mimmy calls two more times. Noah texts me a picture of a vegan cheesesteak he had for lunch in Philly during his lesson break. I remind him that our plan for the Fourth is the same as always.

But I can't stop thinking about the conversation. Frank. Wondering versus knowing.

If wondering means this awful endless loop forever, maybe that gives me my answer.

Max is the first to arrive.

The Fourth is the hottest day of summer so far, the air like fierce, hungry flames licking at my skin. I'm sprawled in the hammock when he emerges from the woods, my red-and-white polka-dot dress hitched up around my thighs for an extra sprinkle of air. I yank it down. The sun hits Max straight on, and he reaches up to shield his eyes, looking for me. I give a lazy wave, and he smiles as he starts toward me.

He took Ginger's message to heart, his arms filled with bags—an arsenal of treats that he proudly displays when he gets to the hammock. Red-white-and-blue-iced cupcakes, red *and* blue raspberry Twizzlers, blue corn chips, star-spangled sugar cookies, and an alarmingly bright red soda that most definitely does not come from nature.

"It looks like you cleared out the festive shelves at Walmart."

"It was quite an expedition. I feel like a real suburbanite now."

"Don't be too proud. I'm not sure discovering Walmart is a badge of honor. Mama would kill you, by the way, if she saw those nutrition labels. You're lucky she and Mimmy are at a barbecue right now—some of their yoga students begged them to come. But we have to eat all the evidence before they get home."

"We'll dump any leftover cupcakes off the top of the hill. Promise."

He drops the bags on the ground and sits next to me. I instinctively move closer to the opposite side.

"Do you realize we only met a week ago?" I ask. "And now we hang out every day." I've been thinking about that since my talk with Ginger yesterday—how has it only been a *week*? I've known classmates for twelve years and I know them far less than I do Max.

"No. A week and *two days*."

"How could I forget those two days?"

"Two days can change everything. One day I lived in Philly. The next day I lived here, across the woods from *you*."

I bite my lip. I don't want to overanalyze, but I can't stop myself from saying, "Do you think it's weird, though? How quickly we became friends?"

"Weird? No. Normal? I don't know. What's normal? Maybe sometimes it just happens this way. People just...click."

Something is definitely clicking. I want to say *I feel like I've known you forever*, but I can't stand the idea of sounding so cliché, no matter how true it might be. "I'm okay with not being normal," I say instead.

"Yeah? Good. Me too. I think—"

The sound of a throat clearing cuts in, stopping whatever Max is about to say.

I startle and push myself more upright, nearly toppling from the hammock as it swings back. My dress has hitched up again in the shuffle, my legs flailing in the air. I frantically tug the dress down with one hand as I attempt to balance against the ground with the other. Max is reaching for me to help, but he tumbles over the side, crashing to the ground in a remarkably loud and ungraceful way. We both burst out laughing.

When I finally pull myself together, I realize Noah is standing just a few feet away. He looks like he would rather be anywhere else in the world but here, watching me with Max.

"Noah! Happy Fourth!" I say, too enthusiastically. Noah lifts his hand in a stiff wave.

"Hey, buddy," Max says, still flat on the grass next to the hammock. He gets a subtle nod in response.

I run to Noah, wrapping him in a hug. "I'm glad you could make it."

"It's tradition." He pulls back, his eyes on the ground.

"Ginger should be here soon."

"Cool."

I feel it then, the awkwardness I told Ginger wasn't possible. Not after so many years. But I somehow cannot think of a single thing to say that isn't about the weather. Noah nods listlessly as I ramble on about the heat-wave pattern sweeping in for the week, quoting the meteorologist Mimmy had playing during breakfast this morning. Max sits up, his head tilted in amusement as he studies me with his artist eyes. I turn away from both of them to tear open the cookie packet and shove a patriotic star into my mouth.

Chewing is much better than talking. Noah and Max take my lead.

We're all a few cookies and Twizzlers deep—sugar rushing through my veins—when Ginger emerges from around the side of the house. I run to her and hug her like we're reuniting after months apart. Ginger laughs and picks me up, spins me until we both flop onto the grass.

We carry blankets and snacks and speakers on our trek across the creek and up the hill. Max sings a loud song about tramping through the dark woods that I'm fairly positive he is making up as he goes. Ginger hums along with him, chiming in with her own creative words for the chorus. They swing side by side up the narrow path like old friends. Noah and I follow quietly in their wake.

When we all make it to the top, Ginger and I lay out the blankets. Max sets up the speakers, fiddling with the cord that attaches to his phone. Noah stares out over the valley.

I could pull him aside. Ask what's wrong. But I don't. I'm pretty sure I already know the answer.

Max was smart enough to bring a pack of cards. We play rummy and war and take turns DJ'ing bad nineties songs. I eat more cookies and smile and make jokes. I fill any silences Noah leaves trailing behind him, and pretend that we're a happy group of friends with no awkward complications.

There shouldn't be any complications. There *aren't* any. Noah and Max are both my friends. I'm allowed that, aren't I?

I'm allowed to not feel guilty for not being in love with Noah.

It's a relief when the sun finally dips below the hills on our side of the valley. Darkness settles in thickly around us, a comforting veil of obscurity. I watch as dots of hazy light flick on in town like a giant, messy constellation.

The first firework goes off.

I hear the bang shudder against the hills before I see the spark arching above us. My favorite kind—white-gold shimmers that erupt gracefully into the shape of a sprawling weeping willow. Flickering embers do a lazy dance against the black sky for a moment before slowly blinking out, like they were never there at all.

We rank them, one to ten, though only Max has ever seen fireworks outside of Green Woods. Our scores are relative. I'm still picky, though—I reserve my tens for the handful of other willowlike displays.

It feels like the show has only just begun when the world around us goes silent and dark. The holiday is over.

"Decent year," Ginger says as we pack up our supplies, "though I wonder how many thousands the town shelled out for that? I would have voted for a new town pool or something, personally. But no one asked me, did they?"

Our descent down the hill is more subdued. We're careful to watch our steps, shining our phone flashlights on the rocky path ahead of us.

Noah says goodbye as soon as we're at the bottom.

Ginger follows soon after with a suspicious smirk and a yawn that feels entirely forced.

I feel wide awake still, probably from the overdose of sugar. I'm not ready to end the night. I tell Max he's welcome to stay.

He does.

I unfold the blankets and spread them out in my yard. We lie on our backs, each on our separate blanket. I close my eyes, and this—the night creatures serenading us, the heavy, honeysuckle-soaked air, the person lying next to me—is the perfect ending to a long summer day.

"Even without the fireworks, the sky is pretty magical here," Max says. "I'm not sure I'll ever get used to seeing so many stars."

I open my eyes and stare out at the woods in front of us, the trees wispy silhouettes against the pinpricks of moonbeams filtering through the leaves.

Our woods.

They've always felt like mine—and Mimmy's and Mama's. A magical bubble. But not anymore. These woods belong to Max now, too. The trees, the creek, the hill, the stars. Ours.

Chapter Seven

"**I'M** excited to meet your dad," I say, because it seems polite—and because the silence in this broken sunroom is too deafening.

Max grunts in reply and stares off into the scraggly backyard.

He was unusually sullen this morning when he came over bright and early to invite me to his house for dinner. With his family. His *whole* family. His dad's idea, he made sure to clarify up front. Not his. And he's still sullen now.

It's a Max I haven't seen before. And it's also a stark reminder that although we seem to have a lot in common, there's still a lot you can't know about someone in two weeks. Two weeks to the day—the anniversary of his first appearance in our clearing.

I've always understood Ginger and Noah inside and out, without having to try. But I like this—learning about someone from scratch. Like putting together an infinity-size puzzle.

"Should I go see if your mom needs any help?" I am desperate to make time pass more quickly—I want dinner to start so it can be over. I want Max to be Max again.

He snorts. "Help unpack the takeout boxes? I think she's got it covered."

"Oh. Okay." I pick at the fraying seat bottom of the lawn chair, pulling at a long string.

The front door closes with a loud thud. An unfamiliar male

voice calls out words I can't decipher. Max's whole body stiffens, hands clenching the rusted armrests. Heavy footsteps move through the foyer, start up the creaking stairs.

"Is he really that bad?" I ask quietly.

"*Yes*. No." He shakes his head. "Sometimes. You'll like him, probably. He's charming. That's the problem. He's friendly enough—it's not like he beats us or anything like that. But he's a snake. You've noticed he's never really around?"

I nod. We spend more time at my house than his, but I've been here enough now. Joanie, Marlow, no dad.

"Yeah, well, part of the deal when we moved here was that he'd work remotely, at least most of the time. That hasn't happened yet. He's going in every day, working late. He claims he needs to be there right now to help with some big case . . . I don't know, though. We've only been here a short time, but I'm not convinced he really ended things with his extracurricular special friend. I have no proof. We've just heard it all before. And I am personally over trusting a single thing he says."

"I'm sorry," I say, because I'm not sure how else to respond. The idea of Mimmy or Mama cheating is as inconceivable as the idea of aliens coming to attack Green Woods.

"I'm sorry for my mom. She deserves better."

I blink at a shadow in the corner, the scalloped edges of a broken pane. There's sunlight outside still, but it's dim in here. Like the light is afraid to trespass. I haven't seen any ghosts here yet—though even without this house, Max's family is haunted. They have enough ghosts of their own already.

"Dinner." Joanie has suddenly materialized in the doorway, head cocked to the side as she watches us. Her bare feet made no sound on the hallway floorboards.

We both jump up from our seats. The chairs scratch against the tiled floor.

"Apologies. I didn't mean to scare you." She stops talking, pinches her lips shut. And then she turns and leaves the room.

Max is silent for a moment. I wonder how long Joanie was standing there, and if she heard what we were talking about. I wonder if Max is wondering this, too.

He sighs then, takes a step toward the door. "And so the night begins..."

There's a white man standing by their kitchen table.

He's ordinary looking—neatly gelled salt-and-pepper hair, slight beard, medium build, wearing the standard middle-aged-man work uniform, a plaid button-up shirt and khakis, both slightly wrinkled.

I look from Joanie to Marlow to Max. It's true that they're both lighter skinned than Joanie, but I hadn't thought about their father's genes before now.

"Well, hello there, Calliope." He grins at me. He has a gap between his teeth, too. And Max's pronounced jawline, his heavy brows and wide-set eyes. "Elliot Jackson," he says, extending his hand. "It's a pleasure to finally meet you."

Elliot *Jackson*. Not Martz. Elliot Jackson.

Max is a Jackson.

His family moving to this house wasn't random.

The stories—they must be about his family.

Old Mr. Jackson . . . was he . . . Elliot's *dad*? Max's grandfather?

I look down at Elliot's hand and I remember to put my hand out, too, and we shake.

It shouldn't matter. Martz, Jackson, it doesn't change who Max is. I know that better than anyone. Silver, Smith, *Silversmith*. But I do have questions . . . so many questions—like why Max didn't tell me.

"It sounds like my son and you have really hit it off," Elliot says. "He's probably sorry we didn't move into the family estate years ago now." He chuckles, glancing over at Max with what looks to me like a loving smile.

Max responds with a thin-lipped, "Ha."

"So, you grew up here?" I ask Elliot, still trying to make sense of all this new information.

"I did. Quite a lot of memories here in this old shack."

There's a pause. I want to ask more: *Excuse me, Elliot, but was anyone in your family murdered in this house?* Probably not polite dinner conversation, though.

"Max said you like Mario's," Joanie says then, motioning us toward the table. There's a platter of lasagna, a plate of stuffed shells, salad, garlic knots. "I wanted to cook, but I just can't get used to this kitchen yet."

"You weren't used to our kitchen in Philly after more than a decade," Elliot says, winking at me. I look away, not wanting to displease him or Joanie with the wrong response.

Joanie acts like she didn't hear him, busying herself with setting out five plates. Elliot grabs a beer from the fridge, Joanie pours a tall glass of red wine. We all settle in around the table. Joanie and Marlow sit across from me, and I end up between Max and Elliot. Lucky me.

Elliot at least speaks through most of the meal, which means I can just chew and nod. He talks first about his new passion for long morning runs, since there's no "adequate" gym nearby. And then he's giving us—or mostly me—an intricately detailed account of his job as a lawyer in Philly. Too intricate, maybe. And with too much justification for why it'll be hard to work remotely in the foreseeable future. When he suggests he may need to rent a small studio apartment in the city to use as a "crash pad" on some weeknights, I think Max might choke on his garlic knot. I hand him my full glass of water.

"Let's not get ahead of ourselves," Joanie says coolly, pushing away her half-eaten plate of lasagna. "The drive isn't that far. And I'm sure once this case is done, you and the team can figure out creative ways to stay in touch while you work from here."

"We'll see," Elliot says, digging in for a second helping of shells. "So, Calliope, I've been a windbag long enough. I want to hear more about you."

"Me?" I drop my fork. It clanks loudly against my plate.

"You're a senior, Max tells me. What are you thinking you'll do after you graduate? Big plans? I know when I was your age, leaving Green Woods was about the only thing I cared about.

Dreamed about it every night." He smiles fondly, shaking his head as he takes a large, cheesy bite.

"I actually love this place," I say, which is mostly true.

Elliot puts his hand up. "I meant no offense. My apologies if I misspoke."

"No, it's fine." I pick my fork back up, scrape at some congealing ricotta on my plate. "I just think the simple things in life are the most important parts. And it's easier to keep sight of that here. I'm not saying I definitely want to live in Green Woods forever. Just that it's not the worst place to be. There are far worse in this world, I bet."

Max reaches over, like he's about to grab my hand. But then he stops himself, reaches for his fork instead.

When Elliot doesn't respond, I keep going: "I have two amazing moms who run their own yoga and fitness studio in town—you could try it sometime, actually, if you get tired of running—and have taught me to always be *me*, to think for myself no matter what. I have two best friends I'd do anything for. And I live in a cozy old house in the middle of magical woods surrounded by a creek and a pond and birds and flowers and trees. That—that is what matters to me." I stab at another stuffed shell. "I love to read and write, and I care about nature and our planet. I want to study something useful. Do some good in our too hot, dirty world." I take an enormous bite, signaling that I'm done. We've covered the essentials.

Elliot takes a minute before saying, "Well, then, I'm glad. It sounds like my son has found a strong and grounded person to date. I couldn't have asked for anything better."

I cough, nearly spitting out the shell in my mouth.

"Dad, what the hell?" Max says. "Calliope and I are *friends*. Not dating. And even if we were together, which we're definitely not"—he shoots me a panicked, apologetic look—"I certainly wouldn't need your approval. You don't deserve to have an opinion, not about my relationships. You should focus more on your own."

Elliot turns an inhuman shade of red and stares at his plate like he's fantasizing about smashing it into a thousand tiny pieces. Joanie stands up, too abruptly, rattling the table and knocking over her glass of wine onto Marlow's lap. Marlow yells about ruining her new white romper, directing an ugly string of foul words at everyone and no one. Max is still and silent next to me and I can't bring myself to look over at him.

I stare out the window behind Joanie's empty seat and wish I was on the other side of the woods. I'm pretty certain that Max is wishing the same thing.

Soon it's only the two of us left in the kitchen. Everyone else has scattered. The food is still on the table, looking hard and dry by now. I don't know what else to do, so I stand up and start clearing away the plates.

"You don't have to do that." Max sighs, dropping his head in his hands. "I'm sorry."

"For what?"

"Well, for one, sorry that my dad thought we were dating. I swear, I never said that to anyone. He just doesn't pay attention."

I shake my head. "You don't have to apologize. That's on your dad."

"I feel like I do. I mean, I knew it wouldn't be great tonight. It never is with this family. But this was a low, even for us."

I turn on the tap and water spits at my wrist for a few seconds before there's a long rattle and then, finally, a steady stream of cloudy-looking water. I'm glad I didn't drink any during dinner.

"I do have a question for you, though," I say, because I can't stop thinking about the fact that Max is a Jackson.

"Sure. You earned it, sitting through that dinner."

I finish scrubbing a dish, put it in the drying rack. "Why did you say your last name is Martz? If your dad—and you—are Jacksons?" I turn to face him.

"Oh. Right. That." He looks up at me, almost smiling. Relieved, maybe, that this was the question I needed to ask. "My legal name *is* Max Martz. It's my mom's last name. She hadn't been with my dad long when she got pregnant, and the relationship wasn't exactly smooth sailing in those early days. Let's be real—it's never been smooth sailing for them. So when she had me, she wanted me to keep her name. Just in case she kicked him to the curb, I guess. Didn't want him tied to me, or her, forever. Even when they ended up getting married, she kept Martz. Too much of a hassle to change, she says, and who cares what the legal name is? Marlow is a Jackson, though. They fight about it sometimes, my parents—my dad wants ours changed. Wants us all to be the *same*. But nope, hasn't happened. Never will."

"Ah. Got it." It's just a name, I know that. A word. But still, I can't imagine not sharing a last name with Mama and Mimmy. "You like to go by Martz, though?"

He laughs. "I like to be as different from my dad as I can be. So, yes. I pick Martz. I pick my mom's blood whenever I can."

I nod and turn back to the sink. Start on another dish. There's still something niggling at me, though. "Why did you never mention your family history, when the house came up? Or when I told you about your grandfather dying here?"

He pauses, and then, "I guess I didn't want to scare you away." He says it so quietly, I have to turn off the water to hear him.

"What?"

He stands up, takes a few tentative steps toward me. "I should have been honest with you. But... I'm ashamed, Calliope. Of my dad. This house. Our family history. I was worried you wouldn't want to be friends. Not with a *Jackson*."

"Of course I still want to be friends with you."

"You sure?"

"I'm sure."

He grins at me. Childlike. Simple. The Max I know. The Max he is when he's away from this house. Max Martz.

There's a radio on the counter that looks like it might have predated the invention of television. I switch it on, shocked when music actually plays. Laced with static and a strange humming noise, but still—music.

I don't recognize the song, something old and jazzy, but I hum along as I fill the sink with more hot water and soap. Max picks up the dish towel and starts improvising lyrics to the song—one of his finest talents, I'm learning. We wash and dry and I stop humming so I can just listen to him.

I forget where we are. I forget about any ghosts.

The rest of the night falls away.

Max walks me home through the woods. I tell him I'm fine on my own—I've walked these woods my whole life—but he insists. It's after midnight, and who knows what kinds of creatures might lurk in the shadows.

When we reach my porch steps, he asks if he can hug me good night.

I say yes.

The hug feels good. Not everyone is a great hugger, but with Max—it's like pulling on your favorite sweater on the first cold October day. I savor it for a moment before I let him go.

It's sweltering when I get upstairs to my room, and I push my window up higher, hoping to catch more breeze. Or any breeze at all. I undress and lie in bed, but I can't sleep.

My mind plays back through the night. The hug good night. The dishes. The dinner. I think about Elliot, and how much power he has to make Max unhappy. Joanie and Marlow, too.

Meeting Elliot—meeting a dad like *him*—has me thinking about Frank again, too.

Eighteen. In less than two weeks. Eleven days, to be exact.

If there are dads like Elliot in the world, maybe I'm better off never knowing Frank.

But then ... there are lots of great dads, too. I just haven't met that many of them. Noah's dad is pretty decent. And I like Ginger's dad way more than I like her mom.

Eleven days.

It's true, I can make the decision anytime I want, ten months from now, ten years. I can keep making lists in my notebook for days on end. I can keep thinking of more cons, more reasons to preserve everything exactly as it is now. Perfect. Mostly perfect.

Eleven days.

It's like a clock ticking in my ears, though, an alarm that I can't turn off, even if I can temporarily hit snooze. And instead of some normal beeping sound, it's playing Frank Zappa's "Don't Eat the Yellow Snow" and "I'm the Slime" on loop—songs I can't really stand, for the record, they make my eardrums weep, as most of his music does. Which maybe is a sign? I don't know.

Breathe in, Calliope. Breathe out. I try some of Mimmy's meditation exercises, picture orbs of light traveling from my toes to my calves to my knees ... but it's not working. My brain refuses to stop.

Eleven days.

Chapter Eight

"**So** still nothing on the murder?" Ginger asks, licking pink smears of melted ice pop from her wrist.

"God. *No*, Ginger. No juicy murder updates for you. I should never have told you that Max was a Jackson. You're too obsessed with that house. It's unhealthy." I splash her from the other side of the green turtle-shaped pool. Even that takes too much effort in this heat. I say it every year, but this time it feels especially true: it's the hottest summer yet. Even Mama was looking at air conditioner sales the other day. Global warming might undo her resolve after all.

"I just can't believe you've been friends with Max for what, almost three weeks, and even now that you know he's an actual *Jackson*, you still don't have any more intel on whether or not there was a murder in that house. We've been wondering about that place for most of our lives and the answer is right at your fingertips."

"Maybe Max doesn't even know. It's not like he and his dad communicate much. He doesn't seem like he'd be super-interested in learning about the Jackson family tree."

"But everyone knows at least something about their grandparents, right?"

"Maybe it was his grandparents' parents, or it happened

before they lived there. Or, here's a wild and crazy idea—maybe it's all just Green Woods gossip. Maybe it never happened at all."

"No way. I believe this one." She sucks down the last bit of her ice pop and drops the stick into the grass behind her. "When do I get an invite over there? I want to sense it for myself. I did see that ghost when your moms took us to Salem—Mimmy's birthday trip that I got to crash. We did that haunted walking tour through the cemetery, remember?"

"Okay, yes. I do remember that there was a white fuzzy spot on the corner of your photo that could easily have been your thumb. I told you that then, too."

She slides her sunglasses down her nose to glare at me. "You were just as spooked as I was. You can't revise history now."

It *had* been a very old, unsettling cemetery. Lots of cracked and crumbling tombstones. But we were also twelve. And had stayed up until midnight the night before reading a Salem ghost book we'd bought from a gift shop. "Well, either way, it's Max's private family business. I'm not prying."

"But you're his *friend*. Seemingly his best friend. It's your right and privilege to pry."

"He's my friend, yes, but he's also my neighbor. Maybe he spends so much time with me because it's convenient. Who knows what'll happen in the fall when he has his whole pick of Green Woods kids. Everyone's going to be hungry for the artsy new boy." I hadn't thought about that until now.

"Please." She waves me away, drops of warm water flicking across the pool. "Neither of us believes that. Let's be real, it's just the two of us right now because he's running errands with his mom."

I open my mouth to deny it—he is out with his mom, but only because I'd told him I was having quality Ginger time this afternoon. I stop, though, when I notice a dangerously bright smile spreading across her pretty pink lips.

"Let's ask if we can hang out at his house tonight," she says. "So I can see it for myself."

"No thank you. We hardly ever spend time there."

"All the more reason! Doesn't his mom want to meet his other friends? Or does she only care about you because you're the *special* friend?" She punctuates the question with an irritating wink.

"I am not his *special*—"

"Just ask. If he says no, he says no. I'll respect that."

"Why can't we all just hang out here? We'll make s'mores. With peanut butter. What else do you want to eat? I'll bribe you with delicious food."

She wraps her legs around mine, pulling herself in closer. "Come on, Calliope. *Please.* We've obsessed over that house for years. I just want to take a teeny peek inside. That's all. It's either this way, or we break in sometime when they're all out." She grins and wiggles her eyebrows, her face so close to mine our noses are practically bumping.

I pull away from her, resting my elbows on the grass behind me. Stare up at the cloudless sky.

"I'll be polite," she says. "On my best behavior. Scout's honor."

"No. And you quit Girl Scouts and left me all alone after two weeks of being a Daisy."

"You like to say we're all friends—that it's not you and Max. This would be a good chance for some group bonding. I'll convince Noah to come, too. He's been pathetically mopey lately. Not that you would know."

A dig. It's not that I haven't invited him to come over here. I have. He's been the "busy" one. Weekdays at Wawa, Saturdays at his cello lesson, practicing—it would seem—every other hour he's not sleeping or eating. I miss him. I miss the three of us. But still, "No."

Ginger laughs, too sweetly. "Maybe I forgot to mention it... I asked Max for some photos he took on the Fourth. I have his number, too."

Ginger races past me and Noah and up the porch steps—nearly wiping out on the second one—and knocks on the front door. Very enthusiastically.

I catch up with her and grab her hand, lean in to whisper: "Remember, best behavior. You promised. If the stories are true, they are about real people. Max's family."

"You do realize I'm not an actual monster," she whispers back huffily. Because she's out of breath or offended, it's hard to say.

I'm still surprised Max agreed to this plan. And even more surprised that Noah did, too. Ginger has a knack for getting her way. That's one thing I've learned many times over in the last seventeen years.

The door swings open, and Max is there. Smiling, but with a nervous edge that's not normally on his face.

"Hey," he says, nodding at me before he steps back to let us in. "So...bad news, I guess. At least for you, Ginger, since you seemed seriously stoked to meet my family when you texted. My sister had a meltdown about some epic party her friends were having in the city tonight. Like a kicking-and-screaming, tear-the-roof-down kind of meltdown. This move has been...hard on her. Anyway, she begged my mom to drive her in. My dad was already there. Working. On a Saturday." His carefully constructed expression droops a bit as he says this. I want to reach out to him. But I don't. "So. Yeah. They won't be back until late tonight."

"That's fine, plenty of other opportunities!" Ginger says cheerfully, pushing past me into the hallway. "I brought chips." She also brought a Ouija board, but that, thank god, is sitting on my kitchen table. That was one battle Ginger did not win.

Max leads us down the hallway, then turns left into the living room. I've only seen the room in passing a few times. Max never seems eager to do much living in there.

We all follow him in, Ginger on his heels, Noah a few feet behind me. He's barely said a word since he showed up on my porch earlier with Ginger. I can't imagine what she possibly said to convince him to come.

I glance around the dimly lit room, an interesting contrast of new and old. The furniture is too fresh and modern, too *big city* for this house. Sleek leather sofa and chairs, an all-glass coffee table, a television that is at least triple the size of ours, hanging up on the wall alongside some expensive-looking abstract paintings. A metal pole lamp that looks cool but gives off very little actual light. And then there's the room itself—more of the floral wallpaper is peeled than not, leaving large patches of exposed plaster. The floors are warped and scratched. One window has a pane covered with cardboard.

"I'm going to go grab some drinks from the fridge," Max says. He's staring at the walls, the window, his lips curling down. "Maybe heat up a frozen pizza if anyone's hungry?"

"Yes!" Ginger says. "That sounds great. I'll come help."

The room is too quiet after they leave.

Noah stands by the doorway, hands jammed in his pockets.

I distract myself with the massive fireplace, easily the best part of the room. Its mantel is a few inches higher than my head, thick slabs of smooth dark wood. I imagine it would be impressively shiny if it was ever polished again. The wood is carved with intricately sprawling trees and leaves and vines, dotted with birds and flowers, stars and sun and moon. The design matches the banister, two pieces of the same set, but this work is much more elaborate. I'm surprised Max hasn't mentioned this to me before. As an artist, I would think he'd appreciate the craft. But then again, I don't think he appreciates anything about this house.

I turn on my phone flashlight for a better view and reach out to touch the wood, running my hand over the finely rounded edges of a cloud near the edge of the mantel. There are nails sticking out at intervals just above my head, empty holes where other nails used to be. They had hung things here once, maybe for Christmas. Pine garlands or strings of cranberries, stockings, greeting cards. The idea warms me. It's a work of art, this fireplace, but someone didn't mind altering it for the sake of festivity. Maybe there *was* some happiness in the Jackson house.

"Look at this," I say, waving Noah over. "I can't imagine how long it took someone to carve this scene. It's so ornate. Somebody put a lot of love into this part of the house. I wonder who. And why." I walk slowly along the length of the fireplace, studying the mantel. There's a house—maybe this house—and people, a man and a woman and a child, sitting beneath a big willow tree. There are tiny details all around them, blades of grass and butterflies, but their faces are oddly blank. Probably worn down by time, but the effect is still unsettling. "You really should come look at it." I turn to Noah and motion him over again.

"Nah. I'm good. I can see it from here."

I don't recognize Noah, not the way he says that. The cool indifference.

Something inside me snaps.

I am suddenly so exhausted by all of it. The awkward silences, the lame excuses he's come up with the past few weeks, the guilt I don't deserve to carry.

"Can we please talk about what's going on?"

"What do you mean?" His eyes are pointedly fixed on the wooden floorboards. Away from me.

"You know what I mean. You're barely even here."

"Obviously I'm here. I'm standing ten feet away from you."

I want to scream. He has never felt more like a brother to me than he does in this moment. A *little* brother. "Why are you making this all so difficult? You do realize me having a new friend doesn't need to change anything between us, right?"

He snorts. "Doesn't it?"

"Noah. You're one of my best friends."

"It's okay. I knew it would happen eventually. I just didn't know when. Or who. But I knew you'd never break the rule for me. Sometimes I wonder . . . if the rule is *because* of me."

"What? *No*," I say, lying to my best friend's face. "But I'm not breaking the rule for anyone."

"You're not?"

"No." I'm not. Am I?

It shouldn't matter anyway. It *doesn't*. Not for me and Noah.

"Calliope . . ." he starts. Stops. *Please god don't let him cry.* I don't know how to handle his tears right now. But I hear the sniffling, the telltale wobble in his voice as he says: "I *love you*."

Here we are then, finally.

The conversation we've been carefully avoiding for so long. Maybe we should have had this discussion sophomore year. Talked about that not-so-anonymous valentine.

"Noah." I take a deep breath, clench my hands into tight fists. "You know I love you like a brother. That's all it can ever be. That won't change. Ever. You need to understand."

The words sound cold. Too cold. And there's so much more I want to say: That my love for him is more important, more permanent than any other kind of love. More special.

But I feel too tired. And frustrated. And this very sensitive conversation feels so out of place in this terrible, lonely room in this terrible, lonely house.

"Well," he says, rubbing his eyes, "that was direct. Message received, loud and clear." He looks up at me finally, and I wish he hadn't. The sadness in his eyes is too big. Too ugly.

"This isn't how this conversation was meant to go." I almost say I'm sorry. Almost.

But I haven't done anything wrong.

I can't make myself fall in love with Noah.

"I shouldn't have come tonight." He takes a few steps back, hovering in the doorway.

"So then why did you? What was the point if you were just going to be miserable?"

"Ginger said I'd lose you—if I kept skipping out on everything. That I had to step up if I wanted to keep being your friend."

"Maybe she's right. You might. You might lose me."

I don't mean that. I don't think I do.

Noah and I are supposed to be forever.

But I have my limits.

"I'm not even dating Max, and this is how you act? What do you want from me, Noah? If I don't love you like that, should I just, I don't know—run off to a nunnery?"

"What? No." He drops his head. "I should go."

"I agree."

I turn away, and I don't look back until after I hear his footsteps move down the hallway, the front door opening and closing.

After he's gone, I drop down on the leather sofa. It's cool and slick and gives no comfort. I feel nauseated. I want to go home. Curl up next to Mama and Mimmy on our lumpy old sofa that feels like a warm hug and watch a marathon of *I Love Lucy*.

"We're back," Ginger announces in a singsong voice, emerging from the doorway with four tall glasses of lemonade balanced in her hands—showing off her waitressing skills. Max is behind her carrying a tray of pizza and chips and napkins.

"Sorry we took so long," Max says, putting the tray on the table and settling in next to me on the couch. "*Somebody* requested a full tour while the pizza was heating up. I'm beginning to suspect tonight was more about checking out the local haunted house than meeting my family." He puts on a pout like he's upset about this, but his eyes look twinkly and amused. Maybe this is good for him—having people over. Making this foreign place feel more like a home.

"Wait. Where's Noah?" Ginger asks, peering around the room as if he might pop out from behind a dark corner.

"He...uh...wasn't feeling well. He needed to go home."

Ginger folds her arms across her chest, frowning. "Is that so? He was *sick*?"

I shrug.

She wants to ask more. Max does, too. He's sitting up straighter, his body tensed.

"Everything is fine. I just don't want to talk about it."

Max nods and reaches for a piece of pizza, jams it into his mouth.

"What really—" Ginger starts, but I cut her off.

"Tell me about the *tour*. You just couldn't help yourself, could you?" I smile as I ask, but my teeth are clenched so hard I must look demonic.

Ginger is distracted then, talking about the sunroom, the staircase, a library upstairs I've never seen.

Max doesn't seem bothered by her obsession with his house. Or maybe he would be, if he wasn't so distracted. Wondering about Noah. What Noah did or said.

We watch a movie after eating. *Wonder Woman*. Ginger's pick. I hope she at least got what she wanted out of this night. One of us can leave happy.

When the movie ends, I stand up and stretch, force a yawn. "I'm exhausted." I give Ginger a pointed look, and thankfully she gets up, too. "Thanks for having us, Max. You've made Ginger's summer."

"Of course." He stands up next to me and his arm brushes against mine. He immediately moves away, gives me space. "We can try again sometime when my family's actually around. Mom and Marlow at least. Maybe we could let Marlow tag along. Throw her a bone."

"Sure." I rub my arm where we touched. "That's a nice idea."

"Sorry you didn't see any ghosts, Ginger."

Her mouth drops. "That's so not why I came!"

He rolls his eyes, but he's smiling at her.

Ginger hugs him, and I put an arm loosely around both of them. It's a noncommittal hug, but I'm not really in a hugging kind of mood.

We say our goodbyes, and Ginger and I quietly walk the stretch of patchy lawn and then cross over into the woods. The moon is bright enough for me to make my way, but she lights up the flashlight on her phone.

"Noah and I had the conversation," I whisper then, even though there's no one around us but the trees.

"The conversation?"

"The one where he says *I love you.* And I say *You know I don't love you like that.*"

She gasps. "Oh god. That conversation."

"Yep. That one."

"How did it go?"

"How do you think it went?"

"I'm sorry."

"Me too."

We make our way slowly through the woods. Clinging on to each other as we step over rocks and fallen tree limbs, hold back sharp, prickly branches.

I wonder about Noah, what he's doing now, if he's okay.

I wonder about Max, how he's feeling, alone in that empty house.

And I wonder if anything will ever go back to normal.

Chapter Nine

A few days pass.

Noah doesn't text or call, he doesn't appear in my backyard with a delightful new flavor of iced tea. I don't reach out to him either.

I'm not sure what's supposed to happen next.

Maybe nothing.

"You okay, sweetheart?" Mimmy asks, stopping by the kitchen table to top off my mug with fresh coffee. Mama is honking the car horn from our driveway, yelling out the window for Mimmy to get her "sweet yoga ass outside" because they should have been at the studio five minutes ago. Mimmy ignores her, eyes fixed squarely on me. "You've been a little quiet this week."

"I'm fine." I look up from the spread of college brochures I've been pretending to study. "Just some growing pains, I guess you could say. Nothing to worry about."

Mimmy frowns. "Noah?"

I nod. I want to smile, but my face refuses.

She doesn't ask more about it, just drops a small plate of fresh ginger raspberry muffins on the table as she makes her way to the door. Mama's incessant honking must be scaring off every living creature in a mile radius of the woods. "Think about something happy, my darling. Think about how you want to ring in eighteen tomorrow. What special meals you might want us to make. Mama and I took off the whole day to be here." She kisses the top of my head and walks out the door. The horn stops. I listen to the sound of tires crunching on gravel and then the quiet that comes after.

Ginger has stopped asking about any grand and elaborate plans. I'm not sure I want to acknowledge a birthday without Noah there with us. Birthdays have always been more a celebration of the three of us, a time to honor fate for bringing our mothers together.

I've eaten two and a half muffins and not tasted a bite of any of them when there's a cheery knock at the door.

Max is there when I open it, grinning at me.

"Good morning! I don't think there could ever be a better way to start my day than walking through woods to eat whatever delicious treat Margo might have whipped up since my last visit. And to see you, of course." He winks, that grin growing even wider.

"You have uncanny timing. I was just about to mindlessly inhale the last few muffins when you knocked. Ginger raspberry. The raspberries were lovingly plucked from our backyard yesterday by yours truly."

Max clutches his heart. "Goddamn it, Calliope. I am a *country boy*. It's official. Morning walks through the woods and muffins made with handpicked raspberries. I even fell asleep last night before I remembered to turn on the city-sounds loop. I never thought this would happen...But it *did*." He shakes his head, looking simultaneously bedazzled and bewildered.

I roll my eyes and start back toward the kitchen, Max trailing me. "Hate to burst your bubble, but I'm not sure this is technically considered *country*. Rural suburbs, maybe. That's probably more accurate. I've had this debate with Ginger and Noah too many times."

"Trust me," he says, wagging his finger while chewing the whole muffin he shoved in his mouth, "this counts as country." He picks up a second muffin, eats it more slowly. Savors it with his eyes scrunched up tight. He explained to me the other night that he tastes things more clearly with his eyes closed—he can see and feel the *colors* of each flavor. A bursting, ripe palette on his tongue.

I pick at another muffin, but I don't close my eyes. I watch Max chew with a closed-mouth smile that looks almost reverent on his lips. I'm not sure anyone has ever had such a deep appreciation for Mama's baked goods.

"So, today," Max says, opening his eyes and brushing crumbs from his hands. "Today, we celebrate seventeen. Not eighteen. Seventeen. The new year always gets all the attention, but I say we honor this old one properly first. The last three hundred and sixty-four days."

I smile, dropping the last bit of muffin. "Kind of a pre-birthday birthday?"

"More of a *birthyear* celebration. Not just about one day. Happy birthyear to you!"

"It was a good year, I guess. I got a new neighbor, for one."

"Yep. A neighbor *and* a friend, all wrapped up in one sweet package."

"So how exactly does someone celebrate a birthyear?" I ask. "I'm new to the concept."

"Me too. I invented it yesterday. Just came to me in a flash. I was thinking about you, and how to make this birthday special enough, and *poof.* Genius descended. Don't worry—it might be fresh, but I have grand plans. And I'm all set up for birthyear activity number one, so if you'll follow me..." He waves me out the kitchen door, into the yard, and then he takes the lead. We pass the turtle pool and keep walking toward the woods.

I hope that birthyear activity number one is not taking place in the Jackson house.

"Close your eyes," he says as we step up to the tree line.

I must look uncertain about the idea of blindly traipsing over rocks and fallen branches because he says, "Trust me, Calliope. How about I hold your hand?"

I nod, and he reaches for my hand, his fingers winding around mine. His palm feels familiar and steady and I realize I *do* trust him, fully and completely. It's a jolt—another reminder of how close I feel to Max.

The walk is slow and smooth, and I am aware of little but the feel of Max's hand in mine. He tells me when to step, when to stop, when to pivot, and after a few minutes I almost forget that I'm only seeing through his eyes.

"Okay," he says, squeezing my hand. "You can look."

I open my eyes, and we're at the tree, my tree, but it's more than that. There are two canvases set up on back-to-back easels and a TV tray covered in acrylic-paint tubes and brushes.

"I thought it could be fun to paint together," Max says, watching me nervously, like he's afraid I won't be as excited as he is about this plan. "See your favorite tree in two different styles and perspectives."

I'm too busy taking it all in, Max, the easels, the tree, the sun filtering in through the leaves. It's cooler today, the air is fresher. Everything is so perfect it's hard to find words.

When I don't answer, Max looks down at his feet, kicking a clump of moss.

"This is the best birthyear activity possible," I say, and I hug him. He looks down at me, his face lit up with relief. "Seriously, I feel bad for any other activities you might have planned. This will be impossible to top."

"You scared me for a minute there, going speechless like that," he says as we slowly let go of each other. We both take a step back. "Although I'm sure I have a pretty high bar to hit as far as birthdays go. Margo and Stella seem like the inventive types. Ginger, too. And Noah," he tacks on.

"Mimmy bakes delicious cakes, that's true. And sometimes Mama takes me and Mimmy camping or rock climbing or rafting—some kind of activity that she not so secretly wants to do anyway, and it's convenient to hype it up as a birthday family outing. Ginger always talks big and likes to brainstorm elaborate outings, but usually it just ends up being the three of us and my moms hanging out in the backyard like we would any other night. But with Mimmy's cake."

"So, no real competition is what you're telling me?"

"I'm not making an official declaration until the birthyear celebration is complete."

"Fair enough."

He takes me to the first easel, hands me a wooden palette.

"Do you have advice for me? As the expert?" I ask, running my fingers along the rainbow of paint tubes.

"Nope. Just have fun, birthyear girl. Anything you paint will be a masterpiece with a fine subject like this. But no peeking at each other's work until we're both finished. That's the only rule."

I've never painted outside of art class. And that was always of boring, ordinary things, potted plants and stacks of books, a portrait of the person across from me. Once I was assigned to paint Penelope Park, and Ginger was jealous.

Painting today feels completely different. Max and I don't talk as I first study the tree, looking at every swirl of bark, each knob and hollow and arc of the trunk with new eyes. There are more leaves than I ever stopped to consider before, like a sea of wide green hands waving down at me from up high.

I'm lost in it all, trying to capture each unique shade of brown and black and green and blue. If not perfectly, then adequately enough to do this tree justice. My hand moves painstakingly across the canvas, drawing rough shapes and outlines to start, then filling in slowly from the bottom of the tree to the top. Watching the tree bloom into being on the canvas fills me with a satisfaction I've never felt before. Maybe it's how Mimmy feels when she creates a perfect recipe from scratch, or how Mama feels when she puts together a new yoga workshop. How Max feels every time shapes and colors spring from his hands, or how Noah feels after composing a new piece for the cello.

I lose track of time.

The only reason I know it's passing is because the light takes on a new slant, the shadows shifting and changing.

I add what might be the last bit of shading to the deepest part of the trunk's hole, step back, and squint at the work.

"How does it look?" Max asks, startling me. I glance up at him for the first time since my paintbrush touched canvas.

"Okay, I think? Not perfect. But maybe nice in its own way. Though part of me wants to keep tweaking, see if I can get some of the shadows to look more realistic."

"The hardest part of painting is knowing when to stop." He looks gravely serious as he says it, like an old monk imparting some ancient philosophy. I bite my lip to stop from smiling.

"Then maybe I am done."

"Can I see?"

I nod. I'm anxious, suddenly, about what Max will think. I've seen the Philly mural on his walls, the elegant way the sun glints off the jagged skyline, the streets filled with miniature, lifelike people. His strokes are all grace and precision.

Max doesn't say anything as he takes in my work. I watch his eyes roam around the canvas, analyzing each piece individually.

"Well?"

"It's beautiful," he says matter-of-factly.

"You don't have to sugarcoat for me. It's amateur, I know."

He shakes his head. "No. You know this tree better than any-one and it shows. It's all heart. You're a natural."

I feel myself glow with his praise. The words make me shy. Fluttery. I step around to look at his canvas, and my jaw drops. It's not just the tree. It's *me* painting the tree. More me than the tree, really.

"You were so engrossed, you didn't notice me observing you," he says.

The painted Calliope definitely looks engrossed. Tightly furrowed brow, narrowed eyes, biting down on her frowning lip as she studies the canvas in front of her like it holds all the great truths of the universe. Sunbeams filter down playfully through the leaves—round and swirly sprinkles of yellow and white and gold, ending in a burst of light that centers directly on me. My rosy cheeks and the messy bun pinned up with a paintbrush, the colorful smears of paint on my arms, my fingers, my dress. The tree is secondary. A background afterthought.

This painted Calliope is stunning. Dreamy. A creature of these woods.

"You changed the assignment." It's the best I can manage.

Max laughs. "I did say two different styles and perspec-tives, didn't I? I can't help my perspective. Good thing you're not around every time I paint, or I'd have a very limited portfolio."

"Oh," I say. *Oh.*

I've never understood the idea of *feeling butterflies* when it comes to romance. The cliché of all clichés. I thought it was just something people said, a throwaway line from cheesy rom-coms.

But no—I feel it now. The sensation of actual flapping insects circling and dive-bombing in my stomach. It's a very real phenomenon after all. Because here it is, the truth I've been avoiding: My summer, my friendships, my priorities have changed because of Max. And it didn't require an official title or label. It didn't even require a kiss.

Max walked through the woods to my house in June, and life changed. Simple as that. It was going to happen with or without my permission. How naive, to think it was ever my decision to make.

"Can I keep it?" I ask quietly.

"Of course. If I can keep yours." He pauses for a beat, and then: "What were you thinking just then? Was it really about keeping my painting?"

I shake my head.

"So...?" he asks, taking a small step closer to me. "What then?"

"I was thinking..." I swallow. "Maybe I was wrong to have a rule about dating. To think I could control whether or not I met the right person at the perfect time."

"Are you saying...?" His face is blank with surprise. I can't tell what's buried underneath—excitement or terror or disappointment or hope.

"You? Yes." I breathe out as I say these two words, feeling instantly lighter. Somehow this confession feels like both the biggest secret and the most obvious truth.

"It's funny you say that, because"—he says, breaking out in a smile—"I was reevaluating the idea that high school relationships are silly. Sometimes, sure. But not always."

I take a step. He takes a step. I step again.

He reaches out and takes my hand, twirls me closer until my face is inches from his. My breath hitches.

I lean in before there's any risk of letting this moment slip away.

Our lips meet.

My first kiss. I'm glad it's here, in our woods. I'm glad it's with Max.

I open my eyes for a second, and I am certain the sun is shining brighter than before, the branches radiant and illuminated above us, a grand glowing archway.

The sun is shining for us.

I'm not sure who pulls away from our kiss first. It's short and sweet. Enough to start.

We grin at each other. Wild, loopy grins.

My brain feels pleasantly hazy. Like all of life's edges are rounded and softened. It reminds me of last winter, when Ginger made Noah and me take swigs of her dad's whiskey with her during a bad snowstorm. A foggy, giggly, snowed-in blur.

Max takes my hand and says, "Time to leave these here to dry so we can move on to birthyear activity two."

I forgot there was more. That this day has even more surprises.

We walk farther through the woods. Past the log bridge that leads to the hill.

It's not until I see the vibrant dark green water that I realize where we're going.

My pond. He remembered.

He squeezes my hand. I squeeze back.

This is happening. This is really happening.

"I can't believe you haven't taken me to your second-favorite place yet," Max says. "I had to venture out and find it all on my own. Trespassing on your property, sorry about that. I was proud of my navigational skills, though—only took me about three hours of wandering to find it."

I laugh. "It's six or seven minutes, tops, from your house."

"The trees confuse me! There are so many of them. Everything looks the same. I swear these woods are bewitched, because it feels like they might go on forever. Even though I've seen a map of the town and I know that can't be possible. Still. It's freaky."

"I used to pretend that was true when I was little. That these were endless magical woods. Borders on the outside, but never on the inside. I would wander around for hours by myself."

"Somehow that doesn't surprise me. Sounds very Calliope-like."

The water looks intensely green today. Probably for very unromantic and scientific reasons having to do with the extreme heat and algae growth. Or maybe it's just a trick of the light, the water mirroring the deep green leaves framing the pond. Whatever the cause, it is completely mesmerizing. Almost impossible to look away.

"I hope you're hungry," Max says, motioning to a blanket and basket to our right that I'm only seeing now. "Hopefully no pesky woodland creatures ravaged our goods. I left my bow and arrow at home."

"The idea of you shooting an arrow is terrifying. And I don't mind sharing my birthyear feast with other creatures. Particularly if it's some friendly pixies."

"You're a better person than me. Or at least a less hungry one."

We sprawl out on the blanket, just along the pond's edge. I feel a slow ache building in my neck and shoulders, strain from painting for so long in the same position. But it's a good ache. A happy, accomplished one. Like the feeling I get after doing an inversions class with Mama or Mimmy.

Max unpacks his spread, mostly "heat-resistant" foods—or "relatively heat-resistant" he amends after seeing the way a pile of chocolate chip cookies has turned into a soggy molten brown clump. But the croissants and blackberry jam taste even better warm, and so do the buttery confetti cupcakes that melt in my mouth. He did think to use ice packs to preserve the cheese and grapes, fortunately, and the sweet tea from his thermos is still so cold it shocks my parched mouth.

We eat until there's nothing left, just a few crumbs we sprinkle into the pond for the pixies to enjoy after dark. And then we lie on our backs, staring up at the canopy of leaves.

I yawn, sleepy from my heavy stomach, the warm sun, this day. "Did you pencil any birthyear naps in?" I ask, my eyelids suddenly too heavy to hold up for much longer.

"The next and final official activity requires the sun to go down, so you're free to do as you wish until then."

"I wish for a nap. Here with you at the pond."

"Then a nap it is—whatever the birthyear girl wants."

I kick off my sandals and scoot closer to him, curling up against his side. He tucks his arm under my head as a pillow. It's strange, how *not* strange it all feels. Like we've been in this position a thousand times before. Sun filters in lazily through the leaves above, bright splashes across my closed eyes. Max tucks loose curls behind my ears, humming as he does it, low and steady. Before I drift away, I think:

I hope I dream about this, right here, because it's the only place I want to be.

Max's golden-brown eyes look more gold than usual, flickering in the tall, dancing flames of the fire. He's focused intently on his darkening marshmallow, bubbling and crisping, too close to the heat for a perfect, even roast. I fight the urge to pull his stick back to a safer distance.

Birthyear activity three started off well enough, a campfire Max set up in his backyard with hot dogs and lemonade and, of course, s'mores. But it's as if the house's energy is seeping outside its dark walls, stealing away all his good spirits. Draining him of happiness.

I hope it's the house, at least—not regrets about this day. The kiss. Us.

His marshmallow ignites in a ball of flames. He makes no effort to snuff it out, watching as it burns, bigger and brighter, melting off the tree branch he's using as a fork.

"You must like your s'mores charred," I say, trying to lighten the mood. "A hearty dose of ash with each bite. Delicious."

There's a pause before he says, "Yep. Sure."

"Okay." I pluck the stick from his hands and set it down. "Please tell me what's wrong. Is it . . . what happened in the woods? With me?" The two s'mores I've already eaten feel sickly sweet at the back of my throat.

"No!" He turns to face me, his eyes instantly clearing. "No. Definitely not. Today was the happiest I've been in a long time. Maybe the happiest. Period."

"Oh." The happiest he's ever been. Because of *me*. I'll replay those words at least a hundred times before I sleep tonight. But still, I need to know: "Something changed between the afternoon and now. What was it?"

He looks back at the fire. "It's nothing. I don't want to ruin this amazing day. My parents were just fighting when I ran inside for the food. Same as always. No big deal."

"What were they fighting about?"

"I only heard snippets. I tried to get in and out as fast as I could. My mom's upset he's not here enough, that he's not fixing the house up for us like he should be. She also suspects he's not as monogamous as he's claiming to be, and that's why he's still doing the Philly commute. I don't know. Maybe this will actually be the end. She'll kick his pathetic ass out, or he'll leave on his own.

He was swearing up and down that he's been loyal, that it's not about anyone else. But it's pretty hard to trust anything he says anymore."

"I'm sorry, Max." I cringe, saying it. It's my default. Overused. Those two words, *I'm sorry*, don't say enough.

"Don't be. It's our fault for letting him pull the same shit over and over again. It's like he can't help himself. He can't stop. He messes up, but then he comes crawling back, saying how much he *loves* us." He grabs the stick again and shoves another marshmallow on it so forcefully the sharp tip of wood pokes out from the top end. "If he loved us, he'd actually be here every day, following through on all the shit he promised to do. Making this nasty shack a real home."

I'm desperate to say something, anything, that might be more helpful than *I'm sorry*. "Even if your parents do decide to separate," I start, "maybe your relationship with him would be better off? People fall out of love and get divorced sometimes. But that doesn't mean he'd stop being your dad. I'm sure he loves you, Max. He's not that terrible, is he?"

"Calliope?" His voice is small and low and almost lost in the night. I wait. Frogs sing out from the creek, crickets chirp, an owl hoots somewhere high above us in the trees. "I care about you. I do. I am so happy today happened. So happy to be here with you right now. And I appreciate your opinions. But . . . can you just be angry together with me? Not defend my dad? I'm not there yet. I might never be there. You don't know him like I do."

My stomach coils and burns. "You're right," I say, reaching

up to lay my palm against his lightly stubbled cheek. "You feel whatever you need to feel. I'll shut my mouth."

He smiles, but it's a sad one. The roasting stick slips from his hand.

He's quiet again then, and my mind wanders to the inevitable. I hear *dad*, and I think: the donor. Frank. Even though he's not my dad. Will never be my dad. I still can't stop myself. The thoughts come on their own. I'm powerless against them.

I haven't asked Max for his opinion on what I should do, and I certainly can't ask now. Because at least I still have two parents who love each other. Two parents who would probably die before they'd move away from me, shared blood or no.

"It's okay," he says after a few minutes. "You don't have a dad and you turned out pretty great. So maybe I'll be fine, too. I just know we can't keep pretending like this."

I nod and he leans down, lips grazing my forehead. What he said is true: I have everything I need. Everyone.

Maybe it's selfish to need more. To *want* more.

What would Frank add to my life?

"I'm sorry to ruin your birthyear with this," he whispers in my ear. There's a tickling sensation against my skin that makes it harder to breathe.

"I had the best day. You didn't ruin anything. Being together is just as much about sharing life's bullshit drama as it is celebrating birthyears and birthdays."

"So wise," he says. "And also, you just said we're *together*...?"

I did. Accidentally.

"That slipped out. I'm sorry. I don't want to be...
presumptuous."

"Oh, I want to be. Together. With you. Only you. I was just
clarifying."

"Yeah?" The butterflies—they're back. Fluttering so fast I
can barely catch my breath.

"Yeah."

And then his lips brush mine, and we're kissing, and there's
no room to think about anything else. No family drama, no broken hearts, no disappointments.

When we pull apart, he leans his head on my shoulder. We sit
like that, not talking, for a long time.

It's just moonlight and flames and him, me, us.

Chapter Ten

"**EIGHTEEN!**" Mama cheers.

"Eighteen," Mimmy echoes, sounding notably weepier.

Mimmy has outdone herself this year. Chocolate chip cookie dough cake, with a cloud of marshmallow icing—lightly torched to give it toasty brown tips—and crumbled graham crackers and chocolate shavings on top. My birthday cake is served for lunch, as it is every year—so I can appreciate it fully as a meal of its own, and then have a second serving later at night for dessert. A Silversmith tradition.

Ginger slides an arm around my waist as I lean in to blow out the flickering flames. Two tall, sparkly purple candles—a one and an eight.

Max stands across from me, Mimmy and Mama on either side of him. Three big grins shining down on me, full wattage.

There is so much love here in this kitchen, but I can't help but feel the absence. Noah.

I haven't seen him since the night at Max's. I was hoping he'd come over to celebrate—that we could all act normal. Be normal. At least for this one day. But he told Ginger he had a last-minute Wawa shift he couldn't skip because there wasn't anyone else to sub in. I did get a *happy birthday* text from him this morning. Just like that—no exclamation points, no capital letters, no emojis. It's the first year of my life that Noah isn't here next to me. It feels wrong in the pit of my stomach.

I smile anyway, try to focus on who is here, not who isn't. I have Mimmy and Mama and Ginger like always. I have Max. The boyfriend I vowed not to have, not before college. But no regrets. None at all. Though if I have to hear Ginger gloating about how she was right one more time since telling her the news this morning, I may be tempted to run off to a convent after all.

I close my eyes and think of a wish.

"Sweetie?" Mimmy says quietly. "Those candles might melt all over the cake soon if you don't blow them out."

I take a deep breath. Blow.

I wish to know who Frank is.

Is that true?

Wishes don't matter, though. They aren't real. I've wished to be as good at handstands as Mimmy and Mama both are—never going to happen. I've wished for a trip to Thailand—those plane tickets never showed up. And I remember wishing once that nothing would ever change between me and Ginger and Noah. That was the summer before the valentine, the rule—the first time I wondered if Noah might have too many feelings for me, even if he wasn't bold enough to put it in writing quite yet.

So wishes—wishes clearly mean nothing.

"I hope you picked a good one," Max says, walking around the table to hug me. "I hear wishes for your eighteenth have more power than other birthday wishes."

I wish to know who Frank is.

"Don't you dare tell anyone what it is!" Ginger claps a hand over my mouth. "Can't risk it not coming true if what Max says is right."

"Ha ha," I say, the words muffled around her palm. I lick her hand and she yanks it away, making a gagging face.

"Gross. I don't care if you are the birthday girl. Still gross. Only Penelope could get away with licking my hand like that. Or maybe a cute dog. But it would have to be a *very* cute dog."

Mama goes to the fridge and pulls out a bottle of champagne. "I think the occasion calls for a proper toast, don't you? I'm going to *assume* this is the first toast ever for the three of you," she says, smirking. "But if you're old enough to sign up for the army or get a tat, you're old enough to drink. *Responsibly.* With people you trust. And no fake IDs, please. Ever." She turns pointedly to Ginger, giving her patented scorching squint. "And yes, I'm looking at you, Ginger."

Ginger gasps. "Stella! I would *never.* I can't believe you would even suggest it."

"Right. I'll remember that."

"Besides, I doubt places around here even card all that much, so we should—"

"Nope. Stop yourself right there. Not any better."

Mimmy claps her hands. "Let's eat cake!"

"A toast first," Mama says, gripping the top of the champagne bottle with a cooking mitt. There's a brief moment of struggle before the cork flies off with a loud *pop*, bouncing against the back door.

When all the glasses are filled, Mimmy passes them out.

Mine comes last, and it looks like the fullest of the five. Mimmy winks at me.

Mama lifts her flute in the air: "To my precious eighteen-year-old baby, you have made our lives richer and more meaningful than we ever knew possible."

"You make us complete," Mimmy chimes in. She wipes a tear with the hand not holding her glass. "We were meant to be three. Not two. Three Silversmiths."

"Yes," Mama says. "Thank god for science. And for doctors who helped bring us our miracle baby."

I almost think she's going to thank Frank. But she doesn't go that far.

Or if she's going to say more, it gets cut off, because Ginger adds, "And thank god for Lamaze classes that brought three pregnant women together. Even if one of those women turned out to be a total dud. Because I don't know who I'd be without Calliope holding my hand every step of these last eighteen years. You make living in this small town feel okay. Much better than okay. And you make me happy to be myself."

I'm pretty sure, Ginger being Ginger, she would have found a way to be happy with or without me. But saying so feels like it would take away from her toast.

"And thank god for old family houses." Max steps up to my side, his shoulder pressing against mine. "Because even if that house sucks, the neighbors might not. Maybe you were always supposed to have those neighbors, and it just took nearly eighteen years to find that out."

Tears are springing up—happy ones—and I blink a few times to press them back down.

"Okay, time to drink," Mimmy says, tapping her glass to mine and tossing her head back for a sip.

I drink and let the bubbles float in my mouth. I want to remember this feeling, this taste, everything about this moment with these people.

We all eat cake. Big heavy slabs of it. It is Mimmy's best cake yet.

When we finish the first bottle of champagne, Mama opens a second. Mimmy raises her eyebrows at her, but Mama shakes her off. It's a special day.

Mimmy is being wise, though. Because other than the cake, we haven't eaten since a few blueberry waffles for breakfast. My birthday requests other than the usual lunch cake—Mimmy's waffles for breakfast, Mama's grilled pizzas for dinner.

They kept insisting on some fancy restaurant in Philly, or a night away at a bed-and-breakfast in the Hudson Valley, and I had to refuse no less than ten times before they believed me. That there's nowhere I'd rather be than here.

The afternoon is warm and fuzzy. Time seems to pass like a slow, lazy leak, a trickle of drops in a bucket, but every time I look at the clock the hands have sped ahead. We spend most of the hours laughing. Mama and Max in particular, as she tells him story after story about my childhood and he soaks it all up. It's good to see them bonding, even over the more embarrassing details. Mama approves, I can tell. She and Mimmy both took the dating news quite calmly when I told them about the birthyear celebration over waffles this morning—"I was wondering when you'd be honest with yourself," Mama had said, rolling her eyes. Mimmy chimed in with, "We're happy if you're happy!" And that was that.

Mimmy passes around fresh glasses of water between sips of bubbles. I notice she's drinking less, a mother hen making sure the rest of us are okay.

Eventually Mama stands up to roll out the pizza dough, wobbling just slightly on her way to the fridge. I want to help with dinner, but I'm not sure my body is in sync with my mind. Instead I watch Max grate mountains of cheese, miraculously with no cuts, while Mama spreads circles of sauce on amorphous blobs of dough. Mimmy chops vegetables, the task that requires the nimblest of fingers.

Ginger sits with me, chattering in a steady stream. I maybe catch one of every few words. Senior year, Penelope, taking a gap year together after graduation to travel the world. *Thailand,* she says. We could do *Thailand and China and Vietnam* . . .

We follow along when the pizzas go out to the grill. I wonder suddenly why we spent the whole blue-skied afternoon inside the stuffy kitchen, under a blank white ceiling. It's cooler out here, easier to breathe.

I splash in the warm dregs of water in the turtle pool. Ginger jumps in, too, dragging the hose behind her. She sprays icy water at my shins and I yelp, slipping and falling on my bottom. I pull her down with me, making a grab for the hose. It's a brutal tug-of-war, water blasting our faces, our open mouths as we laugh hysterically. Max comes over and easily overtakes the hose, squirts us both before turning the stream on Mama. She screams and drops her spatula on the grass, then takes off in Max's direction. They run in circles around the pool, so fast it makes me dizzy.

"I've never seen Stella like someone so easily," Ginger muses, only slightly slurring on the *s*'s. "Though champagne probably helps. But I've seen her tipsy and even tougher than usual before, so it's still a big deal."

"Definitely a big deal," I say as Mama overtakes Max and body slams him to the ground. He throws his wet, grass-stained hands up in surrender. Mama stands, brushes herself off, and tucks the nozzle in her belt loop on her way back to the grill.

"I hope you've learned the hierarchy of this house," she says smugly, giving Max a pitying look.

"This isn't over." He rolls onto his side to face me, propping his head on his hand. "I'm sorry you saw that. My ego is way more bruised than my knees right now."

"Nah. You were the bravest of all of us to even consider taking Mama on. Masculinity never wins around here."

"That's okay. I think I'd rather live in a world where masculinity never wins."

He's frowning as he says it, and I can tell he's thinking about his dad.

"I knew I liked this one," Mama says, sliding the first cooked pizza from the grill.

The pizzas make us all a little steadier. The world gets some focus back, just in time for us to admire the perfect summer sunset above, a blending of deep pink and orange smudges along the treetops. Like blazing fingers reaching out along the horizon, pulling in the last slivers of sunlight until tomorrow. There are second helpings of cake then, too, and between us all we finish every bite.

There is no second round of birthday candles to blow out.

No second wish.

The gifts come next: a hotel reservation for a trip to the Shenandoah Valley this fall and a gold necklace with an oval ruby pendant from Mama and Mimmy; a pair of slip-on Vans that Ginger decorated by hand with metallic glitter; and from Max, a card with a painting of the Philly skyline on the front and a ticket design on the back: *Admission for a day of all the best Philly sights and foods led by the best (formerly) local tour guide.*

My thank-yous are profuse and sloppy. Mimmy pops a bottle of sparkling water for me.

Ginger slips away for a moment, for what I assume is a trip to the bathroom. But she comes back a few minutes later with another package in her hands, a small bag covered in silver and gold smiley-face balloons.

"The sweet shoes were more than enough," I say. "You didn't have to get me anything else."

She bites her lip, shakes her head. "This one's not from me."

"Not from you?"

"Noah. He texted me that he dropped something off. It was at the top of the driveway."

Noah. He was here. "I thought he was too busy with his Wawa shift?"

"Guess not."

My gut feels sour, all that champagne and pizza and cake curdling into a toxic, swirling lump. The unavoidable Wawa shift had felt like a weak excuse. He couldn't see me, not even for my birthday. If it was up to me, I'd choose his friendship over whatever was in that ugly smiley-face bag.

"Are you going to open it?" I can tell Max is trying hard to sound cool and disinterested.

Ginger dangles the bag out, waiting for me to take it from her. I keep my hands at my side. "I don't have to. I can look later."

"No. Open it," Mama says. "It'll determine how mad I am at him for skipping out on my only daughter's eighteenth birthday. I love that boy, but really—time to suck it up. Life needs to go on. He'd be a complete ass to throw away so many years of friendship over a silly little puppy-love broken heart."

"Mama! Please. Stop." My whole body flames with heat. I want to peel my skin back.

I can't look at Max. I can't look at any of them.

Mama shrugs her shoulders. "What? It's true, isn't it?"

I rip the bag from Ginger's hand and stomp over to the hammock. The bag is light, like it's nothing more than the white tissue paper inside. I reach my hand in, feel around. My fingers touch metal strands, and I tug.

It's a necklace set we saw online a few months back—peanut butter and jelly jar best friends charms, something second graders are supposed to wear. I'd adored it immediately, but I'd said I would only want it if it were split three ways. It wouldn't work with just two halves. I was only partly serious, and I'd forgotten all about it. But Noah clearly hadn't. And now he's saying that two halves will be just fine.

We're not *three* anymore.

It's the cruelest gift he could have given me.

A sob rises up my throat. I put my hand over my mouth to hold it back, but it's too late.

Everyone is pretending not to stare at me.

The bag falls from my hand and a note slips out. I don't want to look. But I do.

Happy birthday, Calliope.

I bought this necklace months ago, back when you first saw it. I know it wasn't thirds like you wanted, but I'd found another necklace with a loaf of bread. After all, you need bread to make a PB&J sandwich. It's corny, I know. But you like corny. And apparently you also like jewelry made for kids. (No judgment.)

Anyway, I hope you and G wear the PB&J proudly. Don't fight too hard about who gets to be the PB. Even if it is the best part of the sandwich. Obviously.

Sorry I'm not there today. I thought we'd all be better off if I stayed home.

But I hope it's a great day. The best. You deserve it. Happy 18.

                                    —Noah

I hate that I'm crying. But I'm laughing, too. Noah found a loaf of bread to match. He doesn't say that he'll ever wear it—or even that he'll keep it—but that had been his intention at least. It wasn't just a spiteful jab.

Maybe there's still hope for us. Someday at least.

"Everything okay?" Ginger asks. I can tell she wants to ask much more than that, but she refrains. She glances sideways at Max.

"Yep. It's just the peanut butter and jelly best friends necklaces I saw a while back. Remember? Delightfully kitschy?" I dangle the necklaces in the air to jog her memory.

"Ugh. You expect me to wear that? It's so tacky. Are we back in elementary school?" But she's smiling. Maybe a little hopefully. This summer has been hard on Ginger, too. She walks up to me and plucks both necklaces from my hand. "I'm assuming you're going to make me take the jelly jar, aren't you? It's red at least. Strawberry. Maybe raspberry. Not grape. I would draw the line at wearing a grape jelly jar around my neck. Disgusting." She reaches up to clasp the necklace around her neck, then tosses me the peanut butter jar.

I wear it proudly on top of my new ruby necklace.

I can't pick a favorite.

Mama and Mimmy don't say anything, but they both look as hopeful as Ginger. The sun has dipped completely out of sight by now, and Mama lights the firepit next to us while Mimmy brings out a few citronella candles. They clear away the plates and scraps from the table and then announce they're heading to bed. Time for old biddies to sleep, and young hellcats to keep the party going, Mama says. I don't miss her parting wink.

"What now?" Max asks when it's just the three of us. He sits next to me on the hammock, kicking back to swing. His eyes flick to my necklaces. Away, and then back again. "You still have a few hours of birthday left."

"Don't ask me. The birthday girl can't make her own plans."

"Is it a bad time to say that before I knew Stella was going to get us nice and toasty today, I might have packed a special birthday bottle of my own?" Ginger walks over to her canvas tote she's left by the picnic bench. "And mine might be a tad harder. Just a tad." There's an amber-filled bottle in her hand, glowing in the candlelight. Peach whiskey.

"That's probably a terrible idea." Just looking at it makes me feel woozy.

"One swig. Just us. A toast to all the wild adult times ahead."

"One," I say, already regretting it. "Only one. Don't you have an early shift tomorrow?"

"Nope. Already called in sick. Always thinking ahead." She's dragging a picnic bench to sit directly in front of the firepit. Close enough that stray flames will lick our shins. Max is already scavenging in the brush for additional pieces of wood.

We sit in a row, me in the middle, whiskey in Ginger's hand.

The first few drops go into the fire. The flames flare bigger and brighter, a *whoosh* of intense white light. "To eighteen being as luminous and warm as this fire," Ginger says, raising the bottle in the air. It looks like she's toasting the silhouetted trees beyond the firepit.

"You go next," she directs, handing it to me. I take a small sip, but it still burns hot the whole way down. Max takes a longer swig, and Ginger takes the longest of the three of us. She drops a small splash on the ground when she's finished. "For Noah," she says. "Though he only deserves a half swig."

We're quiet for a while, our eyes lost in the flames. Our minds lost on different thoughts. I mostly wonder about their thoughts. I'm actively trying not to have too many of my own.

"Why is it," Ginger starts, threading us back together, "that sitting around a fire at night with whiskey makes you want to talk about deep, dark secrets?"

"I would guess that's the whiskey magic at work." I feel warmer, looser, but fully here.

"Feel free to share any secrets you might have, though," Max says. "You and I still have some bonding to do. Nothing like embarrassing secrets to seal the friendship deal."

I glance at Max from the corner of my eye. He looks calm, happy, far from the Max who sat around the fire with me last night. Divulging his own deep, dark secrets. Maybe Ginger is right, sitting around a fire at night does bring out something confessional in all of us. Even without whiskey.

"Sadly, neighbor boy, I haven't lived enough yet to have anything that exciting or embarrassing to share. Unless you count the time I shit my pants on a haunted hayride. In eighth grade. That was a low point. Poor Calliope was a witness." Ginger laughs, poking at the fire with a long, forked branch. She pauses for a minute before she says, "My secrets are mostly fears. I hate that I'm eighteen in a few weeks and I've never kissed anyone. Unless you count kissing myself in the mirror. Never gone on a date. Never been asked on one. I talk such a big game and carry myself like I've got more confidence than a wild cougar, but news flash: a lot of it's an act. I guess I hope that if you make believe you're a certain kind of person, that's the kind of person you'll end up being. So far, no positive results in testing that particular theory."

I've never heard Ginger say that before, never heard her voice sound so slight and uncertain. I hate that she couldn't tell me that, at least not without whiskey. Or flames. Or both. "You've never dated," I say, "because Green Woods is a very tiny, very pathetic pool and no one is nearly good enough to deserve you."

"Easy to say. I know that your dream boy appeared out of thin air next door to you like some fairy-tale prince, so your view is skewed. But maybe I'll always be the odd one out. Maybe there's no fairy-tale princess waiting for me."

"Dream boy, huh?" Max asks, puffing out his chest. "Fairy-tale prince?"

Ginger leans around me to slap him on the wrist. "Don't ruin my serious confessional. The spotlight was on me."

"Ginger, please." He grabs her hand, holds on. "Here's what I already know about you: You're going to have to majorly rest up this next year, because once college hits, you'll be on a date with a different girl every night. You'll have *too* many options. You won't know what to do with yourself. Trust that."

"He's right." I put my hand on top of his, a stack of three.

"Whatever you say, Mommy and Daddy." I don't need to look over to catch the eye roll. But her voice is lighter. More Ginger-like. "Okay. Done baring my soul. Who's next?"

"Me," Max says without missing a beat. I turn to him, wildly curious. Our hands all stay together. It feels like a key part of whatever is about to come next.

"My grandmother died in our house. Because of my grandfather."

Just like that, he says it. No lead-in. No softening.

My jaw feels unhinged it drops so low. Ginger gasps next to me.

I don't think either of us breathes as we wait for more.

Surely there will be more.

But then after an unbearable pause Max says, "That's it. Sorry. I don't really want to talk about it more. Not tonight. Not on your birthday."

Max drops his hand, and Ginger and I pull ours back, too. A moment has ended.

Maybe it's all true, what they say about the Jackson house. But it's not some local horror story. It's Max's family. Flesh and blood. Real people, real lives.

"Okay, somebody besides me needs to say something." Max reaches over, presses on my chin to close my mouth. "Calliope. Your turn. Even the birthday girl has to reveal something."

There is no possible follow-up.

"I . . . err . . ." I try to think of words, any words.

What is my secret? Do I have any secrets from these two people?

There is one. My birthday wish.

I open my mouth, and this time words successfully come:

"I want to know who Frank really is."

Chapter Eleven

I wait for Ginger to leave the next morning, after we've success-fully nursed our mild hangovers with pancakes and eggs and coffee. Mama, too—she called in a sub for her first class. But breakfast heals her enough that she can take on her second class, thankfully.

When I'm alone in the house, I walk upstairs and slip into my moms' bedroom. I crouch next to their bed and pull out the locked firesafe chest they keep under it. My birthday is the win-ning combination. It only takes a few minutes of riffling through our official family documents, social security cards and passports and deeds, to find what I knew would be inside: a neat file folder containing the details of the sperm donation.

I take the folder and close the safe, shove it back under the bed where I found it, and then head to my room. I sit down at my desk and flip open my laptop.

My fingers shake as I type in the name of the cryobank and click through to their website.

Cryobank. It's such a sterile word. A sterile place, too, no doubt.

Cryobank. Cryo-: involving or producing icy cold, frost.

Cryobank. I wouldn't be here without one. I wouldn't exist.

I find the tab I'm looking for: *Request Donor Contact.* Because once upon a time, on one particular day in history more than eighteen years and nine months ago, Frank chose to become an open donor, he's obligated to a minimum of one communication with me, upon my request. Unless he's dead. I suppose no one can obligate him in that case. I'm out of luck then. I won't ask if they'll release the name if he is dead, so I can at least read a scrappy obituary summary of his life. I'd rather not consider that possibility yet.

I have to submit my official request in writing. My parents' names, the donor number, some other vital information that is all clearly laid out in my moms' files. I note that I'm open to any kind of contact: e-mail, hard-copy letter, phone call, an exchange of information. Whatever Frank prefers.

I read through it all twice, make sure all the correct information is there. And then before I can stop myself, I click *Submit Request.*

Just like that, I've set it all in motion. It was so fast. So easy.

The cryobank will do the rest. They'll reach out to him. Inform him of my request. He'll choose the form of contact, and then they'll send his e-mail, or letter, or phone number to me. My personal information is confidential until I choose to respond. *If* I choose to respond.

I close out the screen, shove the folder in my desk drawer, and stand up.

I walk downstairs, out through the kitchen door, and flop onto the hammock.

And then I wait.

*   *   *

The weekend is a necessary distraction.

Max picks me up early Saturday morning for our grand birthday Philly tour. He comes to the front door dressed in dark jeans and a checkered short-sleeve button-up shirt with a black skinny tie around his neck. I'm glad I changed outfits five times and landed on the silky green dress that I worried at first would be too fancy.

It's our first time outside of Green Woods together, and the thrill of it thrums in my veins as soon as we pass through the town limits. I put the windows down and turn the radio up and close my eyes as the warm breeze tangles my hair.

There's a palpable buzz of freedom here in this car with Max. Escape.

For the first time, I feel eighteen. I feel different.

We don't talk much during the ride. And we certainly don't talk about our *secrets*. I don't ask about his grandparents, and he doesn't mention Frank. It's like whatever happened around the firepit on my birthday was a contained moment that existed only in that specific time and place, with neatly sealed borders that none of us dare to cross again.

I've been to Philly more times than I can count, but driving into the city with Max makes it feel brand-new. I see it through his eyes. I feel the deep love, the joy.

Our first stop is a tour of Reading Terminal Market. Max had been aghast to hear I'd never been before. It's chaotic and loud and exploding with people and smells—some better than others—aisle after cluttered aisle of vendors and markets, every kind of food one could possibly imagine. Fine meats and exotic produce, honeys and jams and herbs, chocolates, coffee, doughnuts. Max takes me to his favorite stalls, and it's a long list. We split a roast pork sandwich and a grilled cheese with pickled green tomatoes, a cinnamon sugar pretzel and a lemon lavender whoopie pie, an apple fritter. We wash it all down with a minty fresh lemonade.

My stomach aches by the time we leave. "If you leave here feeling healthy, you did the market wrong," Max says, grinning at me.

He takes me to his old neighborhood next, parking the car outside the building he had lived in since he was a kid. Max's family had a floor to themselves. The tenth floor—the very top. It doesn't look like anything special from the outside—pale brown stones, ten stories of white-framed windows, a big green door with a silver 4-1-2 at the top. But the way Max looks at it makes it feel like the most special building on the block. Maybe in the whole city.

"Can we go inside?" I ask, grabbing his hand. "I want to see more. I want to see your old view."

"I doubt the new people who live there would let two strangers poke around their home. But it's okay. I think being in there would make me feel sad and nostalgic and weird, and I don't want to feel that way today. There's no room for any of that bad stuff." He squeezes my hand tight. "I loved it here. It was home. But I'm not sure it feels that way anymore."

We walk for a long time, Max pointing out all his old

favorites—favorite deli, favorite Chinese restaurant, favorite mural, favorite park, favorite bench.

"Favorite bench?" I stop walking and scowl down at the bench. "Do I want to know what happened here?" I picture it before I can stop myself: Max and a pretty, giggling girl, a kiss—maybe his first kiss. A kiss he can't possibly ever forget.

"Stop whatever you are thinking. Please. God. It's where I used to bring Marlow when our mom and dad were fighting and we needed a break from the house. We had a lot of good times here. Probably our best times together. Listened to a lot of music. Mostly me DJ'ing, her listening and learning. Jazz, funk, classical, pop. Played some card games. Sketched people that walked by. It's an excellent people-watching spot. You wouldn't believe the characters we'd see. Philly has some special people, that's for sure."

After we've canvassed the entire neighborhood, we get back into Max's car. We drive, touring one neighborhood after the next, Max keeping up a steady running commentary of the sites. I'm not sure where we're at when we stop to get out of the car again, but after a few minutes of walking, I see it: the *LOVE* sculpture. I've seen it before—everyone has—but I've never actually walked up to it. Never taken a picture with it.

But we do now, in true tourist fashion, asking the most reliable-looking bystander if he'll take our picture. We trust him not to steal Max's phone based on his neat gray comb-over and spiffy white Keds and the fanny pack clipped around his waist.

I try not to read into the photo—Max and I posing in front of bold red *LOVE*.

It's just a thing that tourists do. Being in love is not a requirement.

I'm surprised to find that I'm hungry again, and Max insists we can't leave until we eat a proper dinner. Food we could never eat in Green Woods, he says. He takes me to a Moroccan restaurant, dimly lit and covered in plush cushions. We're served round after round of delicious sweet, spicy food, pies and stew and kebabs and pastries.

We end the day with a stroll along Boathouse Row, charming old houses lining the edges of the Schuylkill River. The sun has just set and the glittering lights framing the houses are reflected in the dark, still water. We stop and hug by the glowing banks and I hold Max more tightly than I've ever held anything in my life.

Philly will never feel the same.

Max and I sit in the parked car in my driveway.

Neither of us is ready to say good night. It's been too perfect a day to end it before midnight. Every last minute of it needs to be fully lived.

Only the porch light is turned on. The windows are all black. Mimmy and Mama didn't wait up. They never do, and I'm glad tonight wasn't an exception.

We're listening to the crickets, Max improvising lyrics to go along with the loud hum of their nightly mating call. *Playing out, into the night, those cricket ladies are lovely all right.* There's a lull in the noise, and Max abruptly stops singing. He turns to look at me.

"Can I tell you something?" he asks. He sounds nervous. His hand feels warm in mine. Too warm. I'm nervous now, too, nervous that we'll cross those boundaries after all, talk about things I'd rather leave unsaid. At least for today. No Frank. No family drama. No murder.

"Sure," I say anyway. The right response, even if it's not the one I'd prefer. It wouldn't be kind to say I'd rather listen to crickets rubbing their wings together than whatever Max would like to confide in me.

"I wanted to say it earlier today. A few times. But the moment never felt right enough."

"You're making me anxious."

"I'm sorry."

"Okay."

"This isn't how I pictured it going."

"It's not how you pictured what going?"

"I love you, Calliope. I know we only met last month, but I do. I've been falling for you since the day I came looking for sugar."

"Oh."

There's not nearly enough air circulating in the car. I jab frantically at the window button to put it all the way down. Then I remember that the car is shut off. The window doesn't move. I open the door instead.

"Uh. Are you running away?"

"No. Of course not. Just getting some more air in here."

"I'm not sure that's the response I was going for."

"You're making me want to faint. That's not a bad thing. Romance can do that to a girl."

"You know you don't have to say it back. It's not like that. I probably just terrified you, saying it so soon. You don't owe me an *I love you* just because I said it to you."

"I know."

"Good."

"But I do."

"You do?"

"I do."

"You do what?"

"I love you, too."

"Thank god." He slaps the steering wheel with his free hand. "You scared the shit out of me. But I wanted to handle myself like a real gentleman. Act all brave and understanding, even with rejection."

It's dark in the car, but I can still see the relieved smile break open on his face.

Maybe this—*love*—happened fast. But that doesn't make it less real.

I love him. I do.

"Can we say it again?" he asks. "Just so I can be sure I didn't dream the last time. And because you kind of took your sweet time getting to it."

"I love you, Max Martz."

"I love you, too, Calliope Silversmith."

* * *

The letter comes on Thursday.

A week after I submitted the request.

The return address is the cryobank.

This feels fast for an actual response from *him*. Too fast.

It could just be a confirmation, I suppose, some official note letting me know that the request is being processed. But I know without opening it—that's not what it is. I know that the answer I think I want will be inside.

I checked the mailbox as soon as I got home from my shift at the studio—I've been tracking the mail obsessively, along with vigilant e-mail checks on my phone. The mail truck comes between 11:13 and 11:48 every morning without fail. Mama and Mimmy are usually at work then, but a few times on off shifts one of them beat me to it. I'm lucky today was not one of those days.

I'll tell them, of course I will. But not yet.

I tuck the letter under my pillow and sit on my bed. It's hot and stuffy in the attic, even with the fan on full blast, like every other day so far this summer. The atmosphere doesn't feel right for this kind of revolutionary life moment. I need to be comfortable. Focused. My best self.

So where do I open it? When exactly? Do I go outside—maybe sit in the hollow of my tree, or climb to the top of the peak overlooking the valley, or sit along the edge of the pond? Drive to a café? Go somewhere outside Green Woods, order a nice latte like an adult and sit there and sip it while I open an envelope that could change everything. Act casual, like it's any other day, and this is any other piece of paper.

Do I wait until dark, when secrets feel more secret?

Mama calls up from the bottom of the attic steps and my heart beats against my chest. I didn't think she'd be home from the studio until later.

"Can I get your help with the garden, sweetie? The weeds are total monsters."

She pops my door open.

I jump up from the bed, my eyes darting back to the pillow. Safe. Fine. No envelope edges peeking out. Nothing to see.

"Everything okay?"

"Sure. Totally okay. I just didn't think you'd be home so early. You scared me."

She glances around the room, like she's not convinced that's all that's going on. Looking for what I'm not sure, Max's foot sticking out from under the bed, a stray marijuana bud. "I gave Marielle my afternoon classes. I need to get some yard work done. We're starting to look like the Jackson house." She shudders at the thought. "Though I haven't seen it in a while, and not since they moved in. Has your boy helped fix the place up?"

"A little." Not really, though. *My boy* thinks it's his dad's duty. His house, his promises. It's more of a standoff than anything. Joanie did at least trim some of the hedges that were starting to grow up over the porch steps.

I change into an old pair of overalls and give one last resigned look at my pillow before following Mama downstairs.

Later. After weeding. There's no rush.

But clearing the garden turns into taking a spin with the push mower, and after that Mama notices weeds growing in the cracks of our front path. I'm sweaty and sunburned and greatly in need of a shower by the time Mama releases me.

Mimmy's home then, too, calling up to me as I'm brushing out my wet hair, asking for help cutting up vegetables for dinner.

Ginger texts asking if she can come over to escape her mom.

Max shows up on the doorstep with some wildflowers he picked by the pond.

And just like that, my day is gone, every minute filled with the people I love. The people I'd like to escape, just for a few hours.

Ginger stays until ten. And it's well after midnight by the time Max slips back through the woods to his house.

My room is still hot, but not quite as unbearable as it was before.

Maybe there is no perfect time or perfect place. Maybe I need to grab the moment whenever it's here.

And here it is.

I sit on my bed, facing the round window. The moon. I take a deep breath.

With trembling fingers, I open the envelope.

The first piece of paper is from the cryobank—they explain that my donor opted to write a letter, which was then e-mailed to their office.

The second piece of paper is from him. Frank. A neatly typed letter that the cryobank printed out.

Before I read a word, I pick up my phone and scroll through my music library. It's only appropriate to have some Frank Zappa on right now. I select "Valley Girl" to start. I know from Mama that Zappa's daughter Moon is featured on that song.

Music playing—volume low enough for me to tolerate—I turn back to the letter.

I start at the top. I want to read all the way through, as it is, not cheat and skip to the bottom. The name that I'm hoping I'll find there.

Hello,

I'm not sure how to address a letter when I don't know who you are. What your name is. A simple hello will have to suffice. But really: hello. I mean it. It's good to "meet."

Though it's strange to make contact. To acknowledge your existence. I'm sure it's just as strange for you.

I have to admit, I'd long forgotten the decision I'd made nineteen years ago. Or not forgotten. Never forgotten. That's not possible. They alerted me at the time to a confirmed pregnancy, but that was the last update I received, so I didn't know if the pregnancy was viable or not. I pushed it away after that. Deep into the back of my mind. I made myself busy with other things.

I was still young at the time, trying to make it in Philadelphia with heavy student debt, and I needed money. (I won't pretend my motives were purely altruistic.) And I was so certain about so many things. One thing I was especially certain about was that I would never have children of my own. I figured that donation—helping other people to have the children they desperately wanted to have—was also a decent thing to do. I kept the donation open because I knew I would be too curious otherwise. I would wonder. Maybe no one would be out there. Or maybe somebody would be.

Here you are. Nineteen years later.

I hope that you've had a good life. That your parents gave you the home and the opportunities you deserved.

In case you're wondering, I ended up having children of my own after all. Soon after the donation. Life laughs when we try to make plans. I don't think I was meant to be a dad, but so it is. You were better off to not have me in your life. I do believe that. You should, too.

I'm not sure what else to say now. I don't know that I can offer you anything that you want or need. In fact—I know that I can't. But if you are still curious about any family history, I'll put my cell number below.

I really do hope you are well. And happy. Above all, happy.

Best,

I close my eyes before I can see the name. My stomach swirls—with anticipation, with dread, with guilt.

It is just a name.

A name will tell me nothing. The name has no power until I search for it online or call his number.

It is just a name.

I open my eyes. The words on the page loop and swirl and I grip the letter tighter as I focus on the bottom.

Best,
Elliot Jackson

Elliot Jackson.
Elliot.
Jackson.
Elliot Jackson.
No.

It's a common name.

This Elliot Jackson could live anywhere—across the country, across the Atlantic.

This Elliot Jackson is not my next-door neighbor.

This Elliot Jackson cannot be Max's father.

Chapter Twelve

I drop the letter to the floor. Sweep it under the bed with my foot.

I can't hold it. I can't look at it.

I can't breathe.

I shut my eyes tight, swallowing the first surge of bile that rushes up my throat.

This can't be right.

The Elliot who wrote this letter must be another Elliot Jackson. Or the cryobank has made a terrible, terrible mistake. Crossed wires. Had the wrong donor write to me.

I was not from a bloodline of maybe murderers. Cheaters.

I was not from the same bloodline as Max.

Max.

The next wave of nausea hits with more force. I jump from the bed, throw my shaky legs down the stairs as fast as I can manage without tumbling headfirst in front of my moms' bedroom door. *I will not puke on the steps. I will not puke in the hallway.* I hurl myself into the bathroom, lock the door, and fall to my knees in front of the toilet.

I wretch over and over again. Dinner, lunch, bile. I wretch until there is nothing left inside me. I am hollow. A shell.

I'm too weak to move at first, my arms still hugging the bowl for support. The porcelain feels cool against my hot skin.

The tears come next. I was wrong—there is something left inside me after all. A steady *drip-drip* added to the pool of vomit. I flush the toilet. Flush again. Add more tears to a fresh bowl of water.

There's a knuckle tap against the door. So quiet at first, I desperately hope I've imagined it. I hold my breath, listen.

Another tap. "Calliope?" Mama. Shit. Mimmy would be easier to get rid of.

I slowly let go of the bowl, grab a wad of toilet paper to dry my eyes. Take a deep breath. "I'm okay. I think it's just a little food poisoning or something."

The knob rattles. "You locked the door?"

We never lock doors. Not the front door, not the bedrooms, not the bathroom.

"I guess so. Sorry. I wasn't thinking clearly."

A pause and then, "Can you let me in? I want to help."

I grip the edge of the tub as I push myself to stand. The rows of checkered black-and-white bathroom tiles seem to be moving in a snakelike crawl beneath my feet. One step. Two. Three. I reach the mirror by the sink—I don't want to look but I do. It's a cruel, masochistic urge. I need to see if I look as awful on the outside as I feel on the inside.

I do.

My eyes are rimmed in purple, swollen and squinty. I'm still sunburned in odd spots from my day of enforced yard work, but every other bit of skin is as pale as I've ever seen it—paler than when I had the flu two winters back. My hair is stuck to my cheeks, glued in place by some noxious combination of vomit and tears and sweat.

"Calliope? Please." Mama's voice is less patient now. More knob rattling.

"Coming." I reach for the faucet, splash a handful of cold water on my face. I check my reflection again, and I look just as awful as I did before, only now my hair is even more matted.

I undo the lock. Mama is already opening the door before I can turn the knob myself.

"Food poisoning?" she asks, brow deeply furrowed. "You haven't been out to eat the past few days. We've eaten all the same foods. Maybe it's a bug. Or hormones. Where are you at with your cycle? I'm due for mine this week, and you know that cycles—"

"Mama." A mother's go-to—always, always the cycle. "No. It's not my period. You're right, it's probably just a bug. I'll wake up feeling fine."

She leans in, studying my face up close. "Have you been crying?"

"What? No." I reach up to touch my cheeks, like I'm confused as to why she would ask such a question. "I was puking hard, though, so my eyes were watering up."

"Hm." It's a deeply suspicious *hm*. If it was Mimmy, she would have already sent me back up to bed, and she'd be downstairs making a cup of chamomile tea to fix me. Not Mama. "Listen, sweetheart. If something has you upset to the point of puking and crying, I would love to know about it. I probably don't need to tell you that. But if you're not ready to share . . . I'll respect that, too. Or I'll try to at least. Temporarily. No promises long-term. Okay?"

I nod. She's hoping I'll break down now. Tell her what really had me wrapped around the toilet bowl in the middle of the night. But I don't. I can't.

When I don't say anything more, she sighs and throws her arms around me. "Anything that's going on, you'll get through it. *We'll* get through it. It can't be that bad."

It's hard not to laugh. *Not that bad.*

What would she say if she knew?

The truth? My donor lives next door, and his son is my boyfriend.

No. My *maybe* donor lives next door. I can't be sure. Not with so little to go on.

"Calliope? Hello? Are you still there?"

"Still here," I say. "Just sleepy."

Mama follows me up the attic steps and I silently thank any god and the stars above and the whole almighty universe that I had the good sense to kick the letter under my bed. She punches roughly at my pillow to fluff it before I lie back down. Even though it's a balmy eighty-some degrees in my room, I let her tuck the sheet tight around me, just like when I was a little girl. It feels good to be covered up. Hidden.

"It really will be okay," she whispers, her lips pecking my forehead.

Will it be?

Can it be?

I might be in love with my brother.

Biological brother. *Half* brother. Though I don't think the "half" makes it better in this case. Blood is blood.

Funny that I never thought blood mattered that much. It didn't matter that I don't share blood with one of my moms. Or Ginger and Noah. They were all my family.

But blood matters now.

Blood is everything.

I don't sleep.

How can I?

All I think about is Max—*Max and me.* A constant loop.

How could being together feel so *right?*

If it's true, if we're related, shouldn't I have felt it somehow? Sensed it?

Some primal instinct should have triggered in me—internal red lights, alarm bells, flashing CAUTION signs imprinted deep in my DNA.

But there was nothing like that. It felt happy. And good. And real.

It was real. Still is.

I close my eyes and picture Max, and I don't know how I can possibly un-love him—as if it was a conscious decision to fall in love in the first place. It wasn't a choice with Max. I met him, and I fell in love with him. Rule or no rule. That was just how it was.

My sheets are drenched in sweat, knotted up from my tossing and turning. The sun comes up and I'm still wide awake. The light seems to form a spotlight on Max's canvas, me and my tree. I can't look away—can't stop remembering that golden day. Our first kiss. The painting, the picnic, dozing on Max's shoulder.

No, Calliope. Stop.

I need to get out of bed. Away from this painting.

The smells of coffee and toast rise from the kitchen. I've never been less hungry, but I know Mama will be up to check on me before going to the studio if I don't come down first. Her temporary patience might flag if I don't at least pretend to be recovering. I swing my legs over the bed and stand. Force my feet down both sets of stairs, one step at a time.

Mama and Mimmy are at the table, sipping coffee with their plates of fresh fruit and peanut butter toast.

"Good morning, sweetheart," Mama says, watching me carefully. "Feeling better?"

"I am. Just like we expected." I take a piece of toast and a few scoops of fruit as proof. The bread is too dry in my mouth, but I smile as I chew.

Mimmy reaches over to pat my hand. "I'm sorry I didn't wake up last night when you were sick. I somehow slept straight through it. Want any chamomile? It'll be easier on your stomach than coffee."

"I think I need some coffee," I mumble, pouring myself a full mug of it even as Mimmy pinches her lips in disapproval. Coffee is my only chance of getting through this day.

Hopefully I'll be exhausted enough by the end of it to sleep tonight. Nightmares can't be worse than reality.

I'm halfway through my mug when I realize with a start that Max could show up on our doorstep at some point today. Bright and chipper and fiending for a baked good. And a kiss.

I can't. I can't kiss him. I can't see him.

"I think I might go to the park this morning," I say, putting my coffee down too hard, splashing some onto the table.

"By yourself?" Mimmy asks, handing me a napkin. "No Max? Or Ginger?"

"I'm sure I'll see them at some point. Later. I just want to spend a little time with myself. I haven't had much of that this summer. Maybe I'll bring a book. Journal."

I sop up the coffee, pretending not to see the quick look Mama and Mimmy exchange.

"Everything is fine. Really." I dip the last end of my toast in the coffee, then shove it in my mouth. "You've always said I need to be my own best friend first and foremost."

"That is very true," Mimmy concedes. "Don't forget a blanket. And sunscreen. And water. And snacks. And—"

"I won't."

"You know, some time alone really might be just what you need." Mama takes a slow sip of coffee, her eyes fixed on me as I stand from the table. "I like Max. You know I do. But you're so young. And you two got serious pretty quickly. It's okay to take things slow. No rush. You have all the time in the world."

We have no time, I want to scream. *No time!*

Slow, fast, it doesn't matter.

If my Elliot is his Elliot, there's no time left.

I walk for a while when I get to the park. I walk until I reach the other side of the lake, find a small shady patch between the bank and the woods. It feels more private here.

I flip through the pages of *Sense and Sensibility*. Try and fail to lose myself in the Dashwood sisters' drama. I put the book down. Pick up my phone. I open the internet app and search: *donor siblings meet*.

I read about a donor whose sperm created fifty children. Fifty. That seems excessive—until I find another article about a British donor who says he likely has eight hundred offspring. Maybe a thousand.

This is our reality, according to the articles I tear through frantically, one after another—these kinds of massive, sprawling genetic families, with no precedent or consistent rules and protocols, especially in America, that prevent this kind of disaster from happening: offspring of prolific donors meeting and falling in love, not knowing the truth about their connection. Not knowing the genetic risks that come packaged with their love.

I read more about online registries, and stories of donor siblings tracking each other down through mail-away DNA tests, regardless of a donor's anonymity.

Some also ended up meeting by chance, fate, serendipity, whatever the hell you want to call it. One couple got married before they discovered their common origin. They had kids.

Three of them. They'd felt *connected* from the first time they met. They'd thought that bond was a good thing. Until they found out the truth.

My moms and I had never seriously discussed signing up for the Donor Sibling Registry. But of course I'd wondered about it sometimes, in all my years thinking about Frank—how many donor siblings might be out there in the world. How many other half Franks were wandering around, not knowing about him. Not knowing about me.

It had seemed so hypothetical.

But it would be naive to think I'm the only one. That it's just me and his actual son. And—oh god. *Marlow.* A possible half sister, too.

I drop my phone. I'm at my limit of absorption for the day.

Max texted a few times while I was engrossed in my search, and I read them now. He went to the house, he said, and no one was home. Was I working? The next text said that he drove into town for iced coffee, stopped by the studio with one for me. I wasn't there either.

I deliberate over my lie, and then type: *I had to run some errands today. New school things.*

He instantly sends back a kissy face.

That emoji, a *kiss*, makes me nauseated.

I can't avoid him forever. I do realize that.

Which means there's only one thing to be done right now— I'll call the cell phone number from the letter. The letter I tucked in my bag when I left my house this morning. I'll call Elliot

Jackson. Hopefully not the same Elliot Jackson who's living next door. The one who is biologically half of my boyfriend. I'll listen to his *hello*, or his voice mail message, and either I'll recognize his voice or not and I'll have my answer.

I can't see Max again until I know the truth.

Because if it's a different Elliot Jackson, then we'll be perfectly okay. This will all be over. The most horrific misunderstanding possible, nothing more. Maybe Max and I will even be able to laugh about it someday. In the—very—distant future. Or maybe I'll never tell anyone. It can be my secret. A nightmare that never leaves my own mind, never infects anyone else.

Please let it be a horrific misunderstanding.

I pull my journal out of my bag, find the page where I've neatly tucked away the letter.

And then I pick up my phone. I tap *-6-7 to block my caller ID, and enter his number slowly, carefully. I tap the last digit, hold my breath. Wait.

Seven rings. Eight. Nine. Ten.

An automated voice clicks on: *You have reached the voice mailbox for two-one-five—*

I hang up. Count to one hundred. Press to redial.

The automated voice comes on again and I throw the phone down. I'm not ready to leave a message, because what would I say? The plan was just to hear his voice, either in person or on a recording. That's where my strategy ended.

I try a last-ditch effort—I do an internet search using his number. There's nothing helpful, though, no clear identifiers for an Elliot Jackson. I could wade through useless webpages for hours. It feels like a black hole.

I need a sounding board. A second opinion. Some brutally blunt advice.

I need Ginger.

She doesn't instantly respond to my text asking what she's doing, which must mean she's working at the diner. I gather up my blanket and bag and head to the car.

The roads and signs and cars are a blur. *You are going to tell Ginger everything.* I'm lucky that I pull into the diner parking lot unscathed. I kiss my hand and tap the ceiling of the car, a superstitious and nonsensical habit courtesy of Mimmy. But I don't question it. Just in case. I scan the parking lot and exhale with relief when I see Ginger's bright yellow car.

She's with a customer when I walk in, looking like a perfect pinup retro waitress in her short red-and-white-checkered dress and frilled white apron, red scarf tied around her neck and cat-eye glasses frames that don't hold actual prescription lenses. And red lipstick, of course. It might be the local diner and no one else gives a shit, but Ginger does. Ginger gives a shit. She somehow makes wiping down greasy Formica tables and serving plates of congealed omelets look glamorous. Like the most desirable job in Green Woods.

I sit down at a booth and watch while I wait. Her customer is certainly enjoying his service. A fifty-something man, balding with a denial comb-over, wearing a white muscle tee and acid-washed denim shorts that should have been disposed of several decades ago.

Ginger is smiling and nodding politely as he leers at her, but the second she turns away she rolls her eyes and purses her lips.

I wave from across the room to get her attention. She stops walking when she sees me, clearly surprised—I used to come here all the time on her shifts, but I haven't done it once this summer. My guilt is a prickly, uncomfortable itch. I'm only here now because my life is a disaster. Not because I'm a good friend who wanted to brighten her day with my company.

But she smiles as she starts over toward me.

"Hey," she says, dropping down next to me in the booth. "Fancy seeing you here."

"I know. I'm sorry I haven't visited you yet this summer."

"Oh please." She waves her hand, her nails tipped in checkered black and white. "I don't really blame you. The food is supremely mediocre, for one. And I'd be distracted, too, if my soul mate suddenly moved in next door."

Soul mate.

Did I think that?

Maybe. Deep down. In a place I wouldn't dare let become words before. And certainly not now.

My face must crumble, because Ginger looks panicked.

"What? What did I say? Is everything okay? You and Max didn't . . . ?"

"No. We didn't break up."

"Oh, *thank god*. I was starting to feel positive about love again after the pep talk you two gave me on your birthday. If you two broke up now, we'd both be hopeless."

"Ginger..." I wipe my clammy palms against my dress. My stomach twists. This is Ginger, I remind myself. I shouldn't be nervous. I can tell her anything. Always. "Any chance you have a break coming up soon?"

She studies me for a moment, her heavily darkened eyebrows pulled in a tight line. Then she glances at the clock, sighs. "Give me fifteen minutes, okay? I'll bring you a root beer."

I drain two glasses of root beer while I wait. The bubbles float in my empty stomach.

"Sorry," Ginger says a half hour later, putting a piece of strawberry pie in front of me. It's unnaturally red and shiny and covered in a swirly mound of whipped cream. It's nearly as big as my head. There are two forks on the plate at least. She slides into the booth next to me, close enough that our arms and legs are pressed together. Her apron is off to show that she's on her break, and her glasses are clipped to her collar. "You looked like someone who needed some pie. I have fifteen minutes. Tell me everything." She picks up one of the forks, cuts off a squishy-looking lump of strawberry from the tip of the pie.

"I did it. I requested Frank's name."

She drops the fork, and the sad strawberry, on the table. "You did?"

"He wrote me a letter."

"Oh my god. That was fast." Her red lips are a perfect O. "Calliope. This is so huge."

"His name is Elliot Jackson."

She starts to say something. Stops. Starts. Stops again. It's like the sound our old lawn mower makes when I first try to rev it up.

"Not—it's not—?" She's begging me to fill in the blanks for her.

"I don't know. He gave me a phone number. I tried calling it before I came here, hoping I could hear his voice and figure things out that way, but I got a robot voice. I didn't know what to say in an actual message, so I hung up. I used the number to search the internet, too, but didn't find anything helpful."

She stares at me with wide, unblinking eyes. "How does this happen, though? I mean the likelihood of being *neighbors*. It must be one in a million. A billion even. Don't they have rules in place to stop exactly this from happening?"

I shrug helplessly. "I was researching earlier today. The system has flaws. I'm proof of that."

"But it can't be him. Right? You would know. You just would."

"Would I?"

She nods, but not with her usual Ginger flair of confidence. "I mean, you met Elliot, didn't you? Did you notice any similarities?"

"No. Besides the fact that we're both white, I look nothing like him."

"Okay. Then you probably have nothing to worry about."

"So you think it could be another Elliot Jackson?"

She picks up the dropped berry with her fingers, pops it in her mouth. I don't know how she's eating right now. I want to scream as I wait for her to finish chewing.

"Maybe," she says finally.

"Maybe?" I definitely want to scream now. And I would, if we weren't sitting in Ginger's place of employment.

"I don't know, Calliope. We have no other facts. You didn't get the answers you needed from calling the number. So you can either keep trying until he picks up the phone, or you can put your big girl pants on and walk next door and talk to him."

"Even then, say I talk to him and he tells me he wrote the letter—maybe the cryobank messed up. They could have had a glitch in the system, or the person referencing the donor number was hungover and miserable and not paying attention. It could be a mistake."

"That's why you have to talk to him face-to-face. And look at him. *Really* look at him."

"But we see what we want to see sometimes, don't you think? Or in this case, don't see what we don't want to see. I don't think I can trust my eyes."

"Maybe. But I don't think you have another choice. He's the only way to get answers. He's the key to everything." When I don't have a response, she asks, "Have you told anyone else yet?"

"No."

"So Max has no clue about any of this?"

"No."

"You know you have to tell him."

"If it's true. Only if it's true. Why scare him away if I have it wrong?"

She bites down hard on her lip, smearing her perfectly applied lipstick. Her teeth are now as unnaturally red as the pie. "And you never felt . . . anything off about you and Max? Never picked up on any weird vibes?"

"No, Ginger. Never once when we were making out did I stop and think—*Gee, could this be my biological half brother? Wouldn't that be something?* And then keep going."

"I know that. I'm sorry. I don't know what the right questions are right now."

"I don't know the right words either."

"I mean—your *brother*."

"My half brother."

"If it's true, what would you do?"

"What do I do? I have to break up with him. It's—" I can't bring myself to say it out loud.

Incest. Test-tube incest, maybe, a product of science. But still—incest.

I start laughing hysterically. It's just so ridiculous—I can't not laugh. Ginger's eyes widen with concern. She picks up the fork and cuts off a big chunk of pie, lifting it up to my lips. "Eat. You need pie. Please."

The pie tastes as fake as I expected, the strawberries sugar-soaked and gelatinous. But the whipped cream makes it more palatable. I obediently chew and swallow.

"It would be illegal to ever have sex with him," I say matter-of-factly when I'm finished.

"That's why you were laughing?"

"Yep."

"You didn't, though? Yet? Did you?"

I shake my head. "No. Definitely not. We've only kissed. But we did say—"

She waits, compulsively eating a few forkfuls of pie in the interim.

"We said 'I love you.'"

"When?"

"The day he took me to Philly."

"You said you loved each other and didn't tell me?" Her whole face droops. "That's...kind of a big deal, Calliope. I know we haven't had much—or any—real alone time, just the two of us. But you could have called me."

"I'm sorry. I should have told you. I don't know why I didn't."

She's quiet after that. It's unsettling.

"It was stupid of me. And if I could redo it again differently, I would. I'd tell you right away. But it doesn't even matter now, that I love him and he loves me. If his dad is my..." I close my eyes. *Donor. Frank.* "Then it was all for nothing. I was a bad friend who got swept up in boyfriend land, and I'll end up all alone in the end. Maybe I deserve that."

"You don't have to be quite that dramatic," Ginger says, roughly dissecting the last strawberries with her fork until it looks like a pile of obscene gore in the middle of the plate. "I would never say you deserve to be in love with your half brother. That's way too epically cruel and Shakespearean. I'm not sure I'd wish that on my worst enemy."

"So"—I reach for her hand, forcing her to drop the fork—"you forgive me? You pity me enough to let my bad behavior slide?"

"I didn't say that either." But she's smiling now, red and toothy. "Ugh. It's hard to stay mad at you when you might be in love with your sibling."

"Thanks for that, Ginger."

"Anytime. That's what best friends are for."

I drown myself in more diner food and too much coffee until Ginger is slammed with the dinner rush, and then I drive aimlessly in loops around town, trying and failing to get lost. It's impossible in this town. The sun sinks behind the hills at the edge of the valley, and I keep circling. I don't stop until Mama texts, asking where I am. She never checks in. It's time to give up for the day. Hope that I've stayed away long enough.

I turn my headlights off before turning down our driveway. Added precaution. Just in case the light would carry through the trees to the Jackson house. Max might be watching for me.

I'm walking up to the porch when I hear: "Something wrong with your lights?" I jump.

Mama's in her rocking chair, a tumbler of whiskey in her hand.

"My lights? No. I was fiddling with the brights. And then figured I was at our driveway, so I just turned them off."

"You do know you're a terrible liar. Which I'm glad about, by the way. Better to be a bad liar than a good one. Though better yet not to lie in the first place."

I sit down on the chair next to her. There's no walking away from this conversation.

"I'm assuming the stealth entrance was for the benefit of our dear neighbors. Though really, I would guess they can only see headlights in the winter, when the trees are bare. Maybe not even then." She takes a sip, glances off in the direction of the Jacksons' house. "I don't see any lights coming from their neck of the woods. So, in the future if you're avoiding Max, probably best to keep those lights on. Never know when a deer or a racoon or a kitten will wander in your path."

"I'm sorry."

"For turning your headlights off? Or for lying?"

I sigh. "Both."

"Good."

"It's complicated."

"I'm sure it is."

"I'm not ready to talk about it."

"That's fine. I don't need specifics. But you can be honest about hiding out. Would have saved an awkward conversation when Max came poking around the studio today. And then again at the house earlier this evening. He said he'd figured you'd be finished picking up new school things by then."

"Oh god. What did you tell him?"

"That you weren't at the studio. Or at home."

"Where did you say I was both times?"

"I said I wasn't sure. That you might be running some more errands."

"Thank you."

"You're welcome. It's what moms do."

We sit in silence for a few minutes, staring out into the dark, and I almost say it. I almost say: *I found Frank.*

But then Mama speaks. I swallow the confession. "Listen," she says. "I won't ask questions or make any grand speeches, but I will tell you this: Whatever it is that's got you so upset? It won't just go away. I'm glad you could have time to yourself today. But, darling—you have to face it. Whatever it is, whatever the implications are. Face it head-on. Be brave. You'll figure it out. I know you will."

"I don't think it'll be as easy as you think."

"I never said it would be *easy*. The most valuable things in life rarely are." Mama takes her last swig of whiskey and stands up. "We should get to bed. I suspect you didn't sleep a wink last night."

I follow her in and go through the motions, brushing my teeth, washing my face, putting on pajamas. I lie in my bed, steeling myself for the morning.

Ginger and Mama are both right. I need to face it straight on.

Face *him* straight on.

No more calls, no more automated voice mail. To be honest, I'm not even certain I'd recognize his voice over the phone well enough, not after one dinner. Even if he picked up, I would need more evidence. A more definitive answer.

I can't be stuck in this loop, wondering, worrying, lying.

Elliot runs in the morning. That's my best shot at catching him alone. Because I can't exactly knock on the door, say *Oh hello, Max, can I talk to your dad? Privately?*

I'll wake up early. Wait by the top of their driveway. Hope he doesn't take a break day.

That is the plan.

Please don't let it be him.

I'd rather he was cruel. A thief. A murderer. A convict of any kind, really.

I'd rather he was anyone else in the world.

Because anyone else means it's okay to love Max.

Chapter Thirteen

THE next morning my alarm goes off at five. For a groggy, dream-laced moment my brain can't comprehend why it's happening: It's summer. My moms never give me the opening shift at the studio. There is no sane reason for me to be awake before the sun is up. Is my alarm clock glitching?

And then it all comes back to me at once, a sad, heavy wave. Max and Elliot. The need to get to the bottom of everything. The need to know.

It's hard to decide what to wear when you might be meeting your father—*donor*—for the first time. Our dinner meeting doesn't count. Those stakes were very different. But at five in the morning, I conclude anything goes and throw a yoga hoodie on over the shorts and T-shirt I slept in and shove my feet into the glitter slip-ons Ginger made for my birthday. The extra sparkle gives me a small flare of courage. It's almost like Ginger will be there next to me, letting me borrow some of her shiny confidence. Though Ginger would never approve of waking up at this ungodly hour for anything other than a diner shift. Even then, she usually pulls an all-nighter instead, preferring to stay up late rather than wake up early.

I take the steps down as quietly as possible, one cautious tiptoe at a time. I'm expecting to breeze out the front door, but my plan is thrown off by a rattling sound in the brightly lit kitchen. Somebody is making coffee.

I'm wondering if it's possible to still slip out the door unheard and unseen when the last stair gives an unfortunate squeak.

Mimmy pokes her head out from the kitchen doorway. "Calliope? What are you doing up so early?"

"I woke up and couldn't fall back asleep, so—" My morning brain whirs, clunky spinning gears not yet in sync for the day. Mimmy watches me curiously. "So—so I thought maybe I'd watch the sunrise from the top of the hill. Start the day on a positive note."

Mimmy nods and smiles in approval, which only makes me feel worse about the lie.

"That sounds like the best way to start the day! Very grounding. I'd offer to keep you company, but we have an early training session at the studio this morning and Mama and I have to scoot soon. She's just upstairs wrapping up her morning inversions."

"That's okay," I say, hoping she doesn't hear how relieved I am to be rid of them. "I've never watched the sun come up alone. Maybe it's time at eighteen."

"Maybe it is." Her voice sounds odd as she says it—a little sad, a little proud. "Wait there just a minute." She disappears back into the kitchen. I hear cupboards opening and shutting, liquid splashing. "Coffee for your sunrise," she says, reemerging with a tall green thermos in one hand. "Vanilla coffee, a healthy pour of oat milk, spoonful of stevia. And a blueberry oat bar in case you get hungry after the walk. I made them yesterday—it's my first attempt at the recipe, so go easy on the baker if it needs work."

"Nothing you make ever needs work."

She shushes me and gives me a quick hug. "You're too biased. Now get up that hill before you miss the best part."

I leave through the back door, walk in the direction of the woods until I'm far enough from the kitchen window, and then skirt the side of the house. It's mostly dark still, though the sky is streaked with the first hints of light. I tread along the grassy edge of the gravel driveway to avoid any crunching sounds, lucky that I know every twist and divot between our house and the road. A few early birds chirp from the branches above me, but otherwise the world is silent. Even the woods still seem to be asleep.

I realize, with sinking dread, that if I don't see Elliot today, I'll have to pretend to become an avid sunrise watcher so I can try to catch him another morning. It's that, or I call the number and leave a voice mail if he doesn't pick up. Wait for a call back.

Please, Elliot, go for a run this morning. Please.

I pick up my pace. The Jackson house is to the right once I hit the road. My moms will be driving to the left to get to the studio.

I don't pass any cars on the short walk. But still, just in case, I hug tight to the tree line. My choice in sweatshirt color—black—and shorts—dark gray—was slightly questionable for a predawn trek.

The Jacksons' mailbox looms in the dim light. They haven't replaced it yet—it's the same mailbox I've been passing my whole life. It looks like it was once white, based on the few flecks of paint still left, but it's mostly exposed metal now. There's a massive dent on the side, maybe from a car, and the pole is slanted dramatically. Like it's a gust of wind away from toppling over. I assume it's just one more item on Elliot's long list of household to-dos.

I choose a spot between two thick tree trunks. There's some privacy if I need to hide—what if Marlow or Joanie are, unbeknownst to me, devoted morning runners, too?

Mimmy's coffee is a godsend. As is the granola bar, which—as expected—tastes perfect even if it's Mimmy's first go at a new recipe. I'm surprised I'm hungry enough to eat, but my stomach seems confused by the time of day and the unprecedented early movement. I drink the coffee slowly, just in case I'm here for a while. It didn't occur to me in my sleep haze to bring my phone, which means I only have the sun to mark the passing of time. I watch as it creeps higher above the treetops, golden light chasing shadows from the woods. Morning dew sparkles. Squirrels and rabbits and other tiny creatures stir.

An hour goes by, maybe an hour and a half. Leaning against the tree trunk has me dangerously close to sleep. I force myself upright, alert. A few minutes later, I hear it: the sound of sneakers grinding down on gravel. I push off the grass to stand.

I get my first glimpse through the trees. Elliot, in a gray T-shirt and shorts, coming up the driveway. Surprisingly quickly. Earbuds in, mouthing along to whatever music is playing from his phone. Frank Zappa would be appropriate.

I take a deep breath and step onto the road.

My heart races, an unsettling *thump-thump-thump*. It's like I not only climbed the hill, but ran the whole way to the top.

Elliot reaches the end of the driveway, eyes widening when he realizes he's not alone. He slows, then stops, staring at me as if he might be imagining that I'm here. "Calliope?" he says, too loudly, overcompensating for his music.

"Hello." I lift my hand to wave, but it stalls somewhere in the middle, stiff and unmoving.

"Uh, can I help you?" He takes out one earbud, then the other, and shoves them in his pocket. "Are you on a morning run, too?"

"No, I'm no runner." I laugh, an awkward, high-pitched sound, and force myself to move closer, cross over the rest of the road to the start of the driveway. I don't stop until I'm standing right in front of him.

Even with the smattering of grays, I can tell that his hair had been dark, brownish black, not auburn like mine. His nose is strong, angular, as different from mine as a nose could be. My face is heart shaped, his more triangular. But he's watching me with clear blue eyes, and his smile shows two deep dimples. His lips are full like mine, too, especially round on the bottom, and with two distinct points at the top, like two mountains on an otherwise flat plain. It's not everything—eyes, dimples, lips—but it's something.

"Calliope? Are you okay? Do you need anything?"

"Did you write me a letter?" I blurt out. I don't have the energy for subtlety or nuance.

"Did I—?" His wide eyes study me, searching for greater meaning.

It's fascinating in a purely objective sense, the way his face plays out the complex chain of emotions that come in rapid succession—bewilderment, recognition, shock, and, lastly and most emphatically, horror.

More subjectively, I feel every reaction in every bone and cell of my body. Especially as I start to recognize tiny, painful familiarities in the planes of his face. The lift of his brows, the twist of his lips, the crinkling of his chin. I've seen those same expressions in photos. In mirrors.

"No." He says it loudly. Like volume will somehow make it more resolute. More true. I swear the leaves around us tremble in response.

"No, you didn't write me a letter?"

"I did write a letter." His fingers tear through his hair, leaving it sticking up in all directions, like he's been shocked. Which, I suppose, he has been. "But it wasn't to you. It couldn't have been to *you*."

"How do you know? If it's the letter I received, there was no name at the top. You didn't know my address. You knew nothing about me. Only that I existed."

"But . . . it could have gone *anywhere*. The other side of the country. Hawaii. Alaska. Not to my next-door neighbor. Not to my son's—" His mouth hangs open, slack, his whole face seeming to lose the elasticity needed to hold everything in place.

"Girlfriend." I finish for him.

"Maybe they made a mistake. Switched names in the system."

He's staring at me, waiting for me to respond.

I say nothing.

"You can't be sure." His last attempt. "We could do a paternity test. You can order them online. Do it at home."

I wonder why he knows this. I don't think I want to know the answer. "If that's what you need to be sure."

"And you don't?"

"I think the cryobank would go out of business if they were keeping bad records."

He reflects on this, *really* looking at me, maybe for the first time. And then he nods, defeated. "I just can't believe it's . . . you. After all these years. That you're my *daughter*."

I stiffen at the word. "Not a daughter," I say, correcting him. "Donor offspring. Those are two hugely different things."

"Right. Yes. I'm sorry. Your moms—do they know?"

I shake my head.

"And Max?"

I shake my head again.

He nods slowly. "Okay. When will we tell him?"

"Not *we*. Me. I will tell him."

"He loves you, you know. He hasn't told me, but I can tell."

I rub my foot against the gravel driveway, watch the glitter catching in the morning sun. "Promise me you won't tell him. Please. It needs to come from me."

He sighs, the kind of racking full-body sigh that would usually be exaggerated, but in this moment, it's the only kind of sigh there is. "Fine. I promise. I'll let you tell him."

I nod, still not meeting his eyes. They look too much like mine.

"I don't need to go on my run, if . . ."

I glance up, curious.

"We could go to the diner or something? If you want to get breakfast. Talk."

It's too much. At least right now.

"Not today. But . . . maybe sometime?"

He nods. "You know my number."

"I do."

"I'm glad you told me."

"Not really a choice, was there?"

"I guess not. But still. I know this had to be hard. Maybe the hardest thing you've ever had to do. I hope things get easier, once you tell Max. I bet you can still be good friends."

Easier.

He says it like he knows me. Understands me

I turn my back to him, pick up the thermos, and start walking home.

I call the cryobank as soon as they open for the day, even though I'd acted so certain for Elliot.

Even though I *am* certain.

They assure me they don't make mistakes about donor

matches. The system is "foolproof." The calm, patient voice on the other end of the line checks, though, referencing both files, just to be certain. I'm not sure if she's technically allowed to do this, but she does. Possibly because she hears my desperation and feels pity. And because I obviously know his name, his identity. We've talked. We're neighbors.

"Neighbors?" she asks, sounding dumbfounded. "We've heard of some interesting coincidences, but . . . neighbors. Wow."

"Neighbors." I leave it at that. For her sake.

The phone call ends then. There's nothing left to ask.

I text Ginger an update: *It's him.*

When she tries calling less than a minute later, I press Decline. I'm not ready to dissect all the gory details. Not yet.

Instead I practice the confession in my bedroom mirror—stare at myself, study what it will look like when I tell Max. My expression. The shape of my lips as I try to form impossible words. The words get harder every time I repeat them. Never easier.

I'm your sister. Half sister.

Your dad is my dad. My donor.

We have to fall out of love.

Max and I didn't grow up together. We didn't share our childhood. We didn't take baths together, or cry about our nightmares, or bandage each other's skinned knees. That was me and Noah. Noah is a brother to me. In every way but blood.

But it all comes down to blood, doesn't it?

I would be *allowed* to fall in love with Noah.

I don't have the same allowance with Max. My heart was wrong for ever letting that happen.

I need to end things. Today.

A letter—I'll put all the truths and feelings into black-and-white for him to process. Write down the things that are too hard to say out loud.

I take out my journal from the drawer and start writing.

Page after page ends up scribbled over and crumpled on the floor. There are no perfect words. Jane Austen herself would have been at a loss for how to express these sentiments with any grace and delicacy. The truth is too ugly for grace. Too harsh for delicacy.

Two hours in, the morning is gone and I'm down to the last three pages of the journal. The final attempt. What will be, will be. Fate has intervened. This is it.

It all started with another letter, I write. *And my own curiosity.* I painstakingly copy Elliot's note. I don't leave anything out, not even the part about how certain he was he would never have kids. *I don't think I was meant to be a dad, but so it is.* Max won't disagree.

Copying is the easy part. Writing my own words after— breaking down the consequences of this first letter—is much trickier. It all feels like overstating the obvious: *You are my half brother. This, us, must end. Immediately.*

I say these things because I have to. But I say much more than that.

I write that it was all true. It was all real for me. Every kiss, glance, word. He is—or *was*—the only boy I've ever loved. More specifically, *been in love with*. *Love* and *in love*, the difference is a hungry, gaping canyon. *Love* is still okay. *In love* will never be okay again.

I remind him of the conversation we had earlier this summer about how quickly we became friends. That sometimes people just click. That moment on the hammock, the easy happiness—it feels like another era. I have aged centuries since then. But I smile as I write this, because the heart of our exchange is still true: Maybe we clicked because we're two souls cut from some of the same cloth. But much more literally than we thought, or ever would have chosen.

When I'm done I fold the letter into careful thirds without rereading, because I need to be finished. I tuck it tightly inside my copy of *Sense and Sensibility* and carry it downstairs.

I make more coffee, graze on some nuts and dried fruit. I'm not hungry, but I need to fuel myself for the torture that lies ahead.

And then I pick up my phone to text Max. Push it all into motion. He'll inevitably come by the house to see me at some point, but I need this to be over with. And better to do it before my moms are home and potentially in hearing range. It will be a separate—also unpleasant—conversation with them. After.

Are you free now? I type, and click send.

I go outside and lie down in the hammock. I toss the book—with my letter—onto the grass below me.

It's a perfect afternoon. Too perfect. Maybe the bluest, clearest sky of the summer. Low humidity. Hot but not scorching. The perfectness is too at odds with the events of my day.

I'm staring at my phone, waiting for a response, when I hear the crunching of gravel. A car in our driveway. *Damn.* I should have had hours still before Mimmy and Mama got home. I'll have to ferry Max away when he gets here, keep a straight face until we're somewhere more private. The hill or the pond or my tree. I hate to destroy our happy memories in those places with this terrible one. But privacy is essential.

I'm feeling solid about this plan when I first see him rounding the corner of the house.

Not Mama or Mimmy. Not Max.

Noah.

He stops abruptly when he notices me watching. Lifts one hand up in a tentative wave.

I wave back, and he must take that as a sign that I won't snap his head off for proceeding. He takes slow steps in my direction. It's hard to keep my patience. A sloth would beat him in a landslide victory. When he's a few feet away, he pauses. Hovers. Still uncertain if it's okay to join me on the hammock.

"Hey," I say, shifting to the top of the hammock and patting the empty space next to me.

"Hey." He sits down carefully, making sure to leave enough space between us that we don't risk skin brushing skin.

He won't look at me. That much is obvious. But I study him. I try to decide if he looks different after this much time apart. We haven't gone this long without seeing each other since I was a newborn and he was still in the womb. His hair is particularly unruly today—his golden-brown curls in clumps sticking out in odd directions, like a tufted bird. He's in his usual uniform, white T-shirt, denim shorts, slip-on sneakers. The same Noah on the outside. But on the inside? I'm not so sure. I don't know what to think anymore.

"How are you?" What I want to ask is: *Why the hell are you here?*

"I'm okay."

I wait for him to pick up the reins of the conversation, perhaps ask how I'm doing. When a few minutes pass and he's made no progress, I say: "I'm surprised you're here. It's a Saturday, too. Don't you have your cello lesson?"

He turns to me, his blue eyes meeting mine for the first time. His cheeks are flushed. There's a strange look on his face. Guilt. Or pity.

I know then, before he says it—why he's here. What he knows. How.

It's a betrayal that slices deep at my core, stealing my breath. Ginger told him.

I won't make this easier for him. He needs to say the words himself.

"Ginger told me your news," he says finally. There's a nervous twitch in his right eye, a rapid flutter. I've never noticed that twitch. I suppose our lives were always too easy before this summer. Straightforward. No twitch-inducing moments of revelation.

"Obviously."

His cheeks turn an even deeper shade of red. Maroon almost. "She called this morning. But she didn't want me to say anything."

"Of course she didn't. It was supposed to be a secret."

"I couldn't not talk to you, though. I couldn't stay away. So I called my instructor and said I was sick today. And then I spent the rest of the morning talking myself into actually driving over here and facing you."

"You've been staying away most of the summer. Why stop now? Don't skip your lesson on my account."

"That's not fair."

"Isn't it? You're punishing me for not being in love with you." Noah flinches at those words, his body curling as far along the opposite end of the hammock as possible without tumbling off the edge.

"Listen, Calliope. I'm sorry. I am. I know I've been shitty this summer. Seriously. Mega-asshole. Total wanker. Me." He points to his chest with both hands, looking down at himself with a disgusted lip curl. "I was hurt, and I ran away. It seemed...easier? But it was dumb. I don't know what I thought—it's not like I could stay away from you forever. You're my best friend."

"Am I?"

"You know you are."

"You have Ginger."

"It's different."

"Is it?" I shake my head. Messy curls fall over my eyes and I don't bother to push them back. Better to be shielded. "Never mind. This doesn't matter. It's not why you came over—to apologize. Don't act like that's the reason."

"It's part of the reason. Hearing about what you're going through—"

"What? You wanted in on the soap opera, too? Didn't want to be on the sidelines of my wild drama? I mean—*incest*. Come on! Doesn't get juicier than that, does it?"

He frowns, looking genuinely wounded. "You know that's not what I'm thinking. I'm here because I couldn't stand knowing you were hurting. I *had* to come. Even if you did end up tossing me out on my sorry ass. I had to try."

"Interesting. You couldn't show up for my eighteenth, though?"

"You're right. I threw myself a pity party after that night at Max's house. And I didn't want to see you and him together. I'm not proud of that particular decision. I was being selfish."

"Incredibly selfish."

"That's true. But don't act like you've been having a miserable summer without me. Not until now." He takes a deep breath, closes his eyes. Preparing. He must find whatever courage he's searching for, because when he opens his eyes again, there's no guilt there, just resolution. "I have to say this, Calliope. And then I'll leave if that's what you want me to do. I know you can't choose to love me like that, and I get it. I do. But you do realize it goes the other way, too, right? I can't choose to not love you, or to stop because that's the more convenient option. Trust me, if I could not be in love with you, I'd be all about it. Unrequited love? Let me tell you. It's the fucking worst. So as hard as love has been for you this summer—not loving me, loving Max, discovering you *can't* love Max—I get it. Not quite like you do. I'll give you that. But it's all hard, isn't it? I needed time to mourn. Time to get over myself."

It's true, what he says. I know it is. There are things in life you can't control:

Falling in love. Falling out of love.

Who and when and why.

"I'm sorry that you love me," I say. And I mean it. It doesn't excuse his icing me out this summer for having another boy in my life. But I am sorry.

"You could be more terrible, you know. Make it easier to not love you." He's smiling.

I smile, too, and push my hair back off my face. He edges closer to the middle of the hammock.

"Really, though," he says softly, "how are you holding up?"

"It's hard to say. I don't think it's fully hit yet. That'll come after I tell Max. Seeing his reaction will make it feel more real."

"When's that happening?"

"Today."

"Shit."

"Yeah."

"Do you think you'll be friends still?"

"I hope so. Because we're more than friends, aren't we? Just not the *more than* I had thought this summer."

"I still can't wrap my head around it—of all the men who donate, your moms picked the guy who grew up next door. I mean, what the hell? Life has strange plans sometimes."

"Strange is putting it mildly."

"Is there anything I can do?"

"No. Thanks. This is my disaster to untangle. I just…" I pause for a moment, try to focus all the questions spinning through my mind. "I keep thinking about family, and what it means. What makes a family, how much blood matters—and if not blood, what does? You've always been the brother to me. We have that history. That bond. Max and I, we have none of that shared past. So how is he more of a brother than you?" I stare at Noah, willing him to give me a good answer. Because I need it—I need an answer to this question, so badly.

Noah shrugs, looking down at his sneakers. "There are different kinds of family, I guess. Some share DNA. Some don't. I don't think one is better or more real than the other. Just because people share DNA doesn't mean they always get along, right? There's more to it than genetics. Families come together in all different ways."

"But why isn't it like that for you?" I reach out, put my hand on his knee. He looks up, first at my hand, then at my face. "I mean—why am I not like a sister? How are you in love with me? Why are things different for you and me?"

Noah winces, looking like he'd rather slip through the holes in the hammock than have this conversation. But even still, he answers. For me. He must sense my desperation. "I guess all the things that make me feel like a brother to you—everything we've done together our whole lives, all the memories, sleepovers by the magic tree, getting our braces on the same day, holding your hand during my grandmother's funeral—just made me feel even more connected to you. You get me. I get you. When you're in a relationship, isn't that person supposed to feel like family? Eventually, anyway. When you settle down and make a life. All that. That's what I want, anyway. Some day."

What he says—it makes sense. It does. Mama and Mimmy are family. Of course they are. We're all Silversmiths. You find someone, you build a life together, you make them your family. Maybe you mix your blood, maybe you don't.

"What about physically, though?" I ask because I can't stop myself—because this is what it boils down to, isn't it? The chemical sensation that comes from deep under your skin. The part we can't control. "I'm sorry. I know that's . . . personal. And weird for me of all people to ask. But I want to understand."

"Jesus, Calliope. You're asking why I'm attracted to you?"

I bite my lip. "Yeah. But if it's too weird, you don't have to answer."

He shrugs. "It's hard to put into words. I just . . . am." He's quiet for a minute, and I'm about to tell him to forget it, that it was an awkward question, when he says: "All the little things, I guess—your laugh sounds like a happy bird chirping in the spring. Your eyes are like the color of the ocean, or at least how the ocean *should* always look. How messy and wild your hair gets, especially in the summer. Case in point: right now." He smiles and flicks a finger at one of my stray curls.

I asked for this, but I'm not sure what to do with the

information now that I have it. It doesn't change how he feels, and how I *don't* feel. Nothing will.

"Thank you for that," I say, standing up from the hammock. "I hate to kick you out, but...Max should be over pretty soon. I think it's probably best if you're gone when he gets here. No offense."

Noah gets up, too. "Yeah. Of course."

"But seriously, thanks for...checking in. I appreciate it."

He nods. He lifts his arms like he's going to hug me, but then he jams his hands in his pockets and starts off toward the driveway.

I watch as he disappears around the side of the house, and then fall back in the hammock. Close my eyes. Breathe.

Wait.

A few minutes later, I hear a snapping twig. Rustling brush.

I open my eyes and Max is there, stepping out from the edge of the woods. His face lights up with a happy boyish smile, and I worry that I'm going to be sick.

I make myself stand. My legs feel weak.

Before he can say anything, I announce: "There's something you need to know."

His smile fades. He walks faster, closes the gap between us. When he reaches out to me, I put my hands up to stop him.

His brows furrow as he frowns. "What's going on?"

"I wrote you a letter. That says it so much better."

"A letter?"

I nod.

"You're scaring me, Calliope. Your face right now—" He shakes his head, looking as sick as I feel. And he doesn't even know yet. "Please just tell me."

I take a deep breath.

"I found my donor."

"Okay? And that's . . . a bad thing?"

"Your dad, Max. My donor is your dad."

Chapter Fourteen

HE follows me up the hill. *Sense and Sensibility* is tucked under my arm with the letter.

We don't acknowledge each other.

After I dropped the bomb, I asked if we could go somewhere more private—just in case my moms got home sooner than I expected. I'm not sure how long this conversation will take.

He nodded. No words. He looked too shocked to articulate whatever might be happening in his mind.

I walk without seeing, grateful my feet know the path so well. When we get to the peak, I sit on a large flat rock, large enough for Max to sit next to me. But he chooses the ground instead, mostly dirt and pebbles with a few blades of sad, scraggly grass, a few feet away from me.

I lean across the rock, letter in my hand. He makes no motion to take it from me. I let it flutter to the ground next to him.

We sit without talking for a long stretch, staring out over the valley. I can't appreciate the view this time. I'm not sure I ever will again.

"I can read the letter to you if you prefer that," I say finally, unable to bear the silence any longer. "It was just…easier to put everything into words this way. There's a lot to say."

Another beat, and then—Max picks up the letter. He unfolds

it slowly, holding it out at arm's length as if the words are too toxic to touch.

And then he reads it. All the way through. Once. Twice.

"How long have you known?" he says finally, the letter falling to his knees. His eyes are still on the valley, the peaks and slopes of the hills across from us.

"Not long. I only got your dad's letter two days ago."

"So that's why you were *busy* yesterday."

"I needed to process. To be sure."

"And are you? Sure?"

I nod for a moment before realizing he won't see. "Yes."

"How?"

"I called the cryobank. They assured me they don't make mistakes, that the records are correct. And I—I also talked to your dad. This morning. I had to make sure he was the one who wrote it. I needed to know it wasn't another Elliot Jackson. He wanted to tell you, but I said it had to be me."

"My dad knows? He knew before me?" His voice cracks now, like this is the worst part of it all, the biggest injustice. "You should have told *me* first."

"I needed to be one hundred percent positive. I didn't want to plant the idea in your head, make you change your mind about me. About us. Not until it was absolutely necessary."

"Who else? Who else knew before me?"

"Ginger." I sigh. "I told her yesterday. When I was trying to process. And then she told Noah."

"Not your moms?"

"Not yet."

He drops his head into his hands, clawing at his hair so hard I wouldn't be surprised if he leaves clumps behind on this hill. "You don't look anything like him. How is it possible?"

"Don't I, though? I didn't think so either. Not at first. But if you really look. There's something there."

"I don't want to believe it, Calliope. I can't. I just can't. I mean—how does something like this even happen in real life? The odds are too crazy."

"I know. I don't want to believe it either. But we have to. It's the truth."

His face is still down, covered by his palms, but I don't need to see tears to know that he's crying.

I've never seen Max cry before.

But I suppose it would be strange if he didn't cry now. I should be crying, too, but I feel too broken for more tears.

"Everything I wrote in the letter is true. I just . . . need to learn how to love you without being *in* love with you. I don't have all the answers. But I know I still want you in my life." I almost reach out to put my arm around his shoulders. I stop myself, though. Pin my hands under my thighs. It feels like I should be doing something more than sitting here and staring at him crying, but I can't. There's nothing I can do to comfort him.

"You should have told me yesterday," he says finally. "As soon as you found out."

"I was still hoping I was wrong. That it was all a horrible mix-up. I was trying to protect you. Me. Us."

I slide off the edge of the rock and crawl on the ground to be next to him. Max pointedly turns his head farther in the opposite direction.

"Talk to me, Max. Please."

The sun is beating down on me, but I feel cold. So cold.

"I can't. I can't talk to you. Not right now. I am so—" He pushes roughly up from the ground, scattering small pebbles in his wake. I watch them bounce and skid off the top of the hill, start their descent to the valley below. "My heart feels like someone pummeled it with a hammer. I'm so damn sad. But I'm so angry, too. I'm angry at life for putting me in this terrible old house we never should have come to—and I'm angry that you, out of every person on this planet, had to be my neighbor. I'm angry that we fell in love. I'm just... angry. So angry."

"I'm angry, too," I say quietly. But I don't stand up next to him.

And I don't try to follow when he starts back down the path.

"I can't believe you didn't tell us," Mama says. I don't think she's blinked in the twenty minutes since I started talking.

"Which part?" I ask. "Me not telling you how much I really wanted to know about Frank, and requesting to be in touch after my birthday—or that Frank is actually our next-door neighbor and Max's dad?"

"I'm going to say: both. All of it."

Mimmy still hasn't said anything. She's staring into her nearly empty wineglass, processing.

I threw open the kitchen door after my walk down the hill, hoping they would both be there. And they were, laughing and sipping wine, nibbling on the rest of Mimmy's blueberry oat bars. They looked so happy and calm. I hated that I had to ruin it.

"I have to tell you something." I practically shouted it. A declaration.

"Oh Jesus, she's pregnant," Mama said, spilling a heavy pour of deep red wine down her—white, unfortunately—Hot Mama Flow T-shirt.

She was temporarily relieved at my insistence that I'm still a virgin. I wouldn't normally want to discuss that kind of intimate detail so readily, but it felt important, knowing what was coming next.

The rest tumbled out after, sloppy and disordered, too many cluttered details. It's a wonder they could make sense of it all.

"Elliot Jackson is your donor. Max is your brother. Your half brother." Mimmy says it now like the words are just clicking into place, minutes after she first heard them.

"Yes."

"How did we pick our neighbor? How is that possible?" She turns from me to Mama, back to me again.

I shrug. "Technically he wasn't your neighbor at the time. He was already gone. Living in Philly. Only old Mr. Jackson—his dad—was there."

"I'm not sure that changes anything," Mama says. She shifts her chair closer to Mimmy's, wraps an arm around her shoulders to keep her sturdy.

"Do you hate me?" I can't look at them. Instead I pick at a stray blueberry on the plate of granola bars, mash it between my fingers.

"How can you even say that?" Mimmy asks. She lays her hand on the table, and I reach out to hold it. She doesn't flinch at the sticky berry film on my fingers. "Look at me, sweetie. Please." I lift my gaze to meet her eyes. Brown eyes. Not blue like mine— or blue like Mama's. Or Elliot's. "This doesn't change anything about our love for you. It doesn't change anything about this family. You are just as much ours. Always a Silversmith. Always."

"But you're not upset that I asked to make contact in the first place?"

"Of course not. You had every right. I only wish you could have felt comfortable telling us your decision. But I understand why you didn't. You needed to do it for yourself. I respect that. We both do, don't we?" She gives Mama a quick glance.

"Yes."

"Yes?" I say, needing more.

"I understand." Mama puts her hand on top of mine. "I respect the decision. I don't love it, but—I respect it. And I love you so damn much and all I can think about right now is how much I'm hurting for you. How unfair this is. Every man on this green earth and we picked the neighbor. You said he's a serial cheater, right? And a terrible dad?"

I nod, inwardly flinching at the description. "Hopefully I only got the good genes. He's a lawyer, you know. Probably had to put himself through school—I think he had a rough family life." I leave it at that—decide not to elaborate on my potential murderer of a grandfather right now. One too many anecdotes for today, and my moms have heard the stories. *Rumors*, they always insisted, even if Mimmy was spooked by the Jackson house, too.

"Did we make the wrong choice?" Mama asks. "I don't even remember why we picked his particular sperm now. It was probably no better than any other sperm in the bank."

"Of course it wasn't the wrong choice!" Mimmy slaps the table hard with her free hand. "If we'd picked any other sperm, we'd have a completely different daughter sitting in front of us. Or son. Who knows? It wouldn't be Calliope, though. So no—no matter how awful everything seems right now, it wasn't the wrong choice. I'd make it over and over again if it meant having *you*."

"Thanks, Mimmy." I give a weak smile. Just because it's true doesn't make it any less odd to think about—I am only here, I am only alive, because of Elliot Jackson.

"You're right," Mama says, "that was idiotic of me. I just can't shake the guilt. I feel like we were in some way responsible. Our decisions led to this point. Maybe we could have picked a different house. A different town. I don't know. Done *something* differently—just one thing. And then my baby girl wouldn't have a battered heart right now."

"You couldn't have known," I say. I feel drained. Defeated. "And no one could have suspected sooner and stopped us from getting to this point. It's not like Max and I look anything alike."

As soon as the words are out, I wonder if that's true. I haven't let myself think about it before now.

It's easy to say we look totally different. He's Black and I'm white. He's masculine, I'm feminine. But of course that's too simple an answer. A cheap, lazy default. There is so much more to both of us. But analyzing all the other details—nose, eyes, lips, teeth, ears, hair, fingers, toes, bone structure—it's too much. It's one thing to find myself in Elliot. It's another thing altogether to see those same things in Max.

"What can we do to help you right now?" Mimmy asks. Mama has taken her hand away, busying herself with sweeping up granola crumbs from the tablecloth, but Mimmy still grips me tight.

"I don't know. I don't think there's anything any of us can do. Right now I just want to give Max a few days. He's angry, I know. But hopefully once it all settles . . . we can be friends again." Friends. It sounds so flimsy, even to my ears. Were we ever really just friends?

"He has no right to be angry, not with you," Mimmy says, a subtle edge to her voice. "And you have absolutely nothing to apologize for. You do know that?"

I nod. She's right. Of course she is.

"I'll talk some sense into that boy if he doesn't come around," Mama chimes in, the edge in her voice far less subtle. "And what about Elliot? Should we talk to him, Mimmy and I? Have some kind of, I don't know, introductory conversation?"

The thought of that introductory conversation makes me cringe. "No. Not yet. Maybe eventually we can all meet. But it feels too soon. There's nothing to say to him."

"Okay. Well. We could go on a trip somewhere, just the three of us, maybe camping in the Poconos," Mama says, "even if it means closing down the studio for a few days. August is always a slow month." Now that the crumbs are all cleaned, she's unfolding and refolding a pile of linen napkins.

The idea is certainly appealing—running somewhere far away from our woods and the Jackson house. Pretending none of this is happening, that life is still good and normal. But Mama herself told me I can't escape my problems. I'd always have to end up here. In this place, surrounded by these people.

I shake my head. "A wise woman once said that if something's upsetting me, it probably won't just go away. I need to be brave. Face it head-on."

"That *is* wise. I don't know if I've ever been prouder of you than I am in this very moment. Come here." She opens her arms, and I rush toward her.

I fall into her lap, and she and Mimmy surround me with their arms.

I cry, and they cry with me. And then Mimmy makes banana waffles with her homemade maple whipped cream for dinner. We sit in front of the TV watching our old *Anne of Green Gables* VHS tapes until I fall asleep—dreaming of wild cherry trees and Haunted Woods and a magical place far away from this one I'm living in now.

Chapter Fifteen

MY moms suggest I skip my shift at the studio on Sunday, but I insist on working. I need to be busy, even though I've barely slept in three nights. I need to not be in the house. And coffee. I need lots of coffee.

But the usual studio chores aren't enough to distract me today. My mind continues to dissect all the terrible particulars of my life. One by one, slowly, over and over again.

When Ginger walks in halfway through the shift, I'm relieved.

Until I remember—she told Noah.

"Hey," she says, not meeting my eyes. Her outfit is more subdued today, black yoga pants and a plain green T-shirt.

"Hey."

I try to decide, quickly, if I'm mad at her. I'm feeling so many things, it's almost like I'm actually feeling nothing. Just a blur of loud, constant emotions rumbling in the background. Like crickets buzzing all night long, so noisy and persistent that after a while it starts to sound like silence. This is my new silence. My new state of being.

"I shouldn't have told him. It was your secret. Not mine. It's just—" She looks up finally, her green eyes rimmed with deep purple circles. Her whole face is tired, her freckles oddly dark and pronounced against her pale skin. It's a rare sighting of Ginger with no makeup. No dark mascara on her white-blond lashes. No pop of red or pink or purple on her lips. She looks so young and innocent. Vulnerable. I don't think it's possible to be mad at this Ginger. "It's just that it was such a crazy big truth. I didn't know how to hold it in by myself. It was wrong to tell him, but I was going to explode without anyone to talk to about it, and I couldn't bother you with all my questions. I'm so sorry, Calliope. I understand if you want to kill me. On top of everything else going on right now, you didn't need me to be a shit friend."

I walk around the side of the counter, stopping a few inches in front of her. She takes a sharp inhale, waiting.

"It's okay." And it is. I don't have it in me to fight with Ginger. Without her, life would be definitively too empty.

"No. It's really not. I shouldn't have said a word to him."

"Maybe not, but it's done." I reach out and take her hand. She tightens her fingers around mine, latching on like she's afraid if she lets go, I might change my mind. "It's over, no going back. I told Max everything. So the secret's out."

"Wait," she says, holding up her free hand. "So much to process. Max knows he's your half brother?" Hearing it out loud—*half brother*—is still a cold slap.

I nod.

"Wow."

"Yep. *Wow* sums it up."

"I'm stunned that, between you and me, you're the one with the colorful shit show of drama in your life right now. Guess I always thought that was more my territory? Huh. Well, definitely a summer to remember."

I dig my nails into her palm. "How sweet and sensitive of you. Personally, I think it's a summer I'd like to immediately forget."

She digs back, and—given her nails are much sharper than mine, filed into perfect mini-talons—her punishment is more effective. "It's my job as your best friend to make jokes when I can. You need to laugh. This will destroy you if you can't find a way to laugh sometimes."

"You didn't do a good job then. You didn't make me laugh."

"Don't worry. I'll keep trying until it works."

"We'll see."

And then, before I can stop her, she has her fingers dancing in my armpits, on my neck, in my ears. I try to resist, not give her such instant satisfaction. But I'm weak when it comes to tickling. I hate it, always have—it makes me feel so powerless. And it also makes me laugh. Every time.

I let out a breathless cackle before I can stop myself.

Ginger squeals, victorious, and doubles down even harder.

I tickle back, and soon we're on the floor, faces covered in tears, holding our stomachs from too much laughing. My abs burn. I feel like I just did one of Mama's core-power routines.

The class ends then, and a few women trickle out, giving us amused glances. Mama is there, too, looking down at us, shaking her head as if she could possibly be angry. She spills a few drops of ice water on us from her thermos before chatting with some of the women.

"Tickling doesn't count as real laughter," I say, gasping for breath. "That was cheap."

"I'll take cheap laughter over no laughter."

"Thank you. I love you." I take her hand.

"You're welcome. And I love you, too." She squeezes my fingers tight.

"It's your birthday in less than two weeks. We should do something fun."

"Um. Duh. That's kind of assumed."

"Do you think Noah will come?"

She's quiet for a beat. And then: "I sure hope so."

The next day I sit on the porch for hours. Flipping through my moms' yoga magazines without reading. Willing Max to step out from the woods. I feel restless without more resolution. I can't stand to leave things like we did. So much anger and resentment. It feels cruel, unfair. Max is better than this. At least I hope he is.

He does come, finally. Just as pink and orange streaks are swallowing the sky.

It seems too early for the sun to be setting, but that's how it goes, isn't it? This summer will end, one way or another. That much is inevitable. Life will go on around us.

Max sits in Mimmy's yellow rocking chair.

"I wasn't sure you'd ever come here again," I say, watching him. He stares straight ahead, off toward the trees. "But I'm glad you did."

He nods slowly. "I wasn't sure if I would either. I haven't slept since you told me. I haven't done much of anything. Cried. Punched my pillow. Almost punched through your tree painting, but I stopped myself."

"Yeah. I haven't been sleeping much either. I think I've drunk more coffee in the last few days than the rest of my life combined."

"Same. Black. All day." He's rocking hard in the chair, the back-and-forth making heavy, rhythmic thuds against the wooden boards. "I'm afraid to dream. Before, I dreamed about you every night."

He dreamed about me every night. The thought makes me nauseated.

"I told my moms," I say. "Saturday. After you and I talked."

"Yeah? How did that go?"

"Oh, you know. Shock. Horror. Sadness. How about you? How are things at your house?"

"Pretty ugly."

I wait for him to say more. But when the silence stretches and it's clear that's all I'm getting, I take a deep breath and clench my hands around the arms of the rocking chair. "So...what's next then? Who are we to each other now?"

"I'm so confused." Max sighs. "But sitting on this porch with you? It feels like the most real thing in my life right now. I look at you, and I remember how it felt to fall in love with you. I don't *want* that feeling. It's not right. It's...disgusting." He turns to face me, and his red-rimmed eyes look so empty and hopeless, my breath hitches. "I don't think I can do this. I don't think I can do *us*. Friendship. It's too hard."

"But—" I reach, grasp. "You've barely had any time to process it all. You said yourself you can't sleep, so nothing is clear right now. We don't have to make any big decisions yet. There's no rush."

"Maybe. But I think it's for the best. Easier in the long run. For both of us."

"Why do we have to take the easy way out? You're my *brother*. Half brother, but still. Doesn't that mean something?"

Max flinches like I've slapped him. "Please don't call me that. Just because we share DNA doesn't mean we get to play brother and sister. It doesn't work that way. Not for us."

"Maybe it *could* work that way, though. If we both try hard enough. I don't want to not know you."

"I'm sorry, Calliope. I really am." He stands up, eyes fixed on the woods ahead. "But I'm not as strong as you."

"So that's it? Just like that?"

"Goodbyes are hard no matter what," he says quietly, still not looking at me. "Let's not make this one harder than it already it is." And then he turns and walks down the porch stairs.

I stare as I did that first day—my eyes tracing his every movement, each graceful swing of his limbs, until he fades into the trees.

I'm sad. I'm angry. I'm disappointed.

I thought the truth had already done its worst. I'd fully understood the consequences. But no.

This—this is the moment my heart fully breaks.

Ginger comes over, and she holds me that night until I fall asleep.

She stays all of Tuesday, too, and sleeps over for a second night.

Mimmy and Mama take turns checking in, but they give me space.

I've never lost anyone close to me—never felt grief in that sense before. But this feels like a death. The funeral has ended. The real mourning has begun.

Ginger and I lie around mostly. Pool, hammock, sofa, bed. She's there for the company, not the conversation. There's not much to say: The entire summer was an ugly mistake. Max is out of my life, and I have to learn how to un-love him. As a boyfriend, as a friend, and as the half brother he was never supposed to be.

Ginger looks guilty this morning at the kitchen table as she scoops a second helping of Mimmy's homemade granola into her bowl. "I could call off my shift if you want. Really. I don't mind. I'll say I caught some weird face rash. They'll beg me to stay home."

I take a small bite of granola and yogurt. My stomach turns as I swallow. "It's fine. Seriously. You gave me a full day of pity party yesterday. That's enough. Life can't be all about me. Your eighteenth birthday is a week from today. Let's talk about that."

"Planning something extravagant will be a great distraction

for you." She gives me a big openmouthed grin, crunching down on the granola. "And by the way, not to make a big deal about this or anything, but..."

She pauses, making a show of her chewing for dramatic effect.

"I didn't want to mention it earlier. Because, well, you know. Didn't feel like the best timing. For example, when you came to the diner to tell me about Elliot. Nope. Not the right moment. And I didn't want to jinx anything. But... I might have met someone. I mean, I definitely met someone. She's real. She exists. She's amazing. But I'm not sure if I'm in the friend zone or there's more. Very early days."

"What?" I drop my spoon. "When did this happen?"

"Last week. She was a customer. Couldn't stop complimenting my red lipstick and my cat-eye glasses. I thought she was just a makeup junkie at first, but then she ordered some pie after she finished her burger and asked for two forks. One for her. One for *me*. And it was key lime, without me telling her that was my favorite pie in the world. Obviously, I took a break. And I left my number on the receipt—for zero dollars, of course, because I picked up the tab. She called me the next day. We've been talking and texting ever since."

I've never seen her face so bright. There's a halo around her goofy grin.

"Wow. I am so happy for you, Ginger." And I am. Mostly. All the best, selfless parts of me. I refuse to acknowledge the tiny evil voice that says, *Why now, why her.* I shove that down deep. "What's her name? Does she live here?"

"Vivi Rodríguez. And no, but her grandma does. Vivi lives a few towns over. But she comes to visit a lot. Her grandma needs help around the house. Which means she's funny, cute, most likely gay, *and* she's a good person who takes care of her elders."

"Will she hang out with us for your birthday? I can't wait to meet her," I say. My voice sounds strained and strangely pitched. Not genuine. I want to take it back. Try again.

Ginger hears it, too. That goofy grin slips and falls. "I'm sorry. I knew it wasn't a good time. It feels like I'm rubbing it in your face, and I'm not, I swear. I shouldn't have said anything. Not now."

"Stop. No. I'm glad you told me. And I really am excited for you. Just because I happen to despise romantic love at the moment doesn't mean you should, too. You deserve this. Plus, you were so patient and good to me all summer."

She reaches across the table, her thick row of beaded and charmed bangles knocking against the wood as she finds my hand and squeezes. "Thanks, Calliope."

The front door opens. A slow creak of the screen door, then a *bang* as it swings shut.

I turn in my chair toward the hall, dropping Ginger's hand. Mama and Mimmy are at the studio. My chest tightens. Max would knock, wouldn't he?

But it's not Max who steps into the kitchen. It's Noah. We haven't talked since his last visit, before I told Max. I wasn't sure where to go from there. Wasn't sure whether he'd only come out of pity, for a one-off conversation because of the dire circumstances, or for a first step back to some kind of normalcy.

"Hey," he says, like it's a casual thing, his being here. Like it used to be. But his smile is too big, more nervous than happy. He sits in the chair next to Ginger. Picks up an extra spoon, taps it against the table like a drumstick. Neither of them can meet my eyes.

I cross my arms and stare them down. "What is this, a changing of the guards? Ginger said I shouldn't be alone?"

"Eh." Ginger twirls her spoon in circles around her yogurt bowl. "No. Maybe. Yes."

"I'm an adult. I can handle myself."

"We're just worried about you, that's all," Ginger says. "I've never seen you so sad."

"*Sad*," I screech, and Noah and Ginger wince. "Well, yeah, I guess I never fell for my biological half brother before now. Or had my heart broken, period. I couldn't even start out with a normal heartbreak, could I? Skipped right past those training wheels. So yes. I am sad. But you don't have to babysit me. I'm not going to do anything drastic. Maybe cry some more. Binge-eat Mimmy's cookie dough out of the freezer."

"So, should I leave?" Noah is already halfway out of his seat.

"Do what you want. I just don't want anyone here out of obligation."

"You are never an obligation." His face is oddly somber as he says it. He sits back down.

Ginger stands then, clearing away her empty bowl and mug, dropping them in the sink. "Just let us love you, Calliope. It's what best friends are for. It's what we've all been doing since the womb." She hugs me from behind, plants a juicy kiss on the top of my head. "I'll call you after my shift. Not to check in. But to ask what plans you've come up with for next week."

The door slaps shut behind her. We hear her wooden platforms clunking on the porch, down the stone path to her car. Noah's playing with a lock of hair, curling it around his finger over and over again. I listen to the hum of the fan. Take a sip of warm water from my glass.

"Are you hungry still?" Noah finally asks. "Looks like you barely touched that yogurt. And from what my informant told me, you haven't eaten much these past two days."

I look at the yogurt. The granola is probably liquefied inside it. The sour smell hits my nose and I push it away.

Noah laughs, and it's such a familiar, joyful sound—I realize how much I've missed it. Missed him.

"I am pretty hungry. Though your *informant* made me take a few bites of her pizza last night. That was about it."

"Okay then," he says, standing up. His chest seems to swell with purpose. "Let's see what you have in the fridge."

I feel hungry for the first time in so long. Ravenous, really.

We assume our old positions. Me perched on the counter. Noah chopping and sautéing, refusing all offers of help. I watch the way he moves gracefully between cupboards and drawers as he cooks. It's like this is his home.

And it is.

Or it *was*. Maybe it will be again.

We eat. We fill up the pool with cold water and go in wearing our clothes. We climb the hill for sunset. We don't talk much. But we're together. It's something at least.

For a few minutes, as I watch the sun slip away, I can almost pretend life is the same as it was before this summer.

Almost.

Chapter Sixteen

MY plan for Ginger's birthday isn't necessarily *extravagant*, but it's the best I can do. And it feels nice to have a distraction, just like Ginger said. Something and someone else to think about.

The morning before her birthday, Noah and I pack up his car with our duffel bags and food supplies—Mimmy made not one but three different baked goods for the occasion—and drive into town to pick up Ginger. She's waiting for us on the porch, Vivi already there with her. A spontaneous invite. Ginger was shocked when she actually said yes. *Still just friends*, Ginger reminded us no less than fifty times, *so you better not make things awkward.* Sophie waves at us from the kitchen window.

It's just two nights at a motel in Wildwood, New Jersey— the only one not completely booked for the week by the time I started searching. But based on the website pictures of fake palm trees and flamingos by the ancient outdoor pool, it has a level of Ginger-approved kitsch that felt suitable for her one and only eighteenth. She'll be completely delighted by the decor.

Vivi smiles at us as she lugs both of their bags down from the porch. She's cute, but in an understated way, far more sub-dued than Ginger's brand of cute. Medium height, medium build, medium length dark hair in a straightforward, simple cut, no makeup or jewelry or bedazzling of any sort. Her denim shorts—not short-shorts, more conservatively cut—plain green T-shirt, and foam flip-flops are in stark comparison to Ginger's cheetah-inspired romper and neon-pink platform sandals. But they look happy walking down the front steps together. I can't hear what they're saying, but Vivi is giggling over something Ginger says. They both blush.

The two days go by too fast. The beach is long and hot and crowded with screaming babies and kids tossing Frisbees in every direction, flinging sand on neighboring sunbathers. The boardwalk is even more hot and crowded. But none of that matters. I'm with Ginger and Noah, and Vivi feels like a natural fourth. She listens and laughs when we go off on long tangents about old memories, and if she's bored, she's polite enough to never let on.

We take a long walk along the water after the masses pack up for the day. It's easy to lose yourself looking out at the ocean—easy to think too much. Max's face comes to me first. Then Elliot's. I close my eyes and listen to the waves, and I think I feel just a little bit better.

I am here. *We* are here.

When Noah puts a lit candle into a funnel cake for Ginger to blow out, she clamps her eyes shut tight and focuses intently on her wish.

Later that night when I see Vivi and Ginger kiss on the moonlit beach, I feel confident that her wish came true.

Eighteenth-birthday wishes really do have a special power.

*   *   *

Thursday night, Noah drops me back off at home. We're sun-burned and sleepy and happy, smelling like salt water and vinegar fries. I don't want to wash the ocean out of my hair. People make fun of the Jersey Shore, but it's the only ocean I've ever known, and ocean is ocean.

I eat dinner with Mama and Mimmy, and after they head to bed, I pick up my phone.

I'm not sure why I do it, but I do.

I call Elliot. I ask him to get breakfast with me on Saturday.

"I didn't think you'd actually call." Elliot is flipping absentmind-edly back and forth through the ten sticky laminated pages of the diner's menu. I've always wondered how they could possibly keep so many different ingredients constantly stocked. Sometimes I want to order the most obscure item on the menu, Delmonico Steak or Dijon Pork Chops, maybe, just to call their bluff. I only ever see breakfast platters and burgers and fries on the tables. And pie. Lots of pie.

Ginger's not on duty today—a fact I knew, of course, when I suggested this morning for breakfast. If she was here and caught wind of our conversation, she'd take a break at the next booth over. She's not really missing anything juicy so far, though. Just a run through the basics: College. My moms. Friends. Hobbies. I'm afraid we've run out of subject material and we haven't ordered anything but our coffees.

"I didn't think I'd call either," I say.

"I'm glad you did."

"Really?" I put my menu down. I always order the same thing: Two poached eggs, two blueberry pancakes, home fries. Extra maple syrup. "You didn't offer out of obligation? I'm not looking for a dad, you know. I don't need anything from you. My moms have it covered."

"I know that. And maybe it was partly out of obligation, at first. Guilt. It felt like the right thing to do. But as soon as I said it, I knew I meant it. I really did want to talk. Learn a little more about you beyond being Max's..." He lets it dangle and die, for both our sakes.

"How is he?" I clench my fists under the table. "Max?"

"Locked away in his room, mostly, sneaking out to steal food at odd hours when he doesn't have to interact with any of us. But he's probably painting up a storm at least—that's his usual fixer-upper when he's down." He frowns. "Though he's never been down quite like this before. If there's a silver lining, it's that he might paint his way into college with all the new material for his portfolio. Quite emotional material, too, I would imagine."

"So, you want him to study art?" I steer the conversation away from how down Max is. My heart is still too sensitive—the messy stitches too loose and easy to tug right back out.

"Sure, if that's his dream. I want him to do what makes him happy. He deserves that, especially after nearly eighteen years of living with me."

I admire his honesty at least. His self-awareness.

"It's none of my business, I know, but—why do you stay?" I

ask. "From the outside at least, it doesn't seem like you want to be there. Maybe you'd all be happier apart."

"Very direct. Must have gotten some of my lawyering genes." I can tell from the twitch of his lips that he hadn't meant to say it—to compare our genes. "Sorry. I don't mean to say you're anything like me. I actually hope you're not."

I shrug. Wait for him to talk more. That's why I'm here. To learn about him.

"Why do I stay?" He laughs, but his blue eyes are sad. "Because I love Joanie. I do. I love her deep in my bones. And the kids, too. They *are* my bones. Funny for a guy who didn't think he'd want kids, I can't imagine a world without them. But I know I have a peculiar way of showing it to all three of them." He pauses, takes a long swig of coffee. Chases it with some lemon water. Clears his throat. "I've never been good at that. Real affection. Commitment. Devotion. I had a pretty poor role model of a dad myself, and a mom who never learned how to stand up for herself. Or maybe she did, ironically, but she picked the wrong time to do it."

This feels like dangerously slippery terrain. We're edging along to what Max has hinted at. The great mystery and horror of the Jackson house.

"I'm sure it's very personal. I don't want to pry—about your family."

"They're your family, too, I suppose? Depending on how you look at it. Biology does matter. It leaves a mark. Nature and nurture, hand in hand."

"Then tell me." I take a breath. "About your parents."

"I haven't talked about it in years."

The waitress comes over then, a tired middle-aged woman lacking Ginger's uniform flare, and I wonder if the moment is lost. She tops off our coffee mugs to the rim.

I order first, and then Elliot says, "Same thing, minus the blueberries."

As she walks away, he looks over at me and smiles. "Good call on the extra syrup. Even if it's the fake plastic-tub kind that's more corn than maple. All delicious in my book. Sugar is sugar."

Mama would of course passionately disagree. I don't tell him this.

He takes a minute, fiddles with the top of a creamer container and then sips his coffee black before saying, "I thought we'd be talking about lighter things today. But might as well dig right in. My dad—your biological grandfather—was a drinker. To put it mildly. Always was, even when I was a boy, but it got worse every year. More constant. He was a mean drunk, as drunks tend to be, headstrong and pushy. Had an opinion about everything. And he was never wrong. *Never.* He found a new reason to scream at my mom every night. She took it. Probably for my sake. I didn't realize that then, though, and got angry at her for being so weak. Some son I was."

His eyes are fixed on mine the whole time he talks, but he's not really looking at me. I could slip away under the booth and he probably wouldn't notice. He's looking backward, into the shadows. A time and place he hasn't thought about in a long time. The expression on his face makes my skin prickle. I asked. I brought this on. This dark, heavy sadness.

"I was fourteen when it happened. It started just like any other fight. I can't remember what they were yelling about, the snippets I heard over my music. I'd lock myself in my room with Guns N' Roses blaring every night. Practically shaking my walls. The fight was so loud, though. So angry. Enough to rattle me, and I had a thick skin by then. I remember feeling so *scared* for my mom—it was just this overwhelming feeling that took over me. Something bad was coming. I knew." His eyes close, deep wrinkles fanning out from the edges. I can see his age in a new way. He wears his experiences—they've left marks, not all invisible. "I watched then, through a crack in my door. They were on the staircase, and Dad was screaming, and for once—for once she was screaming back. He got in her face and she backed away...and her foot slipped, I guess. Missed the next step. There was no stopping her. Or if there was, my dad's instincts were too dulled from all the booze in his blood. She fell backwards, and..." He puts his hands over his eyes, kneads his fingers into his temples.

There it was. The story.

The Jackson tragedy.

Not a murder. But a woman did die.

"I'm sorry. That must have been terrible."

"I'm sorry, too." He lowers his hands. His eyes are damp and red-rimmed. "The cops filed it as an accident. And he didn't push her—not with his actual hands—I could vouch for that much.

But still, it was his fault and we both knew it. We didn't have any family really, and she'd been kind of a recluse, at least in the end. So, no funeral. Just my dad and me watching her get put in the ground. I probably said ten words to him in the next four years. Then I graduated, and I never looked back. College and then law school and then Philly. I put myself through and the bills were real. That's why I—why I ended up at the cryobank. You know the rest: I wasn't dad material."

"Your dad, old man Jackson, as locals called him. I saw him a few times, growing up—at the grocery store, walking down the road. He didn't seem to leave the house much. Or talk to anyone when he did. I know he died, but what happened?"

"Drank himself to death. Seven or eight years ago now? Something like that. No funeral for him either. I suspect some townies would have come out of curiosity, but no one actually knew him. No one cared. Even I didn't mourn. I hadn't talked to him since I walked out the door at eighteen. He didn't know I was married. Didn't know he was a grandfather. Twice over. I thought about calling him the day Max was born, you know. *Thought* about it. Never did. He didn't deserve any life updates." He stares into his nearly empty mug, his knuckles white from gripping it so tight. I take a sip of my own coffee, because I need to do something. Anything. "Anyway," he starts again. Lifts his mug up and drains the rest of his coffee in one swig. "I hired someone to clear out most things from the house, and that was that. Joanie and I couldn't decide what to do with it. We talked about leaving the city so many times. *Fought* about it so many times. I hate that house, I do, but it's more complicated than that. Work was good, I wasn't hurting for money. So, it was locked up, put on hold, until we finally decided to move this summer. And here we are."

I nod. *Here we are.* But instead of moving on, for some reason I think about that fireplace mantel—the nails where somebody might have cared enough at one time to hang stockings and garlands. "I have one more question. Then I'm done, I promise. You can eat in peace. But your dad, did he carve the banisters? The fireplace? Or was that there when they moved in?"

The lines in his face ease. There's a small flicker of light in his eyes. "That was him. It was his wedding gift to my mom. He was so talented, my dad. Makes it all even sadder, doesn't it? I don't remember when he stopped carving, but it was a shame. I think Max inherited some of that talent, though. And that precision and drive. Hopefully that's all he inherited from his grandfather."

"Thank you. For—telling me all that. You didn't have to. I'm sure it wasn't easy."

"It's okay. Being here in Green Woods, in that house, it brings it all back. It's not just you. I haven't faced any of it since I was eighteen. Just a kid. Maybe if I'd talked to people about it more, I'd be less of a mess."

The waitress brings our nearly identical plates. We eat without talking. I don't think either of us is capable of pleasantries.

My grandfather wasn't a murderer after all. But he was an angry drunk. And my grandmother died because of him, just as Max said. It's hard to imagine Elliot, fourteen years old, a boy still, watching his mom die. Spending the next four years with a man he'd never forgive. None of it's an excuse for being a shitty husband and father. But I understand him more now. I wish he'd worked through his demons sooner, or at least tried. For his family.

Our plates are both empty, and we've drunk more cups of coffee than I can count. I feel the jitters snaking through my veins. I want to leave, but I also don't. Once was one thing, but I don't know that there will be other breakfasts. This could be it.

"Just give it some time," he says, leaving a pile of bills at the end of the table. When I reach for my purse, he waves me off. "I hope you can be friends again someday. You and Max. It'd be a shame if you two had to be strangers after this."

"I hope so, too. But he's busy running away from the truth right now. Away from me."

Elliot nods slowly. "I know. We talked about it. Max and me. The one conversation we did have this past week. We sat down with Joanie to tell her. And then—Marlow."

Marlow.

I've been so busy mourning Max and me, I've almost completely forgotten about the other half-sibling involved. She was only a fleeting thought. I made this all about me and us and tuned everything else out.

Marlow.

"It was a shock. For all of them. As you can imagine."

"Yeah. Max said it was pretty ugly. Do they hate me?"

"You?" He frowns, shaking his head. "Not at all. The wrath is all focused on me, as it should be. Joanie was upset she never knew about me donating, but it was before I met her. Not exactly first-date conversation—explaining I didn't want to ever have kids, but I'd donated so other people could. I knew at that point there'd been a confirmed pregnancy from the donation. It was the only confirmation I ever received, for the record. And then a few months later Joanie was pregnant. Quite the surprise for both of us. That was the only baby I could think about. I should have told Joanie sooner, though. I haven't been honest enough with her, about this, about lots of things. We're not fighting because of you, Calliope. We're fighting because I've had a bad habit of keeping things to myself. Of not putting in the work to be a better partner and father."

I let that sit for a minute. Spin my empty mug in a circle. It's a lot to take in: No other donor pregnancies. Elliot's admission of guilt. "And Marlow? Is she…curious about me?"

"I think so. But she's a tough one. Acts tough, anyway."

A sister. I have a half sister who lives next door. A half sister I know nothing about, except that she loves her shoes and dresses.

"Should we head out?" he asks.

"Sure."

The drive home is quiet. When he pulls up to my house, I'm preparing goodbye lines in my head. He shuts the car off. I turn to look at him, but his eyes are focused straight ahead. "Are your moms home?"

I debate lying, saying they're both at the studio. Most Saturday mornings they do work, but they've been using subs for more shifts. To be around for me, they didn't have to say. Mimmy made a point yesterday of telling me they'd taken off today to tackle some end-of-summer yard work.

"I was thinking," he continues when I don't respond, "that I could pop in and introduce myself. A quick hello, shake their hands. Nothing big. It just feels a bit odd, doesn't it? We're neighbors, too, after all."

He's right. Mama asked again this week about meeting him, and Mimmy shot her a warning glance. Said it was up to me, on my terms. Knowing Mama, she'll ask again soon.

Both cars are parked in the driveway. It would be hard to lie anyway.

"Okay." I'm sweating already, even in the car's lingering AC.

"Okay."

We walk toward the house and I push the door open, hoping fervently that they're strolling in the woods or out on their bikes. But no such luck. Mimmy's cheerful face appears instantly in the kitchen doorway.

"Hey, sweetheart, you slipped out this morning! We were wondering where—" Mimmy's mouth is still open, but the words stop coming. "Oh."

"This is Elliot Jackson," I say awkwardly, as if it's not immediately evident.

"Oh." She is frozen in place, a dishrag hanging from the tips of her fingers. The only movement is the sporadic drip of excess water from the rag. She grips the cloth tighter, more drops falling.

"And Elliot, this is my mom. Margo."

Elliot clears his throat behind me. "I thought it would be nice to drop in and say hello." He steps up to Mimmy, arm extended, reaching for her free hand.

Mimmy looks at his hand for a minute before nodding and putting out her limp fingers. It's a very sad shake. Nothing like the power shake Mama taught me when I was still in elementary school. "Every woman needs to learn to shake with authority. First step to cracking that glass ceiling wide open," she'd said. I hadn't understood. What glass ceiling? And why do I want to crack it? But I'd mastered the shake anyway. Mama had been proud.

"Let me get Stella," Mimmy says, pulling her hand back. "She's out in the garden."

We're alone for a minute, me and Elliot, while Mimmy is outside. "She was the easier of the two," I say. "Just to warn you."

"Excellent. Thank you for the heads-up."

Mama steps through the kitchen door first. Her skin looks pale under the tips of pink on her nose and cheeks, already burning from her morning in the sun. The contrast of color makes her expression even more formidable. She is steeling herself, her face pulled into tight lines to mask the softness underneath. She thinks she's good at pretending the softness isn't there, but she's never as good at it as she thinks.

"Hello," she says with a curt nod. "It was thoughtful of you to stop by." Unlike Mimmy she initiates the shake, and, also unlike Mimmy, her grip is firm and assertive. Too firm. Too assertive.

Elliot winces before he can catch himself. A victory for Mama. She will make permanent note.

"I don't want to intrude. Today, I mean, and also generally speaking. But I was glad when Calliope asked me to breakfast this morning."

"Oh, she did?" Mama lifts an eyebrow, leveling her gaze at me.

"Yes. I thought it would be helpful."

"And was it?"

"I think so. Yes."

"Good."

We are in an impromptu staring match. I will not blink. I will not.

"Anyway," Elliot continues, and Mama breaks, turning back to him. "I won't push for other meetings, of course. It's all what Calliope and the two of you are comfortable with. I'm here if she wants to talk more. Otherwise, I'll keep to my side of the woods. I know what my role is here. And what my role isn't. I don't want you to worry about that."

Mama seems to sag a bit, like some of her fire has dissipated. Mimmy is just nodding, nonstop, a human bobblehead, her arms wrapped tight around her chest.

When no one else speaks, Elliot adds, "I'm happy to know that Calliope has such a strong family. And she seems like an amazing young woman. You two must be so proud."

"Oh, we are," Mama says.

"Well, then…" Elliot glances back over at me, looking flustered. He needs help. I would expect more confidence from a lawyer.

"Maybe we can all have dinner sometime." I say it without thinking, grabbing at the first thought that comes to me.

"That would be nice." He gives me a nervous smile. "Though it might have to wait until my family starts speaking to me again."

"They're mad at you?" Mama asks. Her face has fewer sharp lines now.

"More hurt, I think. Shocked. They didn't know. About me donating. It was before any of them, obviously. I never felt the need to disclose it, but clearly, I should have." He gives a sad, helpless shrug. "I'm hoping they come around. Just like I'm hoping it comes around for you, too."

That last part is directed at me, his blue eyes looking disarmingly sincere and sympathetic.

"Well, I'm sorry to hear that," Mama says, and I can tell she actually means it. "It's no one's fault. And you had a right to donate. I'm glad we picked you, you know. Despite all the horseshit that's come along with it. Without you we wouldn't have our dear girl."

Elliot smiles, and—against all odds—Mama smiles back.

"Yes," Mimmy says quietly, stepping in closer to our circle. She has finally stopped nodding. "Thank you."

All three are watching me now. I feel so strange inside. A blend of too many things, not all of them seamlessly mixing. Like a smoothie with too many fruits and powders and seeds.

"I'm not sure I deserve the thanks," Elliot says finally. "But I'm glad I was picked, too. I wouldn't take it back. Not a chance."

Chapter Seventeen

I knock on their door two days later. Monday morning.

I shouldn't be here. Max said he couldn't do *this*. Us. But I care about him. I have to know if he's okay. Even if it's kinder—more effort—than he deserves right now.

Joanie comes to the door. She smiles, but it doesn't reach her eyes.

"How are you holding up?" she asks.

I shrug. "Not great." I don't have to ask to know she's not so great either. She's wearing sweatpants and a baggy white T-shirt and looks like she hasn't slept since she heard the news. Or eaten. There's a new hollow to her cheeks. She fits with the house, too well. A matching set. They are both empty and forlorn.

"It's certainly a mess, isn't it?"

"Yep. Definitely a mess."

"I'm sorry, Calliope. That you have to go through this. I know it can't be easy."

"No. But I poked around in the past. I started this."

"Well, imagine if you hadn't?" She sighs heavily and reaches out to grab the peeling doorframe, leaning against it for support. "Seems to me we'd all be worse off in the end. The truth has a way of coming out. One way or another. Better to have this truth sooner rather than later, don't you think?"

I nod. She's right. Even if it doesn't make right *now* any easier. "Is Max around?"

She sighs, and somehow manages to look even more exhausted. "He is. But I don't think it's a good time. I'll tell him you stopped by. How about that?"

"I guess. Sure. Whatever you think." I take a step back, the porch creaking loudly beneath my sandals. Maybe this is it—the rotting planks are about to finally cave in. I'll be sucked down with them into the dark underbelly of the house.

"Listen, darling," Joanie says, leaning in closer to cover the distance. "What I *personally* think is that my son needs to come out of hiding and talk things through with you. But he's apparently too old to listen to his mother these days. He says that I'm angry, so he's allowed to be angry, too. But things between his dad and I are... very complicated. I'm not angry that you exist. It was just one more secret. One too many."

I'm not sure how to respond to that—such a raw, personal statement—but I don't have to, because he appears then.

Max. Behind his mom, staring at me from over her shoulder.

Joanie startles. "Max, honey. I didn't hear you come down."

"Obviously. And I wasn't *hiding* upstairs. I was in the sunroom." He doesn't smile as he says it, but I can still hear the sarcasm in his tone. *Sunroom.* We've laughed about that. The idea of actually referring to it as a room, as Joanie does. It feels like a small nod to our summer together.

Joanie steps to the side, and I can see him fully. His eyes are rimmed with dark smudges. He's wearing a plain black T-shirt and boxers covered in UFOs and stars and planets.

He looks like the boy I used to love. He looks like a stranger.

"Hey," I say weakly. Even I can barely hear myself.

"Hey."

"I'll leave you kids to it then," Joanie says, turning and walking toward the kitchen.

"Can we talk?" I ask, my voice louder this time. I straighten my shoulders and look him squarely in the eye.

Max is silent for a beat, and then: "Yeah. Okay."

He tilts his chin toward the yard, and I follow him, jumping down the stairs as he does. He sits on the thickest patch of grass in their meadow, the only part that isn't just spare blades in awkward overgrown clumps. I sit next to him.

"Before you ask how I'm doing, can we just skip that?" He's looking down, away from me, plucking at the grass under his knees. I want to make a joke, tell him that there's not enough extra grass in this dead yard for him to be so destructive. But I don't. I'm too sad to joke. Too frustrated. Too exhausted. Too everything.

"No small talk. Promise. I have a feeling your answer would be pretty much the same as mine anyway."

"Okay. So. What did you want to talk about then? You must have come for a reason."

"Mostly I wanted to check in. Say hello. Unlike you, I don't want to be strangers."

"I told you," he says, shaking his head at the ground. "I can't do this, Calliope. Not today. Maybe not ever. I know this isn't your fault, I do. And I hate that I'm hurting you. My mom isn't wrong—I know I'm not handling this well. But I'm still so mad at everything. I'm mad at the whole damn universe."

"I'm mad, too, you know. Or at least I was. I'm still sorting it out. But I don't want to spend the rest of my life being bitter and broken."

"Me neither. But I don't know how to let go and move on with you still in my life. And I need to—I *need* to move on."

"I'm your neighbor. This is Green Woods, not Philly. We're about to start school together. You can't avoid me forever."

"That might not be true. Because . . . well, because we might not stay."

My chest tightens. "What do you mean, not stay?"

He shrugs. "Nothing definite. My mom hates living out in the woods. She thinks it's time to finally sell this old house, get an actual fresh start somewhere, maybe a new city. My dad isn't fighting her that hard on it because it's his fault we're all going through this shit. He's desperate to get back on her good side."

It's like his words have actual heat to them, they burn so hot in my ears. "This *shit*?" I say, and I'm so outraged, so stunned, that I laugh. "You mean—*my existence*? Is that shit to you, Max? Because can I remind you that I wouldn't be here if it wasn't for him? I would literally not be on this earth. My moms would have had a different baby. You just said this wasn't my fault, right? Well, it's not your dad's *fault* either. It's no one's fault. I'm alive because of what your dad did, and I'm actually pretty damn glad that I'm sitting here right now."

He sinks his head even lower, his body folding in on itself. "I know. You're right. I don't mean I wish you weren't born. Never. I just wish . . . we'd never moved here. I'd never met you. Life would have been much simpler that way."

Even with all the anger I'm feeling right in this moment—all the sadness and confusion of this summer—I don't wish that. Not at all. Maybe life was simpler before the Jackson family came along. But simpler doesn't mean better.

Max doesn't feel that way, though. And I have to accept that.

I'm about to stand when he says: "My dad told me you two got breakfast this weekend."

The change in conversation—the fact that he's starting a conversation at all—catches me off guard. "We did. I needed to have a real talk with him. Try to wrap my head around the fact that he's half of my chromosomes. It was good to hear more about his life growing up. His childhood was pretty shitty, not that it gives him an excuse to be a bad dad. But the things he saw, your grandmother dying how she did, your grandfather . . ." I shiver, glancing up at the house. We are sitting directly in its shadow, darkness that seems to seep like a black fog from the porch, fanning out along the ground.

"Wait. He told you about that?" He turns his head and looks up at me finally.

"Uh, yeah. A little." I want to backpedal. I should have left before this conversation.

"That's private."

"I know, and—"

"My mom's the one who told me about my grandparents. Did he tell you that, too? It was *too much* for my dad, she said. Too much to tell his own son. But his donor daughter? Yeah, that's cool. He'll just run and tell her everything."

"I'm sorry," I say quietly. And I am sorry about this. I'm not sorry I had the conversation with Elliot, but it wasn't my business to bring it up again now, here with Max. "It's not like that. Sometimes it's easier to talk to a stranger. And that's what I am to him. You're his son."

"You're right. I am his son. And my family might be a mess, but they're *my* mess. Just because you inherited a few of my dad's shitty genes doesn't make you one of us. You're not a Jackson. And you should be glad about that. Trust me."

"Max, please, I—"

"No. I need you to go. I might be weak or a coward or emotionally immature or all of the above, and I'm sorry. But I can't do this."

"Okay." I stand up, brushing the dirt and grass from my legs, and walk away.

I don't look back.

When the doorbell chimes and Mimmy calls up for me, I pretend not to hear. I pull my pillow tight around my ears, willing the moment to pass.

But then Mama is there, at my door. It's open a crack, my mistake, so she doesn't have to knock to come in. She edges it open wider, peeks her head into the room. "Sweetheart? You have a visitor."

I sigh, throwing the pillow on the floor as I sit up. "I don't want to see anybody."

"It's Marlow. Max's sister." *Your half sister,* she doesn't say, but we both feel the empty space at the end of her words. She gives me a sad smile.

"Marlow?"

Mama nods. "Marlow."

I look down at myself. I'm wearing a neon-pink XXL Hot Mama Flow T-shirt. After my disastrous talk with Max, I was fully planning on spending the rest of the day in bed.

"Now's not a great time."

Mama takes a step farther into the room, closing the door behind her. "Calliope. I think you should talk to her."

"I will. Just not right now."

She sits next to me on the bed. "Don't you think this must be rough on her, too? Everyone is busy thinking and worrying about you and Max. How you're both coping. But there's a third child involved here. And she's younger and probably just as confused. Maybe her heart isn't broken, not the way yours is, but that doesn't mean it hasn't suffered a bruising."

Mama's right. Marlow is alone here. No friends. Strange town. Scary house. A brother who abandoned her when he fell in love with the girl next door. And now he's locked away in his room, grieving over the fact that the girl is his half sister. *Her* half sister.

"Okay. I'll talk to her. Just"—I point at my shirt—"let me change. Does she look flawless? Nice dress, lace-up sandals, model makeup?"

Mama cocks her head to the side, her brow furrowing. "No? She looked pretty casual to me. I only glanced—Mimmy was talking to her—but I believe she was wearing denim shorts and sneakers. No makeup that I could see. Unless it was an exceptionally natural look."

"Huh. Interesting."

"What? Is that so odd?"

"Every time I've seen her, she's all done up with no place to go. She seems like the type to look her best every day. Spend hours prepping. Even if it's just for bored bedroom selfies."

"I see. Well, then maybe you don't know her as well as you think." Mama pats my knee and stands up. "I'll let you change. We'll entertain her for a few minutes."

She leaves, and I throw on a gray T-shirt and black overalls. I slip my feet into my glitter shoes, swipe my hair into a bun.

I can already picture the scene waiting for me downstairs: sullen Marlow, arms crossed, tapping her manicured nails on the edge of the sofa. Mimmy trying to ply her with iced beverages and sugar-free baked goods. Mama making awkward conversation about weather patterns in Green Woods.

I walk down the stairs, slowly. It's quiet. Too quiet.

The three of them are in the living room, not talking. The moms on the love seat, Marlow by herself on the sofa. She has a full glass of lemonade and a plate of lemon rhubarb cookies that appears untouched on the coffee table in front of her.

Mimmy looks desperately relieved when she sees me. "Oh good, Calliope is here!" she practically sings out, leaping up from the love seat.

Marlow turns to face me, and if Mama hadn't told me who was here, it would have taken me a moment to put things together. A long moment. She looks five years younger, at least, without her heavy-lidded eyes and contoured cheeks. I barely know Marlow as it is, but I certainly don't know this little girl in front of me.

She looks small. Sad. Weak. Timid. The kind of girl regular Marlow wouldn't give the time of day. She'd strut right past her empty table in the cafeteria.

But then again, those were all assumptions, weren't they? Based on nothing but appearance. Ginger likes masks, after all. The bolder, the better. Marlow might like masks, too.

I wish I'd tried to get to know her before now. Before everything imploded.

"Hey," I say, shoving my hands deep in my overall pockets.

Marlow stands, keeping her eyes on the floor. Her plain black sneakers. "Can we talk somewhere?"

The moms start to scuttle out of the room, but I put my hand up to stop them. "Sure. Let's go outside. On the porch. You can bring the lemonade and cookies if you want."

Marlow shakes her head. I see Mama immediately eye the plate—lemon rhubarb cookies are her favorite.

I lead Marlow to the porch, and we settle in the rocking chairs. I let her take mine.

It occurs to me, sitting here in silence with Marlow, that this is where I first met Max. This is where it all began. I'm not sure what this conversation will be—if it's some kind of beginning, or another ending.

"I should have come talked to you," I start, "but I was selfish, caught up in my own drama with Max. And it also didn't feel right, intruding in your world like that. But I'm glad you're here."

She doesn't say anything for a few minutes. Just rocks, her feet only hitting the ground when the chair swings forward.

"Max was really upset earlier, you know. After you left. He wouldn't say why."

"Yeah. I know." *My family*, he'd said. *My mess*. What would he say about Marlow sitting here with me? "It's just... difficult right now. I want to still have him in my life. But I shouldn't have come over today. He needs to do his own processing first."

"He loved you, you know. *Really* loved you. I never saw my brother like that before. It was weird. Kind of gross. But nice, I guess, too. To see him so happy."

"Well," I say, my throat swelling up tight, "I really loved him, too. I'm just trying to rearrange that love. Not erase it. But make it into a different kind."

"Is that possible?"

"I want to believe it is."

"I mean, if someone told me my mom wasn't my mom and

I had to stop loving her like she was, I don't think I could do it. I couldn't stop loving Max like a brother either."

"You wouldn't have to stop. Ever. I love lots of people like family that don't have my blood. It's the being *in* love that makes it messy. Regular love is easier."

"Yeah? Regular love with my dad isn't so easy. I want to love him. I *should* love him. Because he's my dad and all. But he makes me so angry, I—" She stops. I turn to her, and her cheeks are shiny in the sunlight. She makes no sound as she cries. I almost wish she would be loud about it, thrashing and raging. The quiet unsettles me.

"You're allowed to be angry," I say. "And sometimes I think you can love your family even if you don't always like them. If that makes sense."

It hits me suddenly, the full weight of this conversation. This first real moment with my little sister. Half sister. Donor sister. Whatever the proper terminology might be, it all feels the same right now. I've maybe felt like a big sister to Ginger sometimes, but this—it isn't the same, not even close. Anything I say to Marlow today will matter. It will define how she sees me. Our relationship from here on out. *If* we have a relationship at all.

"I'm sorry that my digging around made a mess of everything. For you. For everyone. I've had such a great life with my moms. It shouldn't have mattered, really, who my donor was, because I had everything, didn't I? But I'm glad I did dig. Because we had to know this. As terrible as it might feel right now, it would have been worse if it stayed buried."

Marlow doesn't respond. Doesn't give any indication that she even heard me.

There's a long moment of silence. Too long. But it doesn't feel like my turn to talk.

"I'm not sure what I'm supposed to do or say now," she says finally. "Or what I was looking for when I came here to talk to you. I started walking into the woods without really thinking about it. I feel so . . . confused. Because who are you and what does it mean that my dad is kind of like your dad, too? Is that a good thing? I mean, I always wondered what it would be like to have a sister. But what do we all do now? I don't know." She shrugs, frowning. "I guess I just needed to say something to you. Everyone at home's making this all about Max. But I'm here, too, right?"

"You're here, too."

She gives a little indignant *hmph*, crossing her arms over her chest. The tears on her cheeks are drying. I feel hopeful. The old Marlow is coming back. Or maybe not the old Marlow, at least not the one I thought she was. An altogether different Marlow. One I never bothered to really see before now.

"You didn't seem to like me much," she says, side-eyeing me for a moment before staring out at the trees. "You never tried to talk to me or get to know me. Never asked me to hang out with you and Max or to show me the neighborhood. Not that he ever asked either. He was kind of a crappy brother, too, this summer, if I'm being real with you."

"I didn't not like you," I say quickly, my cheeks burning. "Honestly? You seemed too cool for me. I was intimidated."

Marlow laughs. A real one. Bright and chirpy. It's a good sound. I want to hear it again. "Please. You were scared of a little thirteen-year-old girl? What could I do to you? You're like this wholesome forest-goddess girl who seems like she's never felt out of place in her life."

Now I'm the one to laugh. Loudly. "Forest-goddess girl? And you're way wrong. I feel out of place. All the time. But I guess it sounds silly now. And it's not that I was *scared* of you. You just seemed so miserable here."

"Well, it gets lonely, you know, only having friends you can text, and they're always together, busy doing fun things all summer long. They still invite me sometimes, but it's too far to go much, and I know they'll stop sooner or later. Bye-bye, Marlow." She gives the trees ahead a sad little wave.

"I doubt that. And you're not *that* far. You can visit. They can come here."

She shrugs. "Not the same. Do you forget being thirteen? You're old but not *that* old. I can't drive, and neither can my friends."

"I've only ever had two close friends. I've always known they were lifers." Or at least that's what I thought, before this summer. And hopefully I'm still right. There's a learning curve to everything. "That's the rule when you're pretty much born together."

"Well, you're lucky then. You have true BFFs. And a better family, too."

"Not better. Just different."

She glances at me, just so I don't miss her masterful eye roll. "Whatever you say."

I do it then, because I want this stronger Marlow to stay—I reach for her hand, clasp my fingers tight around hers. She looks down, frowning at first, but she doesn't pull away. Our hands stay together.

"You going all sisterly on me now, or what?" she asks.

"Not sisterly. Just—as a neighbor. Maybe a friend even. I want you to know that I'm here. Just a short walk across the woods. If you need anything. At all. I mean it."

"A short walk, maybe, but I got so many pricklies scraping at my legs on my way here, and you're lucky I wore these old shoes I don't care about. I stepped in *two* muddy puddles. And nearly fell when I tripped over a stupid old branch. Land mines the whole way."

"So, you're saying you probably won't be coming over that often?"

"Probably not." She looks up at me, and I can't be completely sure, but I think she might almost be smiling. "Or maybe I'll ask my mom for some farmer boots. And shin guards or something like that. Keep myself protected. Or I guess I could just use the road."

"Yeah?"

"Yeah."

"I'd like that. Though next time you come, you should try my mom's cookies. You missed out."

"Maybe you can wrap some up for me? I won't tell Max about

them. He ate enough of her treats this summer. He talked about them *all* the time. Never brought me any, though. So selfish."

"I'll get you those cookies," I say, letting go of her hand as I stand. "But do me a favor? While you're not entirely wrong about Max being selfish sometimes, maybe give him a chance to do better? He probably needs you more than ever right now."

"Wouldn't know it. He's barely said two words to me. He's been locked away in his room pretty much every minute of the day. Crying and hitting things from what I can tell from listening at the door. It's not *eavesdropping*. I'm just making sure he's okay."

I hold back a smile. "He needs time. But I don't think he'll want to be alone forever."

"Maybe." She closes her mouth. Then opens it again like she wants to say more, but stops. Bites her lip.

I turn away and walk inside to the kitchen. I empty the rest of the cookie tin into a plastic bag. Mama will be disappointed, but it's a good cause. She can have the cookies from the plate Marlow left in the living room, and Mimmy can always make more tomorrow. I hear voices then—the moms stirring in the living room, a few footsteps coming toward the kitchen. "Calliope?"

"Not done yet," I say, slipping back out the door.

Marlow is still in the chair, rocking, when I come back out. "Thanks," she says, looking down at the bag as I hand it to her. She stays like that for a minute, not moving, and then, "Did Max tell you? We might move away?"

"He did tell me."

"It's not a done deal. But we don't have much reason to stay."

It hurts when she says it, but I try not to show just how much. "What do you want?" I ask. I watch her, waiting.

"I want," she starts, lifting her head up to meet my gaze, and I realize for the first time that she has Max's eyes. Not Elliot's. Not mine. "I want a home and for my family to feel like a real family."

"I want that for you, too."

Chapter Eighteen

TWO days pass with no visits from the Jackson family.

It's eating me alive, wondering if they'll move. Leave Green Woods in the dust forever. I might never see Marlow again. Or Max. Or Elliot. My concern right now lies in that order. Funny, how Elliot is the first one I'd cut, after all those years spent wondering about him. Maybe I'd feel more of a connection with him if we had more time. Maybe not.

"Thank god this summer is almost over," Ginger says to me, dipping her glittery yellow sunglasses down her nose to make her stare more pointed. "Because this funk you're in? It can't go on forever. I never thought I'd say this, but I'm actually excited for us to be back in school. Homework and tests and battling with the school board about helping the environment will do you some good." She pushes her glasses back up, leans against the slowly deflating edge of the turtle pool.

There's a slow leak we can't find despite several intensive searches. The turtle is destined to live for one season and one season only.

"But you'll see Vivi less," I point out.

She waves me off. "That might be good, too. She'll miss me enough to finally try to lock me down. Imagine how much she'll worry, wondering about all the cute girls throwing themselves at me in the halls of Green Woods High."

"Does she know there's only one other out girl in the whole school?"

"Of course not," she says, chuckling. "I play my cards carefully."

"I don't think you have to play anything with her. She likes you."

"She does, doesn't she?"

I toss the stick from my ice pop at her face.

"Speaking of Viv, I should head out soon. Hot date tonight. She's taking me to her dad's old-guy-softball-league game."

"Wow. Cheering for her dad in his sweaty polyester uniform. That's a pretty big deal."

"Right? And who knows, we might even hit up TGI Fridays or Applebee's after." She's smirking, or pretending to, anyway. But there's a glow to her. And not just because we've been soaking in this sad pool for the last three hours.

"I'm happy for you," I say, crawling across the lumpy turtle bottom until we're side by side, our sweaty arms and shoulders sticking together. "You know that, right?"

"I know." She leans her head against my shoulder. It's too hot for this much skin contact, but I don't move away. "I just wish we could both be happy and in love at the same time. Wouldn't that be nice?"

I shrug, staring down at my red-tipped knees. "I'm not *unhappy*." I'm lying through my teeth. Ginger's kind enough to not call me on it, though, even if she knows unhappy is exactly what I am. She just pats my hand sympathetically, and then she stands up, her itty-bitty red polka-dot bikini barely covering her lady bits as she shakes herself dry.

"I love you," she says, sweeping down to kiss my forehead. Her long hair, almost sheer white at this point in the summer, tickles my face. "Call me later tonight if you want. I'll come sleep over after I gorge on chicken fingers and loaded baked potato skins."

I nod, and then she's gone. The water is so low I can barely submerge my toes anymore. But I stay in anyway, because there's nothing else to do and it's too stuffy in the house. Mama and Mimmy won't be home for at least another hour. I'm not hungry for dinner yet. I'm not hungry all that often these days.

Ginger's right. School will be a good thing.

Except Max will be there, too, at least to start the year. Wandering the halls by himself, no one caring enough during senior year to bother with the new kid. Or maybe a cute girl sitting next to him in Art Club will take him under her wing. Show him around, become his new Green Woods guide.

I sink down until my neck hits the water and my legs have to dangle off the edge of the opposite side. My eyes close and I stay like that, not moving, for what could be five minutes or an hour. It's peaceful here. Like nothing else exists around me. Maybe this is what it felt like to be inside Mimmy's body for nine months.

"Calliope? Are you okay?"

I open one eye slowly, then the second.

Noah is standing over me, a giant from my vantage point.

He's studying me with a look of grave concern, thick eyebrows furrowed and lips pulled into a deep frown.

"Hey, Noah. I'm fine. Really. Just a little spaced out."

As I start to sit up, I remember that my bikini is four years old, the last clean one I had in my drawer, and that it's almost as scandalous as Ginger's. Much less intentionally so, but under-sized all the same.

"Could you throw me my towel from the bench? It's getting a little chilly, isn't it?"

It's definitely not anything close to chilly out here. But Noah politely nods and grabs the towel anyway, having the good sense to keep his eyes on the grass as he holds it out to me.

When I'm properly swaddled and sitting on the hammock, I notice that Noah and I aren't alone out here in the yard.

"You brought Harold?" I ask, looking over at the large black cello case propped against the side of the picnic table. Harold the cello. Ginger and I had picked the name, so many summers ago. I don't remember why. Maybe only because it was ridiculous—who would name a cello Harold?

"Yeah," he says, still not looking at me, even though I'm no longer indecent.

I pick at a stray thread on my towel and wait for him to offer up more. He doesn't.

"Okay, so is there something you want to play for me?"

He clears his throat and, finally, looks up at me.

"I wrote something," he says. "A song. For you."

"For me?" I repeat, as if his words weren't clear enough.

"Yes. I've been working on it all summer."

My stomach twists and knots like the thick hammock ropes swaying under me. "Oh," I say. I'm not capable of much else, and it seems kinder and easier than *why*. But I'd hoped any awkward conversations or overtures were behind us.

"Can I play it for you?"

I nod. Hopefully not too reluctantly.

He slowly undoes the case, pulls out Harold, the bow, a creased piece of paper that he smooths between his fingers.

It's an unfathomably long ordeal, Noah setting himself up at the picnic table, making sure Harold is positioned *just so*, as if he hasn't been cradling cellos since he was in third grade. The paper is placed carefully on the grass in front of him, though from the hammock I can see the notations are tiny and scrawled and must be nearly indecipherable from his vantage point. He most likely has it memorized. He usually does—he has the kind of uncanny musical genius that allows him to absorb a song after just a few reads.

Noah starts playing then, bow against the strings, no preamble. His eyes close.

The song starts slowly, deep, rich notes that swirl around us in the fading light, picking up speed as they go. Layers of melody peel back to reveal more layers, smooth and satisfying, like I'm unwrapping a piece of dark chocolate and every bite tastes better than the last. I don't want it to end; I feel like I can reach out and grab it, this feeling, make it mine. Everything is good, so good. Too good. Because then, just like that, the chocolate becomes bitter. Far too dark, not enough sugar and milk to balance out the cacao.

There's no pause, no bridge, but it's a different song. Strident at first, Noah's bow furiously moving across the strings, a slurring of sharp notes. Eruption. Destruction. Chaos. And then, slower again, so very slow, lethargic almost. The notes are flat and low and oddly empty. I feel empty, too, listening to them. I can feel the good draining away, the happy taste disappearing completely from my tongue. It was never there. Never real.

Just as I'm about to ask him to stop, say I've had too much, the song changes again. It's not as happy as it was to start, not as full. But it's not as sad either. There is a bouncing rhythm to it, the notes higher and warmer. My toes tap along.

This section, the last one, I suspect, is meant to feel hopeful.

Noah stops. The final note lingers in the leaves all around us. He puts the bow down on the bench.

We don't say anything.

I should, though. I should say something. Thank him.

I stand up, tucking the towel under my arms, and walk over to him. I stop when I'm a few inches away, our eyes locked.

"Thank you," I say, reaching for his hand. "That was beautiful. I felt . . . *everything*."

He's blushing now, a bright red flower spreading over his cheeks. "I didn't know how to say all of that to you. Not without messing it up somehow. So instead I spent the summer finding a different way to express myself. A more foolproof way."

"Noah," I start, more anxious than ever about finding the right words, the best words, "I care about you so much, I do, you have to know that—"

He puts his free hand up to stop me. "Wait. Before you say *but*, I just need to get something out. I didn't play that song to make you change your mind about us. The opposite, actually. I wrote it so I could purge all those feelings and we could move on. For good. I just wanted you to hear it. So you could... understand me better, I guess."

"Really?"

"Really. I'm not proud of how I acted this summer. I just didn't know how to face it, the truth—that you would never love me like I loved you. But seeing you hurt? It was way worse than seeing you love someone else. I wish things were different for you and Max. And I'm sorry I let you falling in love with someone get in the way of our friendship."

"I forgive you," I say, and I do. Completely. "I'm sorry for lots of things, too. For starters, we should have been honest with each other sooner. Like when I knew you gave me that Valentine's Day card sophomore year. And how the *rule* was at least partly to avoid having a real conversation about it. I wanted to protect us, but maybe that wasn't the best way."

"I kind of figured. Not at first, but..." He shrugs. "I could have said something, too."

I shake my head. "No. That was on me. And I wasn't the greatest friend this summer either. I should have spent more solo time with you. And Ginger. Maybe I'll just never date again, period. That's probably the easiest solution. My rule was pretty smart, after all, only it should go above and beyond senior year."

Noah laughs. "Nah. I don't want that for you. Or me. We both deserve love. Someday. Whenever it's meant to happen."

I nod. And then, "I love you, Noah," the words tumbling out before I have time to be self-conscious—because that's all there is, and it's as true as anything else in my life. I may not know a lot of things about love right now, but I do know this: "I love you in the way that matters most."

"I love you that way, too."

I look around us, my mind running with a nonstop montage of Noah memories from this yard: the three of us trying to hang a swing from one of the trees on our own, Noah—and the swing—flying ten feet in the air on the first trial run; Noah filling an old kiddie pool with strawberry juice ice cubes and blue Kool-Aid packets, his "most greatest idea ever"; Ginger screaming hysterically when she found a half-dead baby bird along the tree line, and me and Noah delicately nursing it back to life in a shoebox.

"Can you promise me something?" I ask, turning back to focus on Noah.

"I can't promise until I know what you're asking. But I'll try my best."

"Promise me we'll always be friends. No matter how complicated life gets around us. We don't give up. Not on *this*."

He nods. "I think that's a promise I can keep."

We both reach out at the same time, our double-pinkie oath. One pinkie each never felt like enough. Two hands, two pinkies, full promise.

His grin is brighter than the blazing August sun, and I throw myself against him for a hug.

"You seem cheerier tonight," Mama says, putting a plate piled high with grilled tofu and veggies on the table.

I shrug, picking at the crispy brown edge of a piece of tofu and popping it in my mouth.

"Did it have anything to do with Noah visiting?" She's trying to sound indifferent, but her hungry, searching eyes give her away. Like if she stares long and hard enough, she'll be able to see the answer for herself inside my mind without me having to say a word. I wouldn't put it past her. I don't doubt Mama has superpowers.

"Maybe. Yes. I feel like we finally understand each other."

"So you're friends again?" Mama asks, smiling extra wide.

Mimmy's smile is just as big as she settles into the chair next to me with a basket of fresh homemade corn bread.

"I think so."

"Good," Mama says, loading up her plate with a stack of tofu. "It wasn't right, the two of you being separate. The three of you belong together."

"I know that. Noah's my blood. Ginger, too. Just like the two of you. And as for Marlow and Max and Elliot...I don't know what they are to me yet. I don't know how to label them."

"And that's okay, my sweet girl," Mimmy says, lifting her palm to rub my cheek. "Give it some time. Maybe your family only got bigger this summer, even if it came about in an unusual way. It's not traditional or normal, but what family is?"

"Ha!" Mama laughs loudly around a mouth full of eggplant and pepper. "I would never want to be normal."

"Good thing, too, since there's no hope for you," Mimmy replies sweetly.

"All I ever want to be is a Silversmith," I say, and looking around the table at the two of them, those words have never felt truer. "I never want to know." The words, the proclamation, they aren't planned. Even I'm stunned by my own conviction. But I have no doubts. "I never want to know which one of you is biologically half me. Because it doesn't matter. It never mattered. I was silly to ever think that it did."

Mama makes a strange sound, somewhere between a snort and a sob, hand pressed against her lips. Mimmy is beaming at me like I just won the Nobel Peace Prize and made her the proudest mother in the universe.

We don't say anything for a moment. We just stare at each other, eyes all pink and shiny with tears. Even Mama's.

"You weren't silly," Mimmy says finally, dabbing at her damp cheeks with a napkin. "You were curious. Exploring your identity. That's nothing to be embarrassed about. Ever."

"Maybe not. But either way, this summer taught me a lot, good and bad. And I know the truth now. The one that matters, at least. You are both my moms, equally. You are my family. Period. No scientific evidence needed."

"We *are* family." Mama stands up, walking over to wrap me up tight in her strong, trembling arms. "And family is everything."

Family.

Not just the family we're born into, a random collection of chance and odds and good old-fashioned luck. But the family we create. The people we choose for ourselves. *Our people.*

That family—it really is everything.

Chapter Nineteen

MAYBE *your family only got bigger this summer,* Mimmy had said.

Marlow is back on our porch the next morning, happily working through a plate of lemon bars. She showed up with no warning, appearing along the edge of the woods as I sat in my rocking chair sipping iced tea. I wondered at first if I was imagining it—if Mimmy's words had forced her into my subconscious. But no, she gave a small wave and walked closer, until she was coming up the steps, then she was on the porch next to me, sitting in Mama's chair. She was real. Marlow Jackson. Dressed in a plain black T-shirt and artfully distressed denim short-shorts, and this time with a hint of mascara on her naturally long lashes. Still subdued, but like her usual life force was slowly recharging.

"No real sugar? You're messing with my head," she says, licking the buttery crumbles from her fingertips. "I feel like I'm dancing in a happy, sunny field of sugar when I eat these things."

"A little raw honey and coconut oil. Magic, right?"

"Total magic." She takes another bite, closes her eyes as she swallows. Just like Max does. I wonder what she sees then—if she sees brilliant swirls of color like he does. I want to ask, but it feels like too intimate a detail. "You know how lucky you are, right? Growing up with a mom who makes food like this all the time? I mean, damn."

Damn. Is she allowed to curse? Did I curse at her age? I'm sure I did. But if I was a real older sister, would it still be my duty to say something?

I'm not, though. Not a real sister. Not even a real half sister.

"My mom hasn't really made anything but microwave popcorn and frozen dinners since we got here. She didn't cook much in Philly either, but at least we had a thousand places that delivered. So her kitchen skills didn't matter much. But now? I ate cold soup straight out of the can yesterday. *Cold soup,* Calliope. It was very sad."

"You must miss the city so much," I say gently—hoping this will steer the conversation to the move without me outright asking.

"Yeah. Most stuff. But..." She stares down at the half-empty plate, an odd look on her face. I wonder if the lemon bars she ate might all come back up. At least the porch is easy enough to hose off. "I don't know. I'm not sure I'm ready to leave either."

I can't help it—I feel myself soar up above this porch at those words. The sky today is an electric bright blue, the kind of sky that makes you believe in all the best things. I should want Marlow to be home, to be happy. But what if Green Woods could be that place?

"Has it been decided? Are you leaving?"

She shakes her head. Takes another bar and jams it in her mouth.

"School starts soon," I say, stating the obvious.

"Dad wants to give it more time. Mom wants to leave." She shrugs, swallowing her last bite and putting the plate down on the porch railing. "Mom usually wins, though she never *really* wins, you know?"

I nod. It breaks my heart for Joanie. For Marlow and Max. For all of them. Being a family shouldn't have to be about winners and losers.

"What do *you* think we should do?" she asks, and I am so startled by the question that I slam the back of the rocking chair against the wall of the house.

Every part of me wants to say: *Stay. Stay here with me. I want to know you.*

Is that purely selfish, though?

Or is that maybe the best thing for Marlow, too? And for Max, even if he's not able to accept it yet?

Maybe we need this chance to know each other. To exist in one another's lives.

Maybe this whole awful summer happened for a very good reason.

It's not what Elliot signed up for when he chose to be a donor. It's not what my moms signed up for either. I realize that. This isn't traditional. But then again, who gets to define what's *traditional* about any of this?

"I want you to be happy," I say, because Marlow is staring at me and I have to say something. And I could stop there. I should, probably. But then: "I really like being your neighbor, though. I like sitting on the porch with you right now."

"Yeah?" she asks, her perfect eyebrows—far more perfect than mine have ever looked in my life—lifting up in surprise.

And then she smiles, and it is the most real smile I've ever seen on her face. "I like sitting here, too."

My heart is so full and whole in this moment, I can almost forget how badly it was just broken. The pieces are finding their way back together, even if they're forming a new and different shape. "After all, I could learn a lot from you. Like how to pluck my eyebrows for one. Your arch is pretty impressive."

She laughs. "Hey, wait a minute. Aren't you supposed to be the one teaching me things?"

"We can teach each other, I guess. You teach me to pluck and contour, and I'll teach you how to light a fire and make lemon bars."

"Hm. Less interested in starting a fire like a Girl Scout, more interested in making myself baked goods." She puts her finger to her chin, like she is solemnly deliberating. "I'm desperate for food," she says, "so you have a deal."

"Deal." I grin at her.

"It's weird, but I think your smile kind of looks a little like mine," she says, studying me with squinted eyes.

"That is weird, isn't it? But maybe a good weird."

"Good weird," she repeats, trying it out. "Yeah. Maybe this whole thing is good weird."

"Maybe it is."

I don't sleep much that night.

I'm too busy thinking, plotting, planning.

The idea came on fast—it struck me like a lightning bolt as

I'd sat on the porch, watching Marlow walk back to her side of the woods. Thinking about how I wanted more time. I wanted to have that eyebrow tutorial, bake those lemon bars together.

What if we could actually make that old house feel like a *home?*

I don't know the first thing about fixing up a building. But we start small: make one room better. The living room. Peel off the ancient wallpaper, paint the walls fresh, some bright, airy color. Order a new windowpane. Polish the carved mantel. Refinish the floors. Make the living room feel like a room where people actually want to *live.*

The sun is only starting to rise, dapples of pink smudging the sky above my bed, but I'm already wide awake. I dress in my ripped overalls I reserve for gardening and a pair of old scuffed boots and head down to the kitchen for coffee.

"What are you doing up so early?" Mama asks, eyes half closed as she sits at the table sipping her coffee. "And looking remarkably perky, too."

"I have a plan," I say, pouring a generous amount of coffee into an oversized Hot Mama Flow mug. More bowl than cup. "A terrible plan, maybe—I'm not sure yet. But a plan."

"Oh? Care to enlighten me?"

"I want to help fix up the Jackson house. And I want Marlow—and Max—to stay in Green Woods. I think Marlow wants to stay, too." And then there's Max. Who's told me he doesn't want to talk to me again. Multiple times. But this isn't all about him. And deep down, I'm hoping that the Max I knew finds his way back—that some time and space has given him more perspective. More acceptance. Either way, I can't worry about it until I try, or I'll lose all nerve. If he chooses to reject this last olive branch, it'll be his loss. That doesn't mean I shouldn't have my chance to know Marlow.

"Calliope—" Mama starts, her voice sounding annoyingly uncertain, and I wave her off.

"Mama. She wants to know me. And I want to know her. Why would life bring them back to that sad house if we weren't supposed to be in each other's lives?"

She sighs. Swigs more coffee. Sighs again. "I don't know, honey, but I think that's for them to figure out, don't you? As a *family*. It's already complicated enough for them, I'm sure. And I don't want to see you get hurt. You've been through enough."

"All I'm trying to do is help them make that depressing house feel a little more like an actual home. Maybe they'll still leave. That's up to them. Or maybe they'll decide to stick it out. At least for Max's senior year. I don't know, but I want to do *something*."

"Are you doing this for yourself? Or for them?"

I gulp a steady stream of coffee, considering. "Both. Is that so terrible?"

Mama shakes her head, but she's smiling. "I want you to listen to your heart, my baby girl. And if that's leading you to this? Well, then, you go over there and try. And you let me and Mimmy know if you need any help. We are here for you. Always."

"I will," I say, putting my empty mug in the sink. "For now, though, wish me luck."

*   *   *

The clerk at the local hardware store is friendly to me, in a curious, amused kind of way. Like a grandfather telling his granddaughter how to tie her shoes for the first time. I'm his morning entertainment.

I end up spending a few weeks' worth of my summer earnings at the studio to leave fully stocked with supplies he says I'll need: plastic sheets and tape, a spatula and knife, sanding paper and sponges, primer, brushes, paint. Picking the paint was the hardest part of the process. I ended up making a decision based solely on the name: Hope Springs Eternal, a light, crystal blue, like water fresh from a winding forest stream.

The anxiety hits as I turn onto our road. I take deep breaths, look up at the bright, cloudless sky. I think about Marlow's smile. *Deal.*

I pull down their driveway, park the car.

He's there, sitting on the bottom porch step, the most secure one.

Max.

There's no turning back now. He's seen me.

I grab the bags from the passenger seat, heavy with supplies, and get out of the car.

His hand is shielding his eyes, like he's not sure if the sun is playing tricks on him, or if I'm actually here, walking toward him with my hands full of white plastic mystery bags.

"Hey," I say, dropping the bags on the patchy brown grass in front of the porch. I sit down on the step next to him.

"Hey."

I'm not ready to look at him. It's hard to say if he's looking at me.

I should have practiced this part. Rehearsed. I had plenty of time, lying awake in bed all night, researching ways to strip wallpaper off old plaster walls. I was too fixated on the practical side of this grand plan, not enough on the emotional.

" 'Rowman's Hardware,' " he reads from the side of the bag. "What's in there?"

"I thought we could . . . fix up the house a little." I turn to face Max, but he's still staring down at the bags. "Make a dent, anyway. I bought stuff to strip wallpaper and paint the walls. I figured we could maybe start with the living room? That is—only if you and Marlow want to. And if your parents say it's okay. I just thought—"

I don't remember what I thought. Max is looking up at me now and his eyes are endlessly deep brown pools that give nothing away. I had thought I knew him so well. There was so much to learn, though. There *is* so much to learn.

"Maybe it's a stupid, insensitive idea," I say, babbling to fill the gaping space between us, "and it is stupid, isn't it? But I know you're thinking about moving away. And I just thought that maybe if the house could feel more like a home, you would all stay. At least for now. But it's not my business, and I'm probably majorly intruding. I just—"

"You what?" he asks, and his face is so damn blank it makes me want to scream.

"I just don't want you to go, okay?" I stand up, because there is too much happening inside me to stay still, too much nervous energy. I walk in circles along the lumpy overgrown hedges. "For some silly reason I'm still fighting for us, even if you've given up. What happened and how it went down sucks, yes, a thousand percent. But the connection we had—it was real, wasn't it? I want more time to figure out a friendship. And I want that with Marlow, too. I *really* want that. If you leave—if you leave, I'm afraid I might never see either of you again."

I finish talking, but I keep pacing. Waiting.

After a few minutes, I start to wonder if I'm waiting for nothing. Maybe silence is the last thing I'll hear from Max. He really is incapable of dealing with this. Us.

But then he stands up, too. I stop to watch him as he picks up the bags, one by one. There's a pause, and I think maybe he's going to hurl them into the woods.

"Okay," he says finally. "Let's do this. If Marlow puts on scrubs and helps, too. She doesn't get to stay clean if I'm scraping down filthy old walls."

"Really?" I ask, too stunned to follow him as he starts up the stairs.

"Really. My goodbyes don't seem to work with you anyway. And I'm glad about that." He stops on the top step and turns back to face me. "Marlow told me, by the way. That she's talked to you."

"Oh." I hadn't asked her this—if he knew.

"I didn't love it when she first told me. I wanted to, I don't know, protect her somehow. From all the baggage. But she seemed happy about it. About you. Happier than I've seen her since we left Philly, to be honest."

"Really?" My heart ticks faster. "Did she say that?"

"No, but she didn't have to. I can see it. And she asked my parents if we could stay. I'm pretty sure that's about you."

"I wasn't trying to meddle," I say, even though I'm glad I did, if that's what it was, my conversations with Marlow.

"I know."

I lift an eyebrow. "Do you? It didn't seem like that. After our last conversation."

He sighs and drops the bags on the porch. "I'm sorry, Calliope. I really am. That wasn't my finest moment. As a matter of fact, none of our last few discussions have been. There's a lot to be sorry about. I was angry, yeah. And sad and horrified and shocked and disgusted and, oh you know, *everything*. Pretty much every emotion in the book. But I shouldn't have taken that out on you. You were right—none of this was anybody's fault. And there's nothing I can do to punish the universe, so I guess that's that? Time to move past it all and see what's next."

"Just like that?" I ask, so much hope filling me up I feel woozy. Maybe he took a long time to get to this place. Too long. But he's here now. That's not nothing.

He nods. "Yep. Just like that. If you can forgive me, that is. Because it should have been me, making this kind of grand gesture. I should have come to you."

"You're not wrong," I say, and I can't fight the smile breaking out on my lips. "But if you stay, you'll have plenty of time to make up for it."

"Then come on," he says, reaching down to pick up the bags. "I've got some serious work to do."

The three of us peel and scrape and sand and patch up scrapes and dents.

Joanie watches silently, her mouth a thin, unreadable line.

I don't notice at first when Elliot comes in. But I turn to get fresh sandpaper, and there he is, standing next to Joanie with an arm draped loosely around her shoulders. She's angled away from him, their bodies making minimal contact.

They both disappear then, up the stairs, and we keep going. We only take a break to microwave frozen burritos and popcorn and spoon some ice cream into bowls, bringing it all back to the living room to eat as we work.

And then suddenly Elliot is here again, too, in faded jeans with holes in the knees, measuring the pane of the cracked window, climbing a ladder to tinker with the broken overhead light.

None of us say anything, but no words are necessary.

We work until the sun goes down and the room is too dim to see what we're doing. Elliot orders a pizza, and the five of us eat outside on the porch, sitting on the drooping wooden planks.

Good weird, I think, looking around me: these people, this house, our woods.

Good weird.

*　　*　　*

I come back bright and early the next day to start painting.

Joanie is in the living room when I get there, draping the sofa in a clear plastic tarp. The rest of the furniture is already covered.

"Your moms called last night," she says matter-of-factly, and I nod, dazed but reluctant to ask more and disturb whatever fragile new peace this is.

But I don't have to wonder for long, because soon Mama and Mimmy are on the porch, a wheelbarrow full of gardening tools between them. Joanie goes out to greet them, and I watch from the window as she points to the hedges and mounds of weeds and dirt that had maybe been a flower bed once upon a time.

Max and Marlow paint alongside me. Elliot makes lists of what needs to be done—lists that I think he'll actually make use of this time.

Because he apologizes to Joanie and Max and Marlow as I paint silently in the background, slow, careful strokes. "I should have done this in June. I'm sorry I've been so distant. Negligent. This house. The memories. But we had some happy times, too, while I was growing up. And I want it to feel happy again. That's why I could never bring myself to sell it after Dad died. This place—it's a part of me. For better and for worse. Hopefully more better from here on out. The three of you deserve so much better. You always have. And I'm sorry it took almost losing you to get me on the right track."

They all cry then, Elliot especially. I stay in my corner, turn my head away as I brush away my own tears.

This isn't my home. I know that.

They are the Jacksons. The Martzes. I'm not. That won't ever change.

But in this moment, here and now?

We feel like one big messy family.

Blood. Not blood.

Family.

Chapter Twenty

"**LET'S** go out," Marlow says to me and Max on Sunday evening, like it's that simple. The three of us—one Jackson, one Martz, one Silversmith—venturing anywhere beyond these woods. "I never leave this damn house. Ever."

Max starts to shush her for cursing, but she waves him off. "Seriously, I feel like I'm tripping from all these paint fumes. Take me somewhere. *Anywhere.* I'm begging you guys."

It's been three days—three very long days—of working on the house. The living room at least is finished. Our job is done. Professionals, thank god, will work on the rest, now that we've made our point to Elliot and Joanie.

"Where would we go?" I ask. I start to undo the old button-up shirt I've used for a painting smock, and every last muscle in my neck and back screams at me to stop moving. "I'd have to shower and change before getting in a car. Unless you want some paint stains to mark up that sweet green dream machine of yours."

Max smiles at that. I hoped he would. "That's not a terrible idea. Just another story to add to all the dents and scrapes."

It's decided then.

Five minutes later we're all in his car. Marlow hopped in the back first, leaving the passenger seat for me.

Max puts the windows down as we drive, letting the smell of

paint diffuse out with the cool breeze. "Am I driving somewhere in particular?" He looks over at me. I shake my head, look back at Marlow. It's her turn to call the shots.

"Do you have anything but pizza around here?" she asks, making a gagging face. "I never thought I'd say it, but I'll puke my guts out if I eat pizza again tonight. Mom has that Mario's place saved as a favorite on her contacts list. She needs more options."

"One Chinese restaurant. And grocery stores. Fast food, too, but I draw the line there. That'll make *me* puke my guts out."

"Okay. Chinese then. To go."

"To go where?"

"I want that neighborhood tour you gave Max when we first got here. Show me that pretty view on the hill he kept going on and on about."

I steel myself and wait for the sadness to hit—thinking about that first day exploring with Max, the beginning of everything.

But it doesn't come.

I don't feel sad.

Instead I feel grateful to be going back there. With both of them this time, Max and Marlow. It should have been that way the first time, too—we should have included her.

"Sure. I can do that. If it's okay with you, Max?"

I glance over at him as he drives. He thumps his fingers on the wheel, nods slowly. "I don't see why not."

Max parks the car on Main Street a few minutes later, and the three of us make our way into the Golden Bowl. It's a tiny place, a few small, sticky-looking tables that no one ever really uses. But it's crowded at the counter with other customers ordering takeout. I recognize a few of the faces. From the studio, school, everywhere in Green Woods, really, because that's how it is in a small town.

"Hey! Calliope!"

I turn to see two girls from my grade waving at me from over by the soda machine. Rory and Bea. We've always been friendly enough, though it's been limited to superficial classroom small talk. The two of them are as inseparable as me and Ginger and Noah. As exclusive, I guess you could say. They almost look like twins right now, with their long dark hair and blunt bangs and short denim cutoffs. I wave back, and they start walking over our way. Curious, I'm sure, about the two strangers next to me. And, I realize—catching a glimpse of myself in the mirror above the counter—probably about our matching paint smears, too. I reach up and pick at a blue clump in my hair.

"Who are they?" Marlow whispers loudly.

Her question makes my heart race. Because I'll have to make introductions. How to put Max and Marlow into neat labels?

My neighbors, I'll say. *My friends.*

No need to tell them more than that.

"How was your summer?" Rory asks, smiling pleasantly. Too pleasantly, maybe. Edging into fake territory. "You look like you've been... busy." She stares pointedly at the streak of paint running up my overalls.

"Ha. Yes. Just doing some painting. It's been a good summer.

Actually"—I step back, gesture to Max and Marlow—"these are my new neighbors, Max and Marlow. We were doing some work on their house this weekend."

"Oh, how nice! I'm Bea," Bea says, waving animatedly. She's the people pleaser of the two. That's always been their dynamic. "And this is Rory. You live out there in the deep woods, don't you, Calliope? I think I was there once for a birthday party when we were little. I remember playing hide-and-seek and pretending there were forest fairies chasing us around the trees."

I nod. "That sounds about right. Ginger and Noah and I were always running from those fairies."

"Sounds like I missed quite a childhood," Marlow says, smirking.

Rory laughs. "I was there for that birthday, too. But I thought it was old man Jackson we were running from? That's before the newspaper delivery boy had to call in the search party for his decaying body."

I gasp.

I can't bring myself to look at Max or Marlow, but I feel them stiffen beside me.

"He was a person," I say, gritting my teeth, "not a monster or a character from a story. A *real person*. You shouldn't talk about him—or anyone—that way." Though I'm thinking about all the times I probably talked about him that way, too. *Old man Jackson*. More lore than human. But I was wrong to do that. We all were.

Rory flinches and steps back, like I've slapped her. "Um.

Okay. Sorry?" She doesn't look sorry. She looks annoyed. Ready to pick up her food and move along.

"You're right, Calliope," Bea says, jabbing Rory's side with her elbow. "You know she didn't mean anything by it. This whole town jokes about that house."

"We actually live in that house," Max says. "Calliope's neighbor, remember?"

"Oh," Bea starts, "I'm so—"

Marlow cuts her off. "Old man Jackson was our grandfather. By the way."

Even Rory has the decency to turn bright pink.

He was my grandfather, too, I want to say. Even though it's only partly true. Biologically, yes. But that doesn't make him family. He's not mine to claim. And neither are Max and Marlow. Especially not in public.

"I was just kidding," Rory says. "I didn't know."

"Obviously." Marlow rolls her eyes.

Bea turns to Max. "Let's all start over. Are you a senior, too?"

He nods, looking disinterested. His eyes flash up to the extensive menu hanging above the register.

"Cool. It must be so sad and weird, moving senior year. Rory and I can help show you around, if you want."

"Thanks." He looks back at Bea. "But I think I'm set. I've got my big sister here to show me the ropes at Green Woods High."

"Big sister?" Rory says, squinting as she turns to Marlow— bare faced today, looking exactly her age. Four years younger than Max.

"Nope. Not her. Calliope." He smiles as he says it, a mischievous, shit-eating one, like he's delighting in the fact that this will implode Rory's and Bea's minds.

Big sister.

My mind is imploding, too.

I laugh so loud every last person in the restaurant turns to look at me. Even the two busy line cooks behind the counter.

Max and Marlow laugh, too. Doubled over. Gasping.

We all have tears in our eyes.

"So. I'm assuming that's a joke then." Rory frowns, like she doesn't like being outside of whatever this great prank might be.

"Nope," I say, wiping my cheeks. "It's true. We're half-siblings. I have two moms, remember? I was a science experiment."

Bea's mouth, which has been hanging wide open during this whole exchange, finally shuts. *"Oh."*

"Yep. Well. Good to see you both! I think we'll order now." I smile sweetly and step around them, motioning for Max and Marlow to follow me.

"Come over anytime—my grandfather's ghost would love to meet you," Marlow says, glancing back at them. And then she takes my hand.

"I'm sorry I blew up your spot," Max says later, as we're sprawled out on top of the hill with our food. "Telling those girls at the Chinese restaurant about our sordid family tree. I didn't exactly plan on it. Something about Rory just made me want to shock her tiny little brain." He bites into an egg roll, closes his eyes.

"What colors do you see?" I ask. I take a bite of my egg roll and close my eyes, too.

"Orange. Bright orange. Tangerine. And a nice light green. Tea green, maybe."

I consider this. "I get what you're saying. But do you only think green because of the cabbage? Does knowing what color the food is affect your opinion?"

"I try not to think about the food color," Max says. "But it's not a perfect science."

"Weirdos," Marlow says, "both of you."

I open my eyes. It's getting dark up here, the sun almost completely hidden behind us. I brought one of our camping lanterns, though, and there's more than enough light to see the happy look on Marlow's face as she digs her fork into more fried rice.

"You don't have to be sorry," I say. "About earlier. I'm glad you told them."

"Yeah?" Max opens his eyes, too. He turns to look at me.

"Let's never tell people about earlier this summer." I cringe. I'll probably always cringe, thinking about *that*. Max, too. We cringe together—and then we move on. "But I'm okay with people knowing that we're related by science."

Maybe more than science, too. Or we will be, after more time spent together in these woods. Silversmiths, Jacksons, Martzes— some strange, unlikely fusion of the three.

"Cool," Marlow says, chewing on her rice, "I can't wait to tell kids at school about my forest-goddess half sister."

"And I'll tell them about my little half sister who is infinitely more glamorous than me, and I'll charge them to come over for makeup tutorials."

"What about me?" Max asks. "I'm the odd one out now?"

I shake my head. "Never. I'll proudly tell people about my half brother who can't go for a walk in the rain without taking a mud bath."

"Really? That's the best you can do?" He tosses his last scrap of egg roll at me. "It's been *twice*. Only twice."

I rub my chin, considering. "I think we've only walked in the rain twice, though. So, two for two."

Marlow chuckles. "I better be invited next time so I can see for myself."

"Oh, most definitely." I grin as I reach for the fortune cookies at the bottom of our takeout bag. I toss one cookie to Marlow, one to Max.

"You know what?" Max catches the cookie, crunching it with his fist. "One sister was already more than enough. I should never have gone public with it today. Can I undo that?"

"Nope. No undoing gossip in Green Woods. I'm sorry, though—you're not just the half brother who falls in the mud." *You are so much more. You are so many things.* "You're the boy who tastes color. And the boy who paints sunlight."

"The boy who paints sunlight?" Max's white smile lights up the dark hillside. "I like that one. I approve."

I crack open my cookie, hold the small slip of paper by the lantern:

Make family your friends, and friends your family.

*　　*　　*

Noah is the first to show up for our Labor Day picnic.

It's early still, an hour before I expected anyone. The moms are on a last grocery store run, and I'm lying in the hammock with some lemonade, wondering how the day will go.

"I made that weird fruit salad you love so much," he says, dropping a plastic tub on the picnic table.

"Strawberry Ambrosia Salad?" I ask, clasping my hands across my heart as I jump up from the hammock to join him.

He nods. "Sounds more like a flower than a salad if you ask me. And if the moms are curious, you have to lie and say I used marshmallows and Cool Whip sweetened with agave."

"Will do," I say, popping the lid off and swirling my finger along the edge of the fluffy pink cloud, scooping up a generous dollop to put in my mouth. It's as sugary as cotton candy and tastes like childhood and summer dreams and breaking rules. I take a second dollop. A third.

"Adequate?" he asks, smirking at me.

I sigh. "Perfection. Thank you, dear friend."

He smiles at me with those deep blue eyes, bluer than ever under today's clear sky. "You're welcome. Dear friend."

Mimmy and Mama bustle into the yard a few minutes later, setting the table and lighting the grill, trays of garden veggies and homemade hummus and fancy cheeses cluttering up the table next to my Ambrosia Salad. Noah is called upon to help make beet burger patties in the kitchen, and soon Ginger and Vivi are here,

279

too, unloading the bag of end-of-summer-blowout-sale sparklers and poppers and firecrackers they bought for tonight.

And then I catch movement along the woods from the corner of my eye. Max steps out first, leading the way. Marlow is close behind him, scowling as she picks some prickly branch off her shirt. Elliot. Joanie.

Mimmy had been the one to invite them—*all* of them—over a pitcher of iced tea after she and Mama had spent hours in their yard pruning shrubs and tree branches and breaking up the old patches of garden, prepping the soil for new life. I assumed Joanie would politely decline. She surprised everyone when she said yes.

Noah and Max give each other a nod of acknowledgment, and Ginger throws an arm around Max like they are best buddies, introducing him to her *girlfriend*, Vivi. Marlow compliments Ginger on her cat-eye frames, and Ginger exclaims jealously over Marlow's yellow pleather short-shorts. Joanie makes small talk with Mimmy as they clear space on the table for Joanie's pasta and potato salads, and Elliot sidles up next to Mama by the grill.

I stand still, watching it all happen around me in disbelief. These people—all in one place. A little awkward and stiff, maybe, conversations slightly stilted, but still together. Trying.

Ginger catches my eye and waves me over. She's in the middle of one of her stories about diner life—Vivi chiming in at the punch lines, Max, Marlow, and Noah all laughing along.

I take a deep breath, close my eyes, etching this image permanently in my memory.

School starts tomorrow morning, bright and early. Senior year. This, right here and now, is our last true moment of summer, no matter what the calendar might say. Our terrible, beautiful summer is going to be over.

But nothing about today feels like an ending.

Nothing at all.

Epilogue
Nine Months Later

"**Is** this the tenth time you've cried today?" I ask, smiling as I lean across the kitchen counter to swipe at the tear running down Mama's cheek. "Or the eleventh? I've lost count. Let's see," I say, holding one finger up in the air. "First time was when Mimmy played 'Pomp and Circumstance' to wake me up this morning, and then you—"

"Ha ha," Mama says, catching my hand in hers and squeezing tight. "Very funny."

"I think it's actually ticked up even higher, sweetheart," Mimmy chimes in from across the kitchen as she spreads coconut crème frosting on her cooled pineapple cake. Cake that we'll be taking to dinner next door shortly, along with the lemon drop cookies Mimmy baked first thing this morning. "You missed at least one good cry during the actual ceremony, and then another during pictures. Unless we just count that whole period as one long cry, because I'm not sure she fully stopped at any point. Did you, Stella?"

Mama frowns. "Would you both rather I was incapable of showing genuine emotion? On my one and only little girl's graduation day? Am I that much of a robot?"

"Of course not," Mimmy says, looking over at us with a wide grin. "I'm always relieved to be reminded that you're human, just like the rest of us."

Mama sniffs. "For today, anyway. Don't go getting used to it or anything."

"We'll see about that. Wait until Calliope actually *leaves* us. That will be even harder." Mimmy's grin fades at her words.

"Um, excuse me," I say, and now I'm the one squeezing Mama's hand tight. "This is a happy day. We're *celebrating*, remember? We have a whole summer before I go anywhere, and Penn State is only a few hours away. You'll barely even miss me."

Mama grunts in response, and Mimmy turns back to her icing.

"You'll be busy with the studio like always." I stare down at the counter, spinning a spoon in circles with my free hand. "And you know, Elliot and Joanie and Marlow are always right there across the woods. I'm sure they'd still like to hang out, even if I'm not around."

I try to say it casually, like the thought is just now occurring to me. But I've been wondering about this for months now—what Max and I leaving will do to this delicate patchwork family unit we've been working on so hard since last summer. It hasn't always been easy. His family has its own deeply rooted issues. Those haven't magically gone away. And Mama's been tough at points, as Mama tends to be. But they've been trying. We all have. Max and Marlow and I are the core, though. This collective family revolves around us. What happens when you take two of us away?

Mama lets out a long, weary sigh, and my stomach twists. Maybe I misread all the interactions this last year. Maybe the adults were just playing nice.

Maybe *family* was all in my head.

I look up at Mama slowly, not sure what to say from here—and am instantly relieved to see the small smile playing at her lips.

"You do realize," she says, shaking her head emphatically at me, "this is absolutely the last thing I ever wanted. *Frank*, having any role whatsoever in my daughter's life."

"I know."

"And not just *Frank*, but his whole damn family. You have a half brother and a half sister, for god's sake, living across the woods from us like we're in some awful reality TV show compound. I mean, of all people in the entire world—our neighbors. Our neighbors, Calliope!"

"I know, Mama, yes, but—"

She cuts me off. "And the funny thing is, I wouldn't want it any other way. Not anymore. This setup we have here?" Mama points her free hand toward the window, the woods that separate us from the Jackson house. "It feels right."

Mimmy turns toward us and drops the spatula she's been using on the floor.

"You really mean that?" I ask, stunned. "It's not just graduation day emotions talking?"

"Well," Mama says, chuckling, "these wretched sappy emotions aren't hurting the cause. But I've felt this way for a while now. Don't get me wrong—Elliot is far from perfect. He's got a long way to go. But he's working on himself, isn't he? Marriage counseling. Therapy. Staying put, at home where he belongs. His heart is in the right place, I do believe that. And he's been good to you. Even good *for* you, maybe. And all his personal failures aside, I do love the rest of his family. He did something right, at least."

"Is this really my wife talking?" Mimmy asks. She takes a few steps toward us. "I've never heard you speak like this. Did you drink enough water today? Is your blood sugar low?"

"Wow. I try to be open and vulnerable for once," Mama grumbles, dropping my hand, "and this is what I get from my—"

Mimmy throws her arms around Mama, squeezing the air out of the rest of her sentence. "No, no, I absolutely adore this new side of you. I hope she sticks around. Because I agree." She reaches out and grabs my wrist, tugs me over to their side of the counter. "Calliope was meant to find her people. *Our* people."

I smile as I step into their hug, wrapping my arms around their shoulders. "So that was a long-winded way of saying you'll still be friends with them after I go?"

"Well, no. I can't promise Elliot and I will be *friends* necessarily," Mama says.

I start to pull back, confused, but she latches on tighter.

"We'll be family," Mama finishes. "And that's what matters most."

The three of us are quiet then. I close my eyes and breathe in the smell of Mimmy's tropical cake in the air, feel their arms pressing firmly against my back. The sun streaming in the window is bright and warm against my eyelids. This moment feels better than graduation. More important.

"Okay," Mama says finally, letting go of both of us as she wipes at a fresh wave of tears. "Enough of this. Let's get to dinner. I need to eat my feelings away with those burgers that Elliot always chars to ash. I ate them quietly last year, when I was still playing nice. But now? Nope. I'm teaching that man to grill, mark my words."

We step out from the woods into the Jackson meadow, and my breath hitches. The transformation still surprises me every time.

The grass is green and thick and freshly mowed, and the hedges surrounding the house are trimmed into neat rectangles. Orange marigolds and red geraniums spring up from small flower beds on either side of the porch steps. Porch steps that are strong and stable now—and freshly painted along with the rest of the porch, the front door, the window trim. The windows themselves are clean and shiny in the sunlight. The porch roof is fixed, no longer on the brink of collapse.

The Jackson house is a home again.

If Max's grandmother ever really did haunt this place, I'd like to think she's long gone by now. She can rest in peace knowing Elliot and his family are happy—or at least getting there, happier every day—under this roof.

"I'm pleased that Elliot is keeping up the hedges so nicely," Mama says, eyeing the lines approvingly. "The flower bed is satisfactorily weeded, too."

"He's certainly very lucky he had you to train him in the fine art of lawn care," I say, climbing the stairs up onto the porch. "He would have been lost without you."

Mama preens as she steps up next to me, her chin lifting like a queen's as she turns to fully survey the landscape. "Too true, sweetheart. He was a clueless city slicker when he got here. Forgot his own roots, that one did. But now almost a year in, and I think he's rediscovered that Green Woods boy buried deep down inside."

"I can hear you, you know," Elliot says, tugging the screen door open to welcome us in. "But I'll choose to remember the compliment, and not the 'clueless city slicker' bit."

"Good," Mama says, clapping a firm hand on his shoulder. "Now, let's talk about your grilling technique, shall we?"

Elliot rolls his eyes, but he smiles at me as he turns to follow Mama inside.

Mimmy heads straight to the kitchen with her three-tiered pineapple cake, and I hear Joanie greet her, exclaiming about the cake's beauty, Mimmy humbly insisting it's nothing special— she was too busy dealing with Mama's tears to frost it as intricately as she would have liked. And then Joanie starts in on some story about her shift at the studio yesterday, where she's working part-time at the counter while she trains to be a yoga teacher. She likes to say that yoga is saving her mind, and her marriage. Yoga, and long walks in the woods. She's a country convert, too, even if she refuses to admit that much out loud.

I take a moment to admire the polished banisters, the vines

and leaves springing to life as they wind up alongside the staircase. The carved wood will always be my favorite part of this
house. I start toward the kitchen to drop off the tin of lemon drop
cookies when I hear a creaking floorboard behind me.

"I spent some time working on my woodblock this morning,"
Max says, and I turn to find him standing in the doorway to the
living room. "I'm nowhere near my grandfather's level, but I can
almost tell what I carved is a flower."

Marlow pushes him aside from behind and beams at me.
"*Almost* is right. I guessed he was carving a booger." She shrugs.
"Sorry, bro. Keep working at it, though. Maybe you won't suck
as much by the end of the summer." She walks up to me with her
arms out for a hug, but she stops in her tracks when she sees the
tin. "Lemon drop?"

I nod.

She grabs the tin from my hands. "Margo made these for me,
thank you very much. I made a special request. I'll be taking them
before Max inhales them all." She dashes up the stairs, presumably to hide them in her room.

Max watches her go, shaking his head. "Wow. I'm the one
who graduated today, but I don't get a single cookie? How fair is
that?"

"Don't worry. Mimmy made the pineapple cake you requested.
Personally, I voted for something s'more themed to kick off the
summer, but oh no. You had apparently told her how much you
were craving her pineapple cake. So pineapple cake it is! How's that
for fair, hmm?"

He laughs. "Sorry, but not sorry. I've been dreaming about eating that cake again ever since my birthday."

"She'll probably let you pick the flavor for my birthday cake next month, too. I've already had eighteen years of her cakes, she says. You and Marlow get to have your say now."

He comes up to me for a hug, patting my back consolingly. "Thank goodness I'm going to Penn State, too, so she can streamline her dessert drop-offs in the fall. Is that why you decided to go there? Scared you wouldn't get as many treats if we split off?"

"Excuse me, no. I decided first. And it's because they have a good Environmental Science program. You could be studying art anywhere."

"Digital Arts and Media Design, *thank you*. Art, but 'practical art.'" He lifts his hands to air quote. "Got to keep Mom happy."

"Mm-hmm." I fake a pout like I'm sad about it. But I was nothing but relieved when Max made the decision this spring. With Noah heading up to Berklee and Ginger to Vassar, I'm glad I'll have a friend on the same campus. And I'm glad that friend is Max.

We start walking toward the sunroom—once again an actual *room*, a fully enclosed glassed-in space with a freshly tiled floor. It's the most impressive transformation of all.

"Are Ginger and Vivi still coming over for a bonfire later?" he asks, flopping down on one of the two new plush sunny-yellow chaises.

"Yep." I drop down onto the other chaise and sigh with

contentment as I sink into the cushions. It's infinitely more comfortable than their sleek city-chic sofa. "And Noah said he might pop by with Penelope." Penelope Park. It's new—Ginger's brainchild, actually, a surprise twist to senior year—but Noah seems happy. And that makes me happy, too.

"Cool. Our first fire of the summer. We'll have to do it every night to make the most of these last months."

"Are you sure you want to see me that much? I don't want you to get sick of me and then avoid me at college. I need you. You know I suck at making new friends."

"Maybe not *every* night then," he says, smirking. "But you don't suck at making friends. Aren't I proof of that?"

"You don't count. Maybe we only clicked because—oh, you know—we share half our DNA. So that was an unfair advantage."

"Hm. True. So maybe you do suck at making friends then? I guess we'll see this fall when you dive into the shark tank." He lets out an evil chuckle, and I toss an oversized chaise pillow squarely at his smug face.

"You," I say, sighing heavily, "are such an annoying little brother sometimes, do you know that?"

"Only because I have years to make up for. You had it too easy being an only child."

I'm opening my mouth to make some kind of scathing retort when Joanie interrupts from the doorway.

"Did you think the table would set itself?" she asks, hands on her hips as she squints in at us. "I see four very capable hands in here."

"Yes, Mom," Max says, springing up from his chair.

"Yes, Joanie," I say, more reluctantly, as I pry my legs one by one from the wonderfully cloudlike cushion.

Before I turn toward the kitchen door, I see Mama and Elliot outside by the grill, Mama seemingly demonstrating something with a pair of tongs and a burger patty. Elliot is leaning in, dutifully listening. If he's annoyed that she's taking over, he doesn't show it.

I smile.

And then I follow Max down the hallway to set the table, because it's time for our family dinner to begin.

Acknowledgments

Every book is its own unique journey, and this has been an especially weird and windy and wonderful one. As everyone in my life well knows by now, I am chronically obsessed with hypotheticals—with asking hard, maybe sometimes even impossible, questions. (Thank you all for putting up with me, by the way.) The particular question driving this book has been with me for a long time now: What if you unknowingly fell in love with a person you're not allowed to love, not like that, not under any circumstances? As I wrote, though, the question became about so much more: What is family love versus friendship love versus romantic love? How are those loves different, how are they the same? How do we define what makes a group of people *family*, and what makes that love so special? These are not easy questions, and it took a village of wise people to get me on the right path.

To my agent (among many other things!) Jill Grinberg, I remember the first time I worked up the courage to tell you about this idea, *years* ago now, over some matcha at Primrose. You listened thoughtfully, quietly, never batting an eye, and then started asking me so many necessary and valuable questions about my intentions and hopes for this book. You have poked and prodded and nudged this story along through so many variations and courses, and for that I am immensely grateful. Denise Page and Sam Farkas, thank you both for reading and sharing your brilliant insights, for helping to make this book richer and rounder and better in all ways. Sophia Seidner, thank you for all the vigilant, empowering work you do behind the scenes. I am thankful every day to be part of the JGLM team, as an author and as an agent—to share all pieces of my working life with such a fiercely talented and funny and kind group of women.

To my editor Margaret Ferguson, working with you feels like earning an MFA in the best, most rewarding way possible. Your wisdom and expertise are unparalleled, truly a vast treasure trove of knowledge, and you make me an endlessly better, more careful, more thoughtful writer with each project I'm lucky enough to share with you. Thank you for pushing me further with each new draft, for asking all the big questions—and the little questions—and for not stopping until the story was as it was meant to be. It is an honor to be on your list.

To my Holiday House team—Terry Borzumato-Greenberg, Michelle Montague, Emily Mannon, and everyone else who helped bring Calliope Silversmith to life—thank you for championing me and this book and for allowing me to bring my hypothetical questions to the world. Thank you to my copy editor, Chandra Wohleber, for your insightful polishes.

To my dear readers and friends, Melissa and Lauren DelVecchio, thank you for helping to make this book better and more accurate, and for sharing your beautiful family with me. Your love is an inspiration, always.

To all of my family and friends who have heard me talk about this book idea for years upon years, thank you for listening.

Thank you for entertaining my absurd questions and ultima-tums. Thank you for accepting and supporting me as I am. I love you all with my whole being. Whether we share blood or not, you are my family. My people for life.

To my parents, Denny and Carol, I will thank you endlessly, because you've made all things possible. This book and every book I've written and every book I'll ever write—they're because you believed in me unconditionally. You let me dream big dreams and you made me keep fighting for those dreams to come true, no matter how scary or distant or impossible they sometimes felt. Thank you for holding my hand through it all.

To Danny, thank you for living and breathing this book with me. All the countless drafts, the constant push to write, write, write through pregnancy (because what if I would never write again otherwise?!), the balancing of momming and revising and working full-time, all from home, all together, every day. Thank you for being next to me for every last bit of it, for being a super-human who keeps our home and family merrily chugging along. Thank you for being my first reader, my caffeine supplier, my master chef. You make every day a good day.

To Alfie, your first acknowledgment! You are my joy and my reason, and you are worth every cup of coffee it takes to write these words. Thank you for teaching me the meaning of motherhood.

And to my readers, thank you for joining me on this unusual journey, for trusting in me, and for, I hope, loving Calliope Silversmith and her beautiful family as much as I do. Thank you for being here. You are my people, too.